P9-DNN-579

The SCHOOL BETWEEN WINTER and FAIRYLAND

The SCHOOL BETWEEN WINTER and FAIRYLAND

HEATHER FAWCETT

Balzer + Bray

An Imprint of HarperCollins*Publishers*

Balzer + Bray is an imprint of HarperCollins Publishers.

The School Between Winter and Fairyland
Copyright © 2021 by Heather Fawcett
All rights reserved. Printed in the United States of America.
No part of this book may be used or reproduced in any manner whatsoever
without written permission except in the case of brief quotations embodied
in critical articles and reviews. For information address HarperCollins
Children's Books, a division of HarperCollins Publishers, 195 Broadway,
New York, NY 10007.
www.harpercollinschildrens.com

ISBN 978-0-06-304331-2

Typography by Catherine Lee
21 22 23 24 25   PC/LSCH   10 9 8 7 6 5 4 3 2 1
❖
First Edition

The SCHOOL BETWEEN WINTER and FAIRYLAND

1

In Which Autumn
Meets an Unusual Magician

The dragon wasn't happy with the roses. No matter how Autumn cajoled and pleaded, Amfidzel refused to leave her garden, declaring that she wasn't going anywhere until she'd plucked all the aphids off the drooping stems.

Jack's round face was pale. "What do we do?"

Autumn tapped her foot, surveying the darkening sky. All monsters in Inglenook School's menagerie had to be stabled by sunset—that was the rule, and there'd be trouble if anyone found out that a dragon had been left to lurk the grounds after dark. Not that Amfidzel was particularly lurky, as dragons went. She'd huff and puff over the dying roses until she huffed and puffed herself out, then she'd fall asleep among the lady's slippers.

Like all dragons, Amfidzel was obsessed with flowers. She spent her days hovering over her honey-scented hoard, pruning and plucking and weeding.

Jack patted Amfidzel's flank. "Can't she stay out a little longer?"

"Oh, Jack." Autumn drew her softhearted brother out of range of Amfidzel's horns. Jack was forever making pets out of the monsters, giving them names and fussing over them when they were sick. When he was little, he used to put rain-coats on the Hounds of Arawn when he took them down the mountain for walks—as if they were real dogs, not ghostly, coal-eyed beasts that howled at impending death. It was a wonder Jack had made it to thirteen with all his limbs.

Autumn was tired. She'd spent all afternoon mucking out the stalls in the menagerie, and she didn't have any patience for dillydallying dragons. She drew a breath and spoke into Amfidzel's mind. *Do you want to get Gran in trouble?*

No, Amfidzel said sulkily. Autumn's grandmother was the menagerie's head beastkeeper, and had hand-raised most of the monsters, including Amfidzel herself. It wasn't entirely accurate to say that Gran was like a mother to Amfidzel, but she was certainly more mother than paid keeper.

Autumn decided to change tactics. *If you're good, I'll bring you a present tomorrow.*

Amfidzel's head lifted at that. She was a snowy dragon, white as milk but for a ridge of golden scales down her back. Snowy dragons were only about twenty feet from nose to tail when full-grown, but what they lacked in size they made up for and then some with their enormous antlers. The tips were poisoned: one scratch and you'd fall into a slumber from which not even the mightiest magician could wake. Amfidzel, though, was only ten years old, or about five in dragon years, and almost sweet, if you looked past the antlers and shadowy red eyes.

What sort of present? The dragon's pointed face brightened. *Another rosebush?*

Autumn didn't have the heart to tell Amfidzel she didn't seem to have a green thumb where roses were concerned. Jack's eyes darted between them, his brow furrowed. He wasn't very good at the Speech—half the time, the monsters ignored him.

I'll talk to Miss Ewing down in the village, Autumn said. *She may have some lily seeds from beyond the Blue Mountains.*

Hmph. Amfidzel cast another mournful look at the roses and followed Autumn and Jack out of the garden. Autumn breathed a sigh of relief.

The dragon's garden was enclosed by three tumble-down stone walls that had probably been a farmer's house long, long ago, back when the Gentlewood had been only a shadow on the horizon. It was a small garden by dragon standards—two neat plots of vegetables, a strawberry patch, and a tangled bed of pansies and sweet violets. The oldest dragons had acres of fragrant flowers, vegetables, blooming shrubs for all seasons, and fruit trees. Amfidzel's mother had turned a slope in the Blue Mountains red with tulips and poppies, and laced the scree with creeping hibiscus and mounds of rhododendrons. Gran had seen it with her own eyes, for she was the one who had stolen Amfidzel for the menagerie when she was just an egg. Dragons protected their gardens more ferociously than they did their children.

Autumn led Amfidzel up the muddy mountain path toward the menagerie. Above them, Inglenook School of Magic gleamed against the twilight. It was nestled into the southern face of Mythroor, the largest of the Taran Mountains, having been enchanted into existence from the stones of the mountains by magicians who knew nothing about architecture but wanted something impressive and grand. Inglenook *was* impressive, in a confusing sort of way: a huge pile of columns and turrets and towers and—unaccountably—a drawbridge (there was no moat); your eyes slid all over the school as if trying to work out an optical illusion.

Smoke puffed out of the turret above the banquet hall, where the windows glowed golden. Autumn wondered what sort of feast the magicians within were sitting down to— cabbage rolls and roast duck? Bacon and sweet potato pie? She shivered in the October air, her stomach knotting with a hunger that wasn't entirely for food.

Autumn had grown up in the shadow of Inglenook, in the little beastkeepers' cottage at the edge of the grounds. She knew it was silly to long for something she could never have— for a place at that banquet table, to be among those students as they swept from class to class in their long cloaks. She wasn't a magician. She was a servant, same as the rest of her family. She could gaze into the world of Inglenook, like gazing into a pond full of colorful fish, but she would never be part of it.

Autumn and Jack led Amfidzel into Inglenook's menagerie,

a large stone paddock with a floor heated by an underground spring. The flagstones had been soaked in seawater, which had a soothing effect on monsters—for the same reason that the sea had a soothing effect on people, Gran thought, but nobody really knew for sure.

Autumn put Amfidzel in her stall, which was roomy and lined with floral tapestries that the dragon had selected herself. The stall was next to the griffin and across from the wyverns, who were already asleep. Not all the school's monsters were housed in the menagerie—there were some that were simply too dangerous.

One in particular.

"Here you go," Autumn said, tipping vegetable scraps into Amfidzel's trough. "Gran will be in later to say good night."

"I guess I'll round up the wisps," Jack said sadly. Rounding up the wisps usually involved hitting the pesky things with a stick to stun them, then shoving them into a sack. Jack hated it.

Autumn sighed. Though Jack was her favorite older brother, he was unquestionably the worst beastkeeper. She should have asked Kyffin or even Emys for help—despite being the world's biggest pests, they could at least be counted on not to waste time coddling things that would sooner bite your arm off than thank you. Autumn often wondered what she had done to deserve the curse of three older brothers and not one sister, but then Gran often said that everyone had their burdens to bear in life.

I'm your brother too, Winter had always said whenever she complained.

You're all right, Autumn would respond. *You're younger. Younger brothers are okay.*

Ten minutes younger, he'd snort.

A person can gain a lot of wisdom in ten minutes.

Mud pies, too. A person can get a lot of those in ten minutes. And he'd scoop up a handful of mud and send it whizzing past her head as she ran away laughing.

At the other end of the menagerie, one of the Hounds of Arawn stirred in her stall, crooning hungrily as she tasted Autumn's sadness. Autumn forced her thoughts of Winter away. It was dangerous to be sad among monsters.

"I'll find the wisps," she told Jack. "You go help Emys with supper. It's his turn, and I'd rather not eat burned potatoes again."

Jack's face lit. He wrapped her in one of his warm hugs and kissed her cheek.

"Yuck," Autumn grumbled. "Go away."

Jack grinned and ran off in the direction of the cottage.

Autumn ghosted into the twilight. She could move as quietly as a pooka and as quickly as a crested dragon when she wanted to.

Part monster yourself, Gran had once told her proudly. *The best beastkeepers usually are.*

The wind was silken against her cheeks, still woven with a trace of summer. Autumn ran to the dark side of the mountain, which stretched its long shadow over the treetops. She found the wisps hovering at the edge of the forest, framed against the black boughs.

The forest that clothed the slopes below Inglenook was part of the Gentlewood, the great forest that surrounded the Kingdom of Eryree on two sides. Every year, the Gentlewood crept deeper and deeper into Eryree, no matter how often the king's soldiers burned it back. All forests got bigger if left to their own devices, but the Gentlewood's growth was fed by the magic of the creatures that made their homes there. The part that touched Inglenook's grounds was a long finger extending off the main sweep of the forest, less dangerous, but still home to a variety of monsters.

From a distance, the wisps looked like little orbs, but close up you could sometimes make out a hint of a grinning face or the flicker of wings. Autumn crept up behind them and pounced, walloping two with a stick and trapping them in her sackcloth net.

Cloud-headed dunce! one of the wisps shrieked at her. *I'll bite your toes off!*

Autumn swung her stick, which connected with a nice *ping*. The wisp went down.

The remaining wisps swarmed, hollering insults and threats. It was the only speech they were capable of—even in a good mood, all they did was jabber at each other. Wisps liked to lure travelers astray in the wilderness by mimicking the distant glow of a cozy hearth, but otherwise they weren't particularly dangerous—just annoying.

Cauliflower hair!

I'll poke your eye out, you duck-footed lummox!

One of the wisps got itself tangled in Autumn's hair, while another flew up the back of her cloak. After dancing about for a moment, giggling uncontrollably, she dropped to the ground and rolled. The wisp up her cloak let out a soft *merp* and stopped squirming, and she stuffed it into the net with the others. It felt like cupping dandelion seeds.

A peal of laughter rang through the shadows. Autumn froze.

Charging out of the forest, cloaks streaming behind them, were two boys. As they neared, Autumn saw that one of the boys was Gawain Gruffid, best friend of Cai Morrigan, the most famous magician in the kingdom. Cai was only twelve, like Autumn, but he was prophesied to one day slay the Hollow Dragon, the deadliest monster in the world. Cai had fought and killed a pooka when he was only ten years old—no one knew exactly how; each story was wilder than the last.

The other boy was Cai Morrigan himself.

Cai paused in the forest's shadow, gazing into the trees. His face in the moonlight was alive with longing.

Who looks at the Gentlewood like that? Autumn thought, neck prickling.

Cai backed away from the trees slowly, as if fighting a retreating wave. Gawain called him, and Cai ran to catch up.

Autumn started and shrank back, hoping to fade into the twilight. But there wasn't anything to hide behind, and the wisps glowed faintly through the sackcloth. The boys came to a halt.

"Who's there?" Cai called, trying to peer into her shadowed hood.

Autumn's heart thudded. She knew exactly who Cai Morrigan was—everybody in Eryree did—but she'd never been so close to him. She was suddenly very aware of her mud-stained cloak, her disheveled hair with a wisp tangled in it, and her handed-down work boots, which had a hole in the left toe.

Cai and Gawain, on the other hand, were resplendent in Inglenook cloaks that might have been cut from the twilight, glossy black with lavender trim. Gawain's tie was askew, and Cai's plaid scarf dragged in the grass, but otherwise they were the picture of two dashing magicians, who, once grown, would be treated as royalty wherever they went. Magicians were the protectors of Eryree, the only ones who could stop the advance of the Gentlewood and its monsters. Only the king and queen were more beloved.

Autumn realized she was staring at Cai and bowed deeply. "Sir" was all she could get out.

"It's just a beastkeeper," Gawain said, in the same way you'd say *It's just a mouse.*

Cai seemed relieved. Given how famous he was, he wasn't much to look at, with a lot of messy black hair that often hid his eyes and a delicate, heron-like frame. His light brown skin was covered in freckles that made him look younger than twelve. But his voice had a mellow, musical quality that somewhat made up for his unimpressive appearance.

Cai squinted at Autumn, taking in her white hair and gangly legs, the only parts of her that showed around her cloak. "You're Winter Malog, right? Could you pretend you didn't see us? We're not supposed to be out after dark."

Autumn stared. Every thought flew out of her head, and it wasn't because the famous Cai Morrigan had asked her for help.

"That's not Winter," Gawain said. He had pale skin and beautiful dark curls that fell to his chin, while his gaze had a cool, hooded quality shared by all the wealthier students at Inglenook. "Winter's the dead one. That's his twin sister—I don't know her name."

Cai reddened. Autumn felt as if she'd swallowed something cold and slimy.

"You didn't see us," Gawain said to Autumn. "Got it?"

Autumn bowed her head. To her horror, her lip was shaking. She was not going to cry in front of Gawain. She was *not*.

Gawain stepped closer. "I said, *got it?*"

Autumn forced herself to breathe, forced herself to murmur, "Yes, sir."

"That wasn't so hard." Gawain turned to Cai. "I wish Inglenook would train its servants properly. Come on."

Cai's cheeks were flaming. He murmured something that might have been an apology, and then he was racing up the mountain after Gawain. He looked once over his shoulder, but Autumn didn't see. She was already gone, fleeing across the mountainside with her heart in her throat and furious tears stinging her eyes.

2

In Which Autumn
Takes the Boggart for a Walk

Autumn had lived beside the Gentlewood for so long that she sometimes forgot it was full of monsters. Monsters of all shapes and sizes, and some with *several* shapes and sizes, or none. Not all the Gentlewood's monsters ate children—some ate sadness or fear; others had a taste for souls or hearts or toenails, especially when accompanied by a lot of screaming. But a few monsters had decidedly unmonstrous diets. Dragons ate berries, apples ripe from the tree, and vegetables they grew in their gardens. Amfidzel was particularly fond of her carrots, which grew fat and luxuriously orange, and would devour them, greens and all, with much gnashing and snorting only once they had reached—in her expert opinion—the perfect ripeness.

The morning after Autumn's disastrous encounter with Cai Morrigan, the entire school was buzzing with the rumor that he had snuck into the forest and fought the Hollow Dragon.

"He's all torn up, they say," Ceredwen said, her green eyes wide. Like her parents, Ceredwen was a housekeeper and heard all the best gossip. "Got a scar from here"—she touched her navel—"to *here*." She tapped her forehead.

Autumn hadn't seen any evidence of terrible wounds last night, but she wasn't about to tell Ceredwen that. "What was he doing wandering into the forest and getting himself cut in half?" she said crossly.

She was in one of the spare paddocks with Gran and the others, replacing rotten fence posts. The paddock lay at the foot of Mythroor, where the shade lingered most of the day, stubborn and clammy, a match for Autumn's mood.

"Dunno," Ceredwen said, chewing on one of her blond braids. Ceredwen's hair was long and luscious, despite how she was always gnawing on it. "Maybe he wanted to fulfill the prophecy."

"I'd like to see that." The idea of the skinny, red-faced boy she'd met last night lasting five seconds against the Hollow Dragon was laughable. The Hollow Dragon had burned whole villages to the ground and destroyed half the king's army in a single afternoon. He'd killed ten different magicians and countless knights who'd tried to defeat him. He was the most fearsome monster anyone in Eryree had ever known. And Cai Morrigan was going to stop him?

Autumn snorted.

Her feelings toward Cai hadn't warmed overnight. Even if

it was Gawain who'd been horrible, all Cai had done was stand there like a dolt. And that was the boy the masters at Inglenook doted on, the boy who would never have to work for anything in his life! All because some seer had made a prophecy about him back when he was a drooly baby. Autumn slammed her hammer into the fence post with another snort.

"Do you have a cold?" Ceredwen asked.

"Does your ma know you're down here, Ceri?" Gran said, squelching up behind them. Gran was stout and broad-shouldered, her hair black but for a big white stripe down the side. She was large enough to wrestle a wyvern into submission, and had more than once, and her clothes were so often caked in mud they had turned brownish, while her boots were steel-toed and went up to the thigh. With her beaky nose and fixed glare from squinting into sun and rain and hail, she looked like an old raven who had stalked out of the woods to pick a fight. And as you did with old ravens, most people stayed out of her way.

Ceredwen looked shifty. "I—"

"Didn't think so," Gran said. "You'll catch your death in that sweater. Away with you."

She said it in the same voice she used with the monsters, and it produced a similar effect—Ceredwen went quiet and hurried off, pausing only to give Autumn a wave and put the braid back in her mouth.

"Why don't you ever worry about us catching our deaths,

Gran?" Autumn said, hammering at the post.

"Good grief!" Gran let out a gusty breath. "You think I'd worry myself about having one less munchkin to mind, at my age? Leave it to those parents of yours to run off when you were a babe and get themselves killed by a sea dragon, saddling me with you lot. More work than a wyvern with a toothache, you are, but then your father weren't never nothing but trouble in life, so why should he be any different when he's dead? Ach, child, give over that hammer—you'll put your eye out."

Autumn brushed her hair back from her sweaty brow. "Gran, can I take the boggart hunting? Master Erethor is showing him to the senior apprentices tomorrow, and he'll be more likely to cooperate if he's eaten something."

Gran gave her a sharp look. "That thing fancies you too much, child. You'd be foolish to return the favor."

Autumn sighed. Gran gave her the same warning every other week. There was nothing Gran could do about Autumn's friendship with the boggart, though—nobody could order boggarts around, not even Gran. Whenever she tried to separate them, the boggart just ignored her and followed Autumn around even more out of spite.

"Please, Gran?" Autumn said. "It's not fair that Emys and Kyffin get all the fun jobs. You *never* let me do anything important. Why can't—"

"There's no need to yell."

Autumn sighed again. She heard that a lot, along with *Hush now* and *Pipe down, Autumn*, and, her personal favorite, *Button it*, as if she were an untidy cloak flapping in the wind. She often tried to be quieter, but what was the point? Nobody ever explained it.

"You can go," Gran said. "If you take Emys or Kyffin with you."

Autumn grumbled—quietly.

"What was that?" Gran fixed her with a beaky glare.

"Nothing, Gran."

"Not giving me attitude, are you?"

"No, Gran. Never."

"That's what I thought." Gran drove the post into the mud in two ferocious strokes.

Autumn headed toward her brothers, who were sawing new posts at the other end of the fence, but before they spotted her, she veered left along the ridge. She had no intention of asking for help, particularly from Emys, her eldest and least favorite brother. She had important business in the forest, and she didn't want any brothers getting in the way.

Ever since Winter disappeared nearly a year ago, Autumn's mission had been to work out what had happened to him. Winter would never have given up on her, and she would never give up on him. Never.

She reached the boggart's pen and peeked through a window. The boggart lived in the old beastkeepers' hut, which hadn't been used in a hundred years. It was only one room of crumbling stone, and it wasn't really a pen at all—they just called it that to make the youngest apprentices feel better.

The boggart could leave whenever he liked, though he seldom went far.

Boggarts were the oldest and most powerful monsters in the world, so powerful that nobody knew the extent of their magic. They delighted in this, for they loved above all else to be mysterious. What *was* known was that boggarts could take any shape they liked, from the smallest fly to the wickedest monster—they had no bodies of their own to constrain them. Having no bodies, they were unkillable, as well as impossible to fight; no enchantment known to magicians had ever worked on a boggart. Unusual among monsters, boggarts were homebodies with a bottomless love for company, and would attach themselves to a family whether the family liked it or not. The boggart wasn't really part of the menagerie; he belonged to the Malogs, but especially to Autumn.

The boggart rose from a patch of sunlight, stretching. He wore one of his favorite shapes, a resplendently plump black cat.

Where have you been? I haven't seen you in— He stopped. The boggart had a terrible sense of time. *Ages. Ages and ages.*

"It was yesterday," Autumn said. She didn't have to use the Speech with the boggart, as boggarts spent so much time around people that they learned their languages—not that they always listened. "I have to go into the forest again. Do you want to come?"

Okay. The boggart minced over to the window. The floor of the hut was strewn with coins and trinkets—boggarts hoarded anything shiny. *But your brother's heading this way. The worst one.*

Autumn groaned. Sure enough, there came Emys, striding down the leaf-painted mountain. Bounding alongside him was their dog, Choo, also known as the least magical dog in the world. Choo was named for his habit of sneezing whenever there was a monster near, but also sometimes when there wasn't, which was bad for the nerves. He was large and yellow and fluffy, and his good looks had blessed him with a sense of entitlement to affection from the world at large. This was handy in a dog who spent most of his time around monsters. Choo was fearless—not because he was brave, but because he had no enemies to be brave about.

Autumn rubbed his ears, and Choo gazed at her with his eternally blissful expression.

"Where do you think you're going with that thing?" Emys demanded, his long, narrow face red from the cold. "Gran said—"

"Gran said I could take the boggart for a walk," Autumn said. Choo sneezed all over the boggart, who responded with a hiss. Choo interpreted this as a request to nuzzle.

"Yes, if I looked after you," Emys said with a dark look. "Come on."

Autumn picked up the boggart and fell into step behind Emys. "Don't you have some important mooning around to do?"

Emys just cast another dark look over his shoulder. He'd fallen for one of the students, a quiet, sullen-faced girl, sixteen like him, and they were always sneaking off together. It would be a scandal if anyone found out, as beastkeepers were among the lower ranks of Inglenook servants.

They slipped beneath the boughs of the forest, and the air went damp and chill. A little path parted the oaks, and they followed it as far as a clearing bright with foxgloves. Two more paths led off the clearing—the Briar Path, laid by magicians long ago, and the Unpath, made by wisps or bogles or worse. The Unpath led deep, deep into the forest, its course so rough and winding that few travelers found their way out again.

Unless they had a guide.

"You can hunt if you like," Autumn told the boggart. "But first, lead me to the creek."

Emys glared. "What are you doing?"

The boggart didn't need to be told twice. He melted into a golden nightingale and flitted through the trees along the Unpath with a lilting song.

"This is about Winter, isn't it?" Emys said. "If you've hatched another harebrained scheme to—"

"I only have one scheme," Autumn said. "And that's finding out what happened to him. You can go back if you like. But the boggart and I aren't going with you."

Emys glowered. It had been several years since he'd shoved Autumn into a mud puddle or dangled her upside down over a dragonpat, but he still had a bit of a bully inside him. And like all bullies, he backed down fast when he came up against someone stronger. Autumn knew he was as scared of the boggart as the students were.

"All right," he said finally. "But Gran's going to hear about this."

"You're my least favorite brother," Autumn said, and they set off after the boggart.

The path wound around a cleft rowan that Autumn didn't remember, which meant the Unpath had changed, as it often did. She soon lost all sense of direction. Emys's hand went to the dagger at his belt, his eyes darting every which way. Choo bounded up and down the path, for he wasn't lost in a dark forest filled with terrifying monsters, but on a happy adventure with two of his favorite people in a place with lots of interesting smells.

The boggart flickered through the trees, and Emys and Autumn followed, making a terrible noise as they crashed through the undergrowth. Being fearful of magicians, monsters didn't often stray into the parts of the forest that encroached on Inglenook's grounds, but that didn't mean they *never* did. She wished Emys wasn't such an oaf.

Autumn was scared. She was scared every time she went into the Gentlewood, but it was a good kind of scared. She knew she shouldn't, but she loved that old forest. She loved the bluebells that drowned the forest floor, the hovering wisps that set the trees aglow at night. She loved when the morning draped cobwebs of fog over the trees, how the boughs creaked and groaned like a deliciously haunted house.

Autumn's foot stuck in a bit of bogland. She and Emys bickered about which way to go—Emys was for looking for a way around the muck, while Autumn wanted to plow through. In the end, she ignored him and stormed ahead, boots squelching and slurping dreadfully in the ooze. On the other side of the bog, they found a perfectly dry pathway of raised ground only a few yards away.

"Good grief," Emys said, flicking mud from his cloak. "You have to do everything in the loudest, most obnoxious way possible, don't you? No wonder that boggart takes such a shine to you."

"You're one to talk about loud. Like a dragon trying to walk on its hind legs, you are."

They came to a cluster of hills where the forest thinned, filled with little clearings crowded with rosebay. Autumn and Emys wove their way between crumbling walls shrouded in moss. Her heart quickened, and even Emys trod more carefully. This had once been the village of Beddle, abandoned a century ago after a dragon attack. Every year, at least one of Eryree's villages was swallowed by the great forest as it continued its steady southward advance. Things had gotten worse, far worse, over the past two decades, since the Hollow Dragon had come down from the north.

A few more minutes brought them to the creek. It wound through a lacework of ferns and ivy, dark and quiet, as if it, too, was fearful of discovery.

Can I hunt now? the boggart asked. Boggarts didn't die without food, but they grew sluggish and more bad-tempered than usual.

Yes, Autumn said. *Eat and come back quickly.*

Don't worry, the boggart said. *There's nobody near, man or beast.* He alighted on the ground and became a griffin with a lashing tail and a mane like a waterfall. Emys smothered a yelp, and the griffin snorted with pleasure and charged into the underbrush with an eerie grace and barely a rustle of leaves. Choo charged after him and was delighted when the boggart vanished like smoke, for didn't such surprises make every game more fun? He trotted back to Autumn and accepted the ear rubs that were his due.

"What exactly are you hoping to find?" Emys asked.

"I'm not *hoping.* I'm investigating."

When Winter disappeared, everyone had assumed it was the Hollow Dragon's doing. They'd found one of Winter's boots in the Gentlewood, burned black and still smoking. It wasn't the first time the Hollow Dragon had taken a child from Inglenook. The magicians all shook their heads—it was too bad about the boy, they said, but beastkeepers died all the time; dangerous line of work, very dangerous—and carried on with things. Even Gran had believed it.

But Autumn never would.

Ever since Autumn could remember, she and Winter had

been able to sense one another. It was as if she carried around a map in her head that showed Winter as a little glowing dot. If someone asked where he was, she had only to open the map inside her, and she would know. When he vanished, the dot hadn't disappeared. The map had, leaving the dot behind. Winter was still there, still *somewhere*, but for some reason, Autumn couldn't find him.

Nobody believed her, and she couldn't really blame them. It sounded far-fetched even to her. So, rather than trying to convince anyone, she set about gathering evidence.

First, she went to the place where the magicians had found the boot and examined the scorches on the forest floor. The Hollow Dragon was surprisingly dainty when it came to fire-breathing—only a patch of grass had been burned. But did that mean anything? She didn't know.

So Autumn started asking the trees.

The Gentlewood was ancient—it had existed before Eryree was Eryree, before the Southern Realms were the Southern Realms. And some of its trees weren't trees at all, but monsters that had fallen asleep in its deep shade, and dreamed there still. Autumn had first woken a misshapen alder that had once been a dragon. It had taken her weeks to do it, visiting whenever she could escape Gran's notice and shouting into the dragon's mind until the bark that had grown over its skin twitched and trembled. While the beast didn't remember much, it was sure it had smelled a solitary boy heading toward the creek on the day Winter vanished.

And so Autumn had gone to the creek, and there she had found a monster that looked like a log but was in fact an ancient ogre beneath a blanket of moss. The ogre hadn't been happy about being disturbed, and if the boggart hadn't been with Autumn, she might have been in real danger. But after much grumbling, the ogre said she remembered seeing a white-haired boy pass that way, and possibly a dragon too. They had been traveling north, along the streambank toward the Gentlewood proper. She knew no more than that.

Then, a few months after Winter vanished, one of the masters had made a strange discovery: she had found Winter's other boot.

Inside the school.

It had been lying in one of the disused passageways, Winter's initials etched plain as day into the sole. Had Winter abandoned the boot and marched into the forest in his sock to be abducted by the Hollow Dragon? If so, why hadn't anyone seen him? Had someone found the boot in the forest and brought it inside? Why?

None of it made sense.

Autumn picked her way along the streambank, over rocks slick with algae and melting leaves, Choo at her heels. There weren't many wisps floating about in the moody forest daylight—they usually slept until nightfall. She passed the sleeping ogre and continued north. She hadn't found another monster to awaken, though she'd been looking for weeks.

She paused next to a snag and rested her hand against the rough bark, listening. Listening, and trying not to let the disappointment well inside her—after all, she'd only just started. But each time she had gone looking for Winter, she'd found nothing, and it was hard not to think that this day would turn out just like the others.

She would never give up on him, but each day that passed made the hope she carried a little heavier to bear, with more sharp edges of sadness.

"What *are* you doing?" Emys's hand was still on his dagger.

"I'm listening for a heartbeat."

Emys stared at her, slack-jawed. "In a tree?"

"They aren't all trees. Some were monsters once. You know that—you've heard Gran's stories."

Emys took a rapid step backward, bumped into a tree, and skipped sideways. "Y-yes."

Autumn kept going. A Hound of Arawn howled in the distance, and Autumn tried not to imagine its burning eyes looming out of the shadows. The forest grew darker the deeper you went into the Gentlewood, thick boughs knitting together overhead, but the undergrowth was less, and Autumn and Emys moved swiftly. Autumn wondered how much time she had before Gran got suspicious and came looking for them. Gran didn't need a boggart for protection when she went into the woods—she could command most monsters with a thought.

Choo stopped, his front half low to the ground as he sniffed at a stump. "Choo," Autumn called, but the dog only wagged his tail. "Choo!"

"Keep your voice down," Emys snapped.

Autumn waded through the bluebells and crouched at Choo's side. Something was buried among the roots and fallen leaves—a blanket, maybe, or clothes? She had walked past this spot a dozen times, yet had never noticed it.

Choo whined. Autumn reached under the roots, pushing through red toadstools that released a sweet-smelling mist as they broke, and hooked her fingers around the cloth.

It was bigger than she had guessed, buried under a layer of old forest, and came loose with a shower of leaves. It was soil-stained and smelled of mold and mushrooms.

"Autumn?" Emys called.

Autumn didn't answer. She fumbled for the collar, even though she knew what she held, knew before she laid eyes on the clumsily stitched *W.M.*

It was Winter's cloak.

3

In Which Cai Morrigan Needs a Favor

Autumn wanted to go straight home to examine the cloak, which she'd hastily stuffed into her pack, but a servant caught up with her and Emys at the forest's edge and told her she was wanted by one of the masters. The servant kept staring, and Autumn realized she was covered in mud. She couldn't bring herself to care.

Questions swarmed her as she followed the winding mountain path. How had the cloak ended up so deep in the forest? Why wasn't it charred like the boot?

The crag where the junior apprentices trained was high above Inglenook, a flat-topped bluff only reachable by a rubbly stairway. From there you could see the dark stain of the Gentlewood going all the way to the northern horizon, the wave-creased sea to the west, and the Twyllaghast Mountains to the east, rocky and trailing mist.

About fifty junior apprentices huddled on the windy mountainside, ranging in age from eight to fourteen or so. Their staffs gave the bluff a pretty glow—at each tip was a small crystal filled with light, for all light was magic, gathered and transformed into enchantments by a mysterious alchemy not even magicians entirely understood. There was star magic, sun magic, fire magic, and moon magic. From what Autumn understood (which was very little), all magicians could cast the same spells, no matter what kind of magician they were, though some spells came off better if cast by a sun magician or a moon magician and so on. Gran had once said that magicians were like musicians, who could play any song they wished, but some songs were written for fiddles and others for harps or drums, and it was harder to play music that wasn't meant for you.

Master Connor waved Autumn aside. The students were practicing enchantments on the menagerie's troop of brownies, small monsters covered in hair who looked like wizened old men. Some brownies were simple household creatures that liked cleaning and cooking, and snuck out of hidey-holes at night to wash dishes and such, but others were troublesome. They had a rudimentary magic that allowed them to leap great distances by summoning wind, and the students had to summon their own wind to oppose it. Autumn's job was to intervene whenever a student looked likely to be hurt, and she soon had her hands full.

"Careful, miss," she called to a little girl waving her staff haphazardly. A brownie snuck up behind her and bit her ankle.

Let go, you, Autumn ordered. The brownie yipped and ran off, but the girl had already burst into tears. Her enchantment shattered, and a glitter of sunlight fell to the grass like rain.

"You're wasting magic, child," Master Connor said. The girl cried harder. Autumn supposed the master had to be strict, though she knew sunlight was the easiest magic to replenish; even on rainy days a little leaked through the clouds.

Normally, Autumn was good at handling brownies—if you could grab them by the scruff of the neck, they went limp as kittens. But she was distracted, and by the end of the lesson, her hands were scratched and bleeding.

After the students had gone, Master Connor lectured Autumn for her inattentiveness. The brownies had gotten into her books and scattered pages across the mountainside, and Master Connor made Autumn clean up the mess, though it wasn't her job. Autumn mumbled her apologies and kept her expression dull. She'd found that to be the best approach—if the masters thought you were a half-wit, they let you off easier. They never seemed to need much convincing on that score.

The sun sank behind the mountains as Autumn chased scraps of paper here and there. The wind had a mean streak that evening, and no sooner had she closed in on her quarry than it drifted off to a precarious ledge or gorse thicket. Soon she was sweating and cranky.

The moon rose in the violet sky. A handful of magicians wandered out across the lawn in front of the school, gathering moonlight.

Autumn paused. It was a little like watching someone swirl a broom through a nest of cobwebs. The moonlight brightened briefly as it drifted into the magicians' staffs. Sometimes, they reached down and scooped it by the handful.

Autumn wondered what it felt like to touch light. She often tried to imagine it. With its silvery hue, she thought moonlight would be cold and a little slippery, like fish. Starlight had the gentle creaminess of bone, and that's how it would feel—smooth and ghostly. Sunlight and firelight would be warm, of course, but firelight would crackle and snap in your hands, whereas golden sunlight would have the sticky ooze of honey.

Autumn's fingers tingled. She made herself turn away from the magicians.

When she had gathered up all the pages she could find, she raced back down to the castle and left them in Master Connor's office. Then she entered the river of students heading down the grand staircase toward the banquet hall and dinner. The fastest way back to the cottage was to cut across the third landing to the passageway that led to the servants' entrance.

A ripple passed through the crowd. Autumn could guess what it meant, and sure enough, there was Cai Morrigan, making his way down the stairs. He was walking with a dark-haired girl Autumn didn't know, except as one of his sidekicks. He never seemed to notice the stares and whispers that followed in his wake, or how the younger students leaped out of his way as if he were the king himself. One girl tripped in her haste, and Cai paused to help her up. Her friends stared at her in awe.

Autumn glared at the side of Cai's face. Head down, she wove through the crowd, jostled and elbowed at every step. A few magicians looked at her askance, but for the most part, they ignored her.

"Autumn?" a voice said. "Autumn Malog?"

Autumn turned, expecting a servant. Instead, she found herself face-to-face with Cai.

The other students swirled around him, cloaks trailing like fins. Cai was halfway down the stairs, looking up at her, but when he turned and made his way back upstream, the students parted to make way for him.

Autumn's face heated. Normally, nobody ever noticed the servants, unless they did something wrong. Now here was a magician—and not just any magician, but *Cai Morrigan*, future savior of Eryree—staring right at her with a slight smile on his face. Autumn felt an urge to run away.

"Are you all right?" Cai asked.

Autumn blinked. "What?" She added quickly, "Sir."

He gestured. "Your hands."

"Oh! I—I had some bad luck with the brownies."

Cai nodded. "I remember. The juniors have to trap them, don't they?"

Cai was already a senior apprentice, which was unheard of for someone so young. Most magicians didn't graduate from junior to senior until they were at least fourteen, and some never managed it at all if their magic was weak.

"Are *you* all right?" Autumn said, looking him over curiously. She could see no evidence that he had recently fought the worst monster in the kingdom. On the contrary, he looked healthy and rested, his cloak spotless and his dark hair at least partly combed. His eyes were the crisp brown of pinecones. Autumn was suddenly and acutely aware of the twigs tangled in her hair.

"Yes," Cai said in a voice that had a question in it.

"I heard you fought the Hollow Dragon last night," Autumn said. "Um, sir. People are saying he nearly killed you, and that you have a scar from here to here." She pointed.

He smiled faintly. "People say all sorts of things."

That wasn't an explanation, but Autumn didn't see what she could do about it, so she just stood there, waiting.

"Listen," he said, "I'm sorry about Gawain. He shouldn't have said that about your brother."

Autumn faltered. She was surprised Cai hadn't already forgotten he'd seen her last night, what with all the heroism he'd been up to. "That's all right."

"No, it isn't," Cai said firmly. "I know you probably don't want to have anything to do with me, but is there a chance we could talk? I have a favor to ask."

Autumn stared. The idea of Cai Morrigan asking her for a favor made as much sense as the headmaster asking for one from Choo.

Unless.

She thought of Gawain. He was cruel, and maybe Cai was no different—maybe this was all part of some prank. The students pranked the servants sometimes, especially the cooks, sneaking into the kitchens late at night to eat all the pudding and replace it with river mud, for instance.

"What sort of favor?"

He smiled as if she'd said yes. "Meet me at the ghost tree tomorrow after class. I won't keep you long, promise."

Autumn tried to arrange her scattered thoughts. But Cai just gave her another of his absentminded smiles and melted back into the river of magicians.

4

In Which Autumn
Doesn't See Herself in the Mirror

The next morning, Autumn was half convinced her conversation with Cai had been a dream. What could Eryree's most famous magician have to say to her?

She gazed up at the ceiling. It was sloped, because her bedroom was in the attic, her bed tucked into the corner. If she rolled too far to the left, she banged her nose against the roof. Winter's bed was opposite hers, the blankets neatly folded and clean, for she took them outside for freshening every week. Autumn hadn't let Gran take the bed away, though Gran had suggested, in a quiet tone quite unlike her usual manner, that Autumn could replace it with a wardrobe all her own.

Autumn didn't look at Winter's bed, with its cold blankets and smooth pillow. The hardest times, she found, were going to sleep and waking up. During the day, she could distract herself from missing him with chores or her schemes in the forest.

But if she woke in the night, or lay there in the quiet of early morning, it was just her and the empty bed.

She rose and pulled on her clothes, gazing at herself in the old mirror, which was scuffed and stained, like her. She wore the blue-gray tunic and trousers that were standard issue for Inglenook's servants. These were presentable enough, with a minimum of grass stains, but her cloak was a mess. It had looked nice once—Inglenook was generous with its servants, and everyone who worked out of doors received a cloak woven with a simple spell to ward off cold, which gave the soft gray wool a telltale shimmer of enchantment. But a beastkeeper's cloak was impossible to keep clean, and the shimmer was dulled by a layer of grime and small tears. One of the top buttons was missing, so Autumn had to fasten it unevenly to keep out the cold. Her white hair, long enough to tuck behind her ears but not long enough to tie back, was unevenly cut.

No, of course Cai would have nothing to say to the likes of her. His friends had probably been watching on the stairs, laughing into their hands. If she went to the ghost tree tonight, Cai wouldn't be there, and they'd laugh harder.

It was Jack's turn to cook breakfast, thankfully, and the cottage was filled with the smell of baked eggs and cockles and buttered toast. It was also filled with the smell of brothers, but Autumn was used to that. She elbowed her way up to the table between Kyffin and Emys. Kyffin smiled at her and ruffled her hair as he always did. Kyffin was fifteen and almost as handsome as he thought he was. They usually ignored each other, though only Autumn did so on purpose.

Autumn kicked Jack under the table. She needed to tell *someone* about Winter's cloak. But Jack's dreamy expression didn't change.

She kicked him again. Jack gazed at her with a look of wounded puzzlement, and then he sighed and passed her the toast. "You could *ask*."

Autumn gritted her teeth. Winter would have known right away what she meant. She wouldn't have had to kick him—he would have read her face and understood.

"You," Gran said, giving Autumn a look that pierced her right through and pinned her to the chair. "You're with me today. The gwarthegs need deworming."

Autumn's jaw dropped in outrage. What had she done to deserve the worst chore of them all, a chore Gran reserved only for grandchildren she wished to punish? Then, of course, she remembered that she'd done a great deal, such as disobeying Gran and sneaking into the Gentlewood with the boggart. She shot Emys a poisonous look, but he was too busy scooping cockles onto his toast with the single-minded focus of a starving wolf.

Autumn sighed. There was no point even talking to her brothers when they had food in front of them, let alone threatening revenge.

Autumn spent the rest of the morning following Gran

around the gwartheg paddock with a bucket of medicine that resembled green snot. The gwarthegs grazed along the lower slopes of the mountain by the Afon Morrel, a lazy river that wound down from the Blue Mountains and through the Gentlewood. You couldn't see the castle from there, though occasionally the wind carried the scent of woodsmoke.

Gwarthegs looked like enormous black cows. Their eyes were black like the rest of them, with an unpleasant intelligence. They fed on flesh, human when they could get it, and moved with a slithery grace. Their hooves tinkled like gentle bells in a way that made you horribly sleepy—or conveniently sleepy, as the gwarthegs surely saw it.

For Autumn, the morning couldn't be over soon enough. It was her job to shove spoonfuls of the awful green stuff down the gwarthegs' throats, inevitably splashing herself in the process, while Gran spoke soothing commands into their minds. Then the gwartheg would begin to cough and cough, until it coughed up something that resembled an emerald snake— monsters, of course, didn't have the same illnesses as ordinary beasts. Autumn had to catch the worm before it escaped and crush its head with a shovel. Half the time, the wily worms escaped into the Afon Morrel, where the gwarthegs drank, ensuring the continuation of the whole hideous cycle. Most monster-related duties were unpleasant, but it was the futility of this particular chore that made Autumn want to tear her hair out.

"Off with you, then," Gran finally grunted. Autumn didn't need to be told twice. She was so relieved to be rid of the hacking beasts that she almost forgot to care that she was covered in green slime.

"Boo!" A figure leaped onto the path. Autumn shrieked and stumbled backward, but it was only the boggart in his boy shape. He grabbed her before she fell.

"That was too easy," the boggart said, looking disappointed. "What's wrong with you?"

"I'm dead tired, that's what," Autumn groused. "Emys tattled to Gran. I'm in for a week of punishment, at least."

The boggart shook his head. He looked like he was twelve—his boy shape had always been the same age as Autumn—and had large black eyes that reflected the light strangely, black curls, and rosy cheeks. The boggart, being vain, never chose an ugly shape. Like Autumn, he was dressed in servants' robes. Standing still, he might have been mistaken for a servant, but he moved like smoke and his feet left no imprint on the ground. His fingernails were long dark claws no matter what shape he took.

"I wish you didn't have to listen to her," he said. "When we're married, you'll be able to do whatever you want."

Autumn rolled her eyes. The boggart often promised—or threatened, depending on how you looked at it—to marry her when she was grown. She had been only four or five the first time he said it. She had been playing in the Afon Morrel with

Winter and cut her foot on a rock. The boggart had made a bandage out of spiderwebs and promised that when they were married, he would make them a castle of stone smooth as glass, and he would order the rocks in the stream to move out of her way when they saw her coming. Autumn had never agreed to marry the boggart, mainly because she had little sense of what marrying someone meant, though there was a part of her that reasoned that if she had to marry someone when she was grown, why not the boggart, who was her best friend?

She wasn't going to tell him that, of course. She didn't know much about marriage, but she knew you were supposed to *ask* someone to marry you. The boggart, like many monsters, thought too much of himself.

"I'm glad you're up," Autumn said, and she told him about Winter's cloak. She hadn't wanted to say anything in the forest with Emys listening, and after their adventure the boggart had gone right to sleep. Boggarts slept more than cats, sometimes for weeks at a time.

The boggart listened with a frown on his face. "Why didn't the magicians find it? They searched the woods."

"Because they *didn't* search the woods," Autumn said. "Not really. The cloak was barely singed—only a little at the hem."

"Like the boot." The boggart's frown deepened. "Whatever happened to Winter, he wasn't burned to a crisp."

Autumn nodded. The path curved over a knoll matted with heather, and the castle came into view. Just below it was

Ravenbrood Tor, a green spur topped with a flat, weathered stone. One of Master Edelmeet's classes was on the tor right now with Amfidzel, practicing shielding spells. Kyffin stood off to one side, ready to leap into action if Amfidzel grew tired of having light dashed in her face and decided to decorate her antlers with magicians.

"That's not all." Autumn's heart was thundering. "It wasn't the cloak Winter was wearing that day."

"Are you sure?"

Autumn bit her lip. "Mostly." Winter hardly ever wore his newest cloak, which he'd been given on the previous Midwinter Eve, when Inglenook gifted every servant with a new uniform and a bottle of cream liqueur—or a satchel of chocolates, if you were under sixteen. He complained that the fresh glitter of the enchantment made it harder to move stealthily through the Gentlewood, which was true enough, though telling anyone that would mean admitting that he and Autumn played in the Gentlewood.

"So," the boggart said musingly, "someone planted one of Winter's cloaks in the woods and burned it a bit to make it look like the Hollow Dragon took him."

Autumn felt a rush of relief that the boggart had come to the same conclusion she had. "Exactly. And if they planted the cloak—"

"They planted the boot too," he finished.

They gazed at each other for a long moment, taking in the

seriousness of it all. "What do we do now?" the boggart asked.

"I don't know." Autumn's hands tightened into fists. She felt a familiar rush of frustration. What *could* they do? They might have found evidence that Winter hadn't been stolen away by the Hollow Dragon, but Autumn had to admit it was pretty spotty. It also wasn't evidence of where he *had* gone.

"The other boot was in the school," the boggart pointed out.

"In the corridor below the Silver Tower," Autumn said. "But you heard Winter in the kitchens."

The boggart nodded. He thought he'd heard Winter's voice once, calling him. Unfortunately, the boggart hadn't been able to work out where the voice had come from. He'd been napping at the time.

"The Silver Tower, the kitchens." Autumn tapped her foot. "It doesn't make sense. I've searched both places more than once. And *you* searched Inglenook from top to bottom after that second boot was found."

"I searched everywhere I could think of," the boggart said. "The school's old, and there's magic everywhere, layers of spells all tangled and hodgepodge. It gives me a headache. I don't think even the masters know about half of them."

Autumn's head was whirling. "Look again, okay?"

The boggart nodded. He became a hummingbird with a ruby breast and flitted up the mountain.

Autumn followed at a slower pace. Inglenook's ghost tree loomed above her. It was a hawthorn, like all ghost trees, twisted with age and hung with ornaments commemorating important events in Inglenook's history. Most schools didn't have their own ghost tree to connect them to their past or store family memories. A school wasn't a house, after all, but the magicians who founded Inglenook had wanted it to feel like a home, and so they had planted the tree the day the school opened.

The ghost tree made her think of Cai, so she looked away. Normally, the servants' path afforded a view over the combe and the hem of the Gentlewood, but the day was misty, and Autumn saw only outlines.

A sheep baaed at her from the slope above. There was a farmstead on the next mountain, which overlooked the pocket-size village of Lumen Far.

"Baa," the sheep said again, peering expectantly.

Baa, Autumn said into the sheep's mind. She'd tried using the Speech on ordinary beasts before, but most took little notice. Autumn imagined the sound sheep made to greet lost members of their flocks. She couldn't say it, but she could think it. *Baa*.

"Baa," the sheep agreed. It minced along beside her, as if pleased with its new friend. Who really knew a sheep's mind, though? Maybe it just wanted to chew on her sweater.

Autumn was happy to have the sheep with her. She and Winter had done almost everything together, including their chores—Gran had long ago given up on assigning them separate duties—and sometimes it still felt strange to do things by herself. She supposed that it was lonelier to be alone when you were used to being two people than it was when you'd only ever been one.

Baa, she told the sheep, hoping it wouldn't wander off. *Baa. Baa.*

"Baa," it replied contentedly, keeping pace with her along the path.

The farmer appeared in the distance and waved to her. Autumn waved back. She wondered how much longer the farmer would stay in Lumen Far. All the other shepherds had moved south or abandoned their farms after losing their flocks to the monsters of the Gentlewood.

"Hi, Autumn," Ceredwen said as Autumn walked into the servants' foyer. She had a broom in her hand, and her lustrous hair was tucked beneath a bonnet, of which one of the strings appeared suspiciously chewed. "Mrs. Hawes again?"

"Mmm," Autumn said.

Autumn worked for Gran—none of the other servants, not even the steward or the keeper of keys, could order her around. Beastkeepers were looked down upon by everyone, but they also stood apart from the other servants due to the importance of their work. If one of the masters wanted the services of a beastkeeper, they notified Gran directly. However, sometimes when Gran didn't have need of Autumn, or when she just wanted her elsewhere, she told her to report to the head housekeeper. Gran and Mrs. Hawes were friends, and given that Mrs. Hawes occasionally sent her own servants—those with a stout disposition—to clean the Malogs' cottage and weed Gran's garden, Gran reasoned that they should return the favor.

For her part, Autumn was fairly certain that Mrs. Hawes would prefer Gran *didn't* return the favor. Autumn wasn't any good at cleaning up. Gran called her the two-legged whirlwind—good at attacking things, not so good at the finer tasks. One time, Autumn had finished cleaning a chimney only to turn around and find that her boots had tracked mud, leaves, and mouse fur—the remains of the gwarthegs' last meal—all over six different carpets.

Today, though, Autumn had no intention of reporting to Mrs. Hawes.

Autumn motioned Ceredwen closer, lowering her voice. "You didn't see me, okay?"

"When? Yesterday? I'm pretty sure I saw you, Autumn. Didn't I say hello? Are you mad at me?"

Autumn smothered a groan. "No, you didn't see me *today*. You *especially* didn't if Gran comes looking for me. Understand?"

Ceredwen's expression cleared. "Oh! Anything you say, Autumn. Hey, do you want to hear the ballad I've been working on? It's based on something the bards played last month during the harvest banquet. You remember the one with the loyal old horse and the prince who lost his way in the Gray Marshes—"

"Later, okay?" Autumn cut in. If Ceredwen wasn't talking, she was singing. Autumn often marveled that such a small person could contain such a large volume of words.

Autumn hadn't meant to make friends with Ceredwen. Three years ago, Ceredwen had been outside hanging laundry when a thick mist crept up the mountainside. Spying it from the cottage window, Autumn had raced up the path and reached her just in the nick of time, for the mist had sprouted horns and fur. It was a pooka, rolling toward Ceredwen with its fanged mouth open like a dustpan ready to scoop her up, and Ceredwen standing there frozen with her eyes buggy and her braid still in her mouth. Autumn had tackled her just in time, yelling into the pooka's mind until it burst into tears and fled down the mountainside. Pookas were great blubberers, though they had nothing on Ceredwen, who had sobbed and clung to Autumn for an hour at least. Autumn had let her because she didn't know what else to do, though her eardrums hadn't thanked her later.

Then, to Autumn's astonishment, Ceredwen had turned to her with a frighteningly earnest look on her tearstained face and stated that her life now belonged to Autumn, and that she, Ceredwen, would remain forever in her debt. It sounded like something out of a ballad, which it probably was. But Ceredwen had made good on her promise dozens of times, keeping Autumn's secrets and lying shamelessly to Gran as needed.

Ceredwen was even working on a ballad about Autumn, which at last count numbered some two hundred verses.

Autumn climbed up the nearest servants' staircase—the school was a warren of staircases and poorly placed corridors. She kept her expression dull, nodding to anyone she passed.

She mounted another staircase, then hurried along a narrow hall lit by a few shivering candlesticks that was used by the housekeepers when they cleaned the magicians' dormitories. Then she climbed another staircase, which led to an empty room with two doors at the back. Inglenook would be a nightmare to map out.

Finally, Autumn found herself in a strange, broad corridor lined with windows overlooking the mountainside. There wasn't much point to them, as they were so close to the slope of the mountain that they saw little light. If you opened one, it would get stuck in the heather.

It was Ceredwen who had told her about this hidden hallway. Ceredwen knew that Autumn was looking for secret rooms and passages, anyplace Winter might have stumbled into and gotten himself trapped by some enchantment. She told Autumn about anything she found or heard from the other housekeepers, who, after all, knew more about secret passageways than anyone in the world.

Autumn had searched a dozen such places over the last year and come up empty-handed. But the cloak had given her new hope.

The problem, of course, was that she didn't know what she

was looking for. What sort of spell could trap a boy for almost a year? Had Winter been turned into a statue? Embroidered into one of the tapestries? Had the spell been a prank gone wrong, or had Winter stumbled into an ancient enchantment?

She couldn't begin to guess.

Autumn spent the rest of the afternoon opening and closing windows, banging on walls, and examining tapestries. She stayed until the shadow of the mountain swallowed the land below. The rainclouds fled south, replaced by lazy white tufts that threw spears of sunlight onto the fields.

Her disappointment grew. It grew so big she could feel it weighing her down like wet wool. She didn't normally get this upset when her investigations brought her to a dead end. It was because of Winter's cloak—she'd been so full of hope when she found it. But beneath the hope, there had been fear.

Because despite what she'd said to the boggart, despite all her theories, her discovery of the cloak in the forest had another, simpler explanation: that Winter had been taken by the Hollow Dragon, like everybody said he had.

Am I wrong?

It was a little voice that said it, buried deep inside her. She didn't normally listen—mostly, she pretended it didn't exist. But now she heard it clearly.

Dizziness washed over her. For a moment, she couldn't sense the little glowing dot that was Winter. But that was only because she was upset—not because the little dot had never been there to begin with.

Wasn't it?

A tear slid down her face and she yanked on one of the tapestries, cursing. The tapestry didn't deserve it, but she couldn't stop herself. When it wouldn't come loose, she kicked it. There was a pressure building behind her eyes, and she knew more tears were about to burst out—they were the bursting kind, not the sniffly type. Something like terror rose inside her like a towering wave.

Autumn?

She whirled.

At the end of the corridor was a bay window overlooking the deep valley between Mythroor and its neighbor, Mynfarn. The darkness made the glass reflective. Autumn's own face stared back at her—her face, with one difference.

The lips were moving.

Autumn's legs wobbled. "Winter!" she croaked.

She raced to the window. She didn't think about the logic of it, what Winter could be doing staring out of a window. The only thing that mattered was that he was *there*.

She ran her hand over the window—all she felt was smooth glass. Winter wasn't standing on the other side—the space there was empty, as was the mountainside below. Somehow, he was *inside* the window.

He gazed back at her. He didn't look upset, or even surprised. He looked *lost*.

"Winter!" Autumn struck the glass with her fists. "Winter!"

Winter's mouth moved again, but Autumn couldn't hear him.

Use the Speech! she shouted. That's how she had heard him before. Winter looked back, as if someone had tapped him on the shoulder.

"Winter!" she sobbed. "Where are you? What's happening?"

Someone *had* put a spell on him—just like she'd thought! But what terrible magic could trap a boy in glass? Winter looked back at her, and then he seemed to take a step away—impossibly, for the window was barely an inch thick.

Then he was gone.

Autumn's own reflection returned—an infinitesimal change; even Gran used to get them mixed up sometimes. Her reflection's hands, though, were pressed to the glass.

"Winter?" Autumn was shaking to her bones. She ran from window to window, tripping over her feet, shouting his name. But there was only shadow and windswept grass.

She went back to the bay window, hands clenched tight. One of the stones in the seat was loose—she wrenched it off, then hurled it at the glass. A spiderweb of cracks formed. The evening wind whistled through, brushing the hair from her forehead. She didn't realize she was speaking at first, a hoarse, murmured chant like the wind outside.

"I'll find you," she said. "I'll find you. I'll find you."

5

In Which a Magician
Comes to Dinner

Autumn dashed home through the gathering dark. Foxes and other small creatures fled before her, for she wasn't careful about avoiding their burrows as she usually was but ran heedless through the night.

A fire burned inside her. She had been right! Winter *was* trapped in the castle. She'd waited by the bay window until she could wait no longer, but he hadn't come back.

She would go back to the window at first light. Or should she sneak into the kitchens? That was where the boggart had heard Winter's voice. Had he been in a different window then? Should she search *all* the windows in Inglenook? What sort of enchantment had done this to him? And how was she to get him out? She would ask the boggart—yes, surely the boggart would have some ideas, despite his dislike of magicians and their magic.

Her thoughts wheeled like birds in a tempest.

She leaped down the mountainside, past Amfidzel's garden and the overgrown remnants of the old beastkeepers' hut. She hopped over the familiar stream and slapped her way through the familiar gorse to emerge behind the cottage, its windows golden and steamed. There she froze in midstep, her breath billowing around her.

Standing by the cottage was Cai Morrigan.

He was facing the Gentlewood, one hand on his staff. In his eyes was the same longing Autumn had seen in him before. He watched the waving leaves as intently as if something was written there.

He turned as if he'd heard her, though she'd been frozen for several heartbeats. "Hello," he said in his musical voice, smiling. He was such an improbable sight—standing there on the overgrown path in Gran's garden in his lightly shimmering Inglenook cloak—that Autumn couldn't speak. He was one too many impossible things in a day.

"What are *you* doing here?" she finally managed.

Cai blinked. "We were supposed to meet at the ghost tree, remember? I came to see if you were all right."

Autumn's jaw dropped. The idea of Cai Morrigan not only waiting for her, as if *he* was the servant, but coming to *check up on her* was too much. Her face hardened. Without pausing to think through the wisdom of it, she grabbed Cai by the cloak and dragged him away from the windows. Then she shoved him against a tree.

"What are—I didn't mean—" Cai sputtered. He was so

startled that he'd dropped his staff. "Autumn—"

Autumn cut him off, her voice low and fierce. "You listen to me, Cai Morrigan. I don't know what sort of prank you and your friends are planning, but I don't want any part in it, see?"

She kept one hand on his chest, pushing him into the mossy trunk, as she scanned the mountainside for Cai's friends. If she saw Gawain, she would throttle him. She would throttle him, then feed him to the gwarthegs. The shock and terror and delight of finding Winter all bubbled inside her, a tangled mess of feelings that felt like it was doing the thinking for her.

"Autumn?" Cai's voice was oddly hesitant. His eyes, some part of Autumn noticed, were a loamy brown. She could have sworn they'd been the color of pinecones before. "I came here alone. I just want to talk to you, honest."

Cai looked not only stunned but *hurt*, and she realized with a start what she was doing. She couldn't push Cai Morrigan into a tree! He could get Gran fired for that—for *less* than that.

Cheeks burning, she stepped back and dropped into a hasty bow.

"I'm so sorry, sir," she mumbled at the ground. "I thought . . . You showing up, out of the blue . . ."

He made a face. "Don't call me that." He frowned. "You thought I came to play a trick on you?"

"Lots of students play tricks on the servants."

"*I* don't," he said, in a voice that made Autumn think she'd offended him, though she couldn't imagine how. He rubbed the back of his head ruefully. The shimmer of his cloak—a much deeper shimmer than Autumn's, due to layers of spells built into the weave—had been creased by Autumn's grip. "You're strong."

Autumn cast around for something humble to say. "Well, compared to you."

She could have kicked herself. But Cai just smiled.

"Look," he said, his face growing serious. "I wanted to talk to you because . . . well, you're clearly a good beastkeeper. Better than your brothers. I saw you handling that snowy dragon the other day."

Autumn gazed at him blankly. "Amfidzel? She's just a baby. Anyone could handle her."

Cai's mouth twisted. "I couldn't."

Autumn was about to snort, but then Cai let out a soft breath and held out his hands. "See that?" he said, disgust in his voice. "Just *talking* about her is enough."

Autumn didn't understand until she realized that Cai's hands were trembling.

"You're—you're afraid of Amfidzel?" Surely it was a joke. Some sort of odd magician's joke that she couldn't understand any more than she understood their spells.

"I'm afraid of all of them." Cai shoved his hands into his pockets. "Every dragon in that forest. I can't get within ten paces of them without embarrassing myself."

"But—" Autumn was lost for words. "But how do you do your lessons?"

"Most lessons are theory, learning how to draw on our

powers without unbalancing the realms," Cai said. "I have permission to skip the ones with dragons. The headmaster knows the truth. So does Gawain. He started a rumor that my magic is so strong that I lose control of it sometimes, and the masters are afraid I'll kill one of their monsters. The other students believe it."

They would, Autumn thought. She would have believed it herself—the real reason wouldn't have even occurred to her. Cai Morrigan, afraid of dragons? Not just afraid, but so afraid that he couldn't be in the same room as a silly baby like Amfidzel?

"But you go into the Gentlewood," she argued. "I saw you the other night."

"I'm not afraid of the forest," he said.

"That doesn't make any sense."

"I *know*." He sounded tired. "I know. Will you help me?"

"Help you?" Autumn repeated. "How am I supposed to do that?"

"Teach me how not to be afraid," he said. "Teach me how to be like you."

All the wind went out of her. In a moment, she would fall to the ground like a popped balloon. Cai Morrigan wanted to be like her? Now she knew he wasn't joking—he was mad.

Into the deafening silence, Cai went on. "I think that if I could get *used* to being around dragons, I'll get better. That's how you're supposed to get over a fear, right? You could show me the dragons in the menagerie. Tell me what they're like, how they think. All we learn in school is how to fight them."

"I'm not a teacher," Autumn said slowly. "I'm just a beast-keeper."

"That doesn't mean you can't help me." Cai gazed at her. "Master Bellows once said that the boggart follows you around like a pet."

Autumn let out a sharp laugh. The boggart, a pet? The boggart had once led a troupe of bards straight into a dragon's garden for singing out of tune. He'd shoved one of Autumn's ancestors into an oven for raising a hand to his wife, the boggart's favorite at the time. A boggart made a fine companion if he liked you; if he didn't like you, he'd be the cause of your untimely and probably painful death and laugh about it afterward.

"The boggart isn't anyone's pet," she said. "We're friends."

Cai shook his head. "Friends."

Autumn remained suspicious, but she hid it behind the dull mask all servants perfected. "I'm not a teacher. You wouldn't learn anything from me."

Cai's face fell. Had she hurt his feelings? Autumn wasn't used to thinking of Cai as someone with feelings. He was like a constellation, distant and remote, not a *person*.

But what did it matter, anyway? She didn't want anything to do with Cai or his world. She'd just found Winter—he was alive somewhere, waiting for rescue. All she wanted was to go get the boggart, and together they could rack their brains.

She bent awkwardly to retrieve Cai's staff. It was warm

against her skin, but perhaps that was just where Cai had been holding it. The crystal at the end was filled with starlight, for Cai was a star magician—the rarest kind, naturally. The kind Autumn would choose to be if she had a choice, which nobody did, least of all her. People said star magicians were more powerful than the rest, because the magic from stars had to be stronger to cross such great distances. Autumn, of course, had no idea whether that was true—what she knew about magic could fill a thimble. But she did know that *all* magicians were rare, and almost all were born to magician parents. They were often called the Minor Nobility, for having magic in your family's veins was almost as good as having royal blood. It also made you rich, for the king and queen paid their magicians handsomely and gifted them with land. The most celebrated magicians, those who had slain terrible beasts or hewn paths through the Gentlewood, had huge estates on the sunny southern coast of Eryree near the capital of Langorelle.

Autumn brushed the crystal with her fingertips, unable to help herself. Its light was cool and silvery, and left traces on her skin like potter's glaze.

The back door of the cottage creaked open. "Why are you lurking out there in the cabbages, child? Dinner's on the table." Gran's voice faltered. "I see you've made a friend."

"Um, this is—" Autumn stopped. She was struck by an absurd but unshakable certainty that Gran wouldn't believe her if she said Cai's name, though he was standing right there—that she would laugh and tell Autumn to stop making up stories.

Fortunately, Cai had his wits about him. "Hello, Mrs. Malog. I'm Cai Morrigan. Sorry for keeping Autumn."

"Cai who?" Gran snorted at her own joke. Then her expression darkened. "You've missed your own dinner, boy, yakking away with my granddaughter. You'll eat with us." The door slammed behind her.

Cai looked alarmed. Autumn didn't blame him—it had sounded more like a threat than an invitation.

"You don't have to," Autumn pointed out.

"That's all right." Cai managed a smile. "It's nice of her to offer."

Autumn suspected it was the first time in recorded history that Gran had been referred to as *nice*, but she didn't argue. Feeling unaccountably as if she were leading Cai to the gallows, or possibly heading there herself, she gestured, and they went inside.

It was a very strange dinner.

Dead silence fell when Cai walked through the door. Emys's eyes went buggy, which Autumn made a mental note to imitate the next time she was alone with him. Fortunately, Choo was there to break the tension, erupting into an ecstasy of full-body wagging at the arrival of another admirer. He threw himself onto Cai, who laughed and patted him and politely ignored the muddy pawprints Choo left on his cloak. Choo sneezed all over him, and Cai ignored that too.

Everything Cai did, Autumn couldn't help noticing, was

polite. He even managed to sit down politely, something Autumn had never seen before. She tried to imitate it, but something must have been off, for Jack gave her a strange look and asked if she needed to use the bathroom.

Her brothers were polite to Cai in a wooden sort of way. They clearly had no idea what to make of him, and apart from a few hellos and you're-welcomes, were as mute as the chairs. Autumn considered this a vast improvement over Emys's complaints and Kyffin's boasting, but Cai couldn't have known what he was being spared from. Gran shot Cai looks out of the corner of her eye that might have been suspicious, disapproving, or curious, to name just a few possibilities. Only Choo was at ease, and he sat at Cai's side throughout dinner like a jovial ambassador.

Autumn wasn't sure what to make of Cai either. He seemed intimidated by Gran, which said something for his common sense, and after giving her a few polite—naturally—compliments about the meal, he turned his attention to Jack. Autumn could understand why Jack would present an obvious conversational target, being close to Cai's age and nonthreatening in a moonfaced sort of way, but Jack just stared at Cai as if he were a species of boy he'd never encountered before. At one point, when Cai asked Jack if he enjoyed working in the menagerie, Jack's spoon missed his mouth entirely and hit his ear. Fortunately, Cai seemed to realize quickly that the small talk he'd learned at fancy dinner parties wasn't going to get him anywhere at Gran's table, and he turned his attention to his meal, like the Malogs.

Autumn found herself seeing the cottage in a new light. She'd always thought it big enough, if she'd given it any thought at all. Now she realized it was small, minuscule even, all of them crammed around the table in the kitchen, where herbs hung in bunches from the ceiling. The cottage had only three rooms, not including the attic—one belonged to Kyffin, Emys, and Jack, and the other was Gran's. Autumn wondered how many rooms Cai's house had.

The food was certainly nothing like what Cai was used to— onion stew and Gran's infamous black bread, sliced thick and ladled with cheese sauce. (Gran steadfastly refused to divulge the source of the black color, which was likely for the best.) There was no meat. Meat was expensive, especially heading into winter. If the fishmongers who made the winding eight-mile trek to Inglenook from the harbor town of Yr Aurymor couldn't offer Gran a good price on herring or rock crab, the family often went without. Cai made no complaints, tucking into his food with a gusto that rivaled Emys's.

Like Gran, Autumn kept an eye on him through dinner. Her opinion of him hadn't changed much—in fact, she found him even less impressive now that she knew he was afraid of drag-ons. She wondered if he was going to slay the Hollow Dragon by choking him. Not in a heroic way—by getting stuck in the monster's throat.

For her part, Autumn could barely touch her food. She kept seeing Winter staring out of that cold glass and counting the minutes until she could sneak back to the castle. Cai kept getting muddled up with Winter in her mind, because he was the thing her eyes kept drifting to, sitting there perfectly improbable at Gran's table. Cai, who knew all about magic and Inglenook, and who had come to her for a favor.

And slowly, an idea took shape.

The sky darkened beyond the windows. Nightfall was when the Gentlewood came alive, full of whispering shadows and sighing leaves. Autumn was used to the sound of it weaving through her dreams. Cai, though, couldn't stop staring at the forest. When he looked at the Gentlewood, he seemed to forget where he was—his spoon drifted back to his bowl, and his face emptied, as if he was no longer behind it but out there in the darkness somewhere. He was motionless for so long that even Emys looked at him askance, and Emys wouldn't notice a pack of howling Hounds if there was a bowl of stew in front of them.

Autumn elbowed Cai. She was mildly worried they'd poisoned him—perhaps the digestive systems of world-famous magicians were so unused to ordinary food that it made them sick.

Cai blinked at her, then smiled. He had a nice smile, though there was something vacant about it. Not because it made him look stupid or foolish, but because it didn't seem to hold any real emotion, as if he was only smiling because he felt he should, because it was polite. Autumn wondered if that was what all famous magicians were like, putting on a show for people all the time, and wondered also why they didn't just grow a backbone and zap people who didn't like them.

She spent the rest of dinner deep in thought. At the end of the meal, Cai offered to help clear away the dishes, but Gran just shooed him out of the cottage without replying to his thank-yous, possibly because she didn't know how to. Gran didn't have guests for dinner, apart from Sir Emerick, a shabby old wandering knight whom Gran had once rescued from a pair of wyverns. And Sir Emerick didn't really count as a guest, for he and Gran had known each other since before Gran's chin hairs came in, as she liked to say. They spent Sir Emerick's visits drinking and arguing about the Old Days until they both fell asleep in their chairs.

"Wait." Autumn ran to catch up to Cai. He turned, his cloak shimmering gracefully. The wind smelled of the night-blooming flowers of the Gentlewood.

"I'll help you," she said.

Cai's face broke into a smile. "Really? Autumn, you have no idea—"

"If," Autumn cut in, and Cai went politely silent.

She regarded him. She didn't like Cai, nor did she trust him. But that didn't have to matter. You could still work with someone you didn't trust, the way Autumn worked with the monsters of the menagerie, and you could work with people you didn't like, such as Emys. What mattered was whether they could help you.

And Cai could help her.

"If," Autumn repeated, "you help me find my brother."

Cai's smile faltered. He gave her that soft-eyed look the

– 60 –

masters wore whenever they accidentally called her Winter. The look that had been on Gran's face when Autumn told her that Winter hadn't been stolen away by the Hollow Dragon, that he was still alive somewhere.

After a long moment, Cai said, "How?"

"I think he's trapped in the school," she began slowly. She didn't know how much she should tell Cai. The problem was that it all sounded like a hallucination. After all, she and Winter were practically identical—who would believe that she hadn't just seen her own reflection and imagined the rest?

"I don't know why he's trapped," she went on, "or how. But you'll help me look for him. You know the school inside out. You're always having adventures there—like when you and Gawain found the hidden tunnel to that old coblynaw's treasure hoard. Plus, people say you're the strongest magician Inglenook's ever trained." Autumn didn't mention how hard to believe she found this. "If Winter's trapped by an enchantment, maybe you can find him."

"Autumn," Cai said slowly, "your brother went missing a long time ago. There's no way he'd still . . ."

"I know it doesn't make sense." Autumn's hands clenched. "But he's alive. He *is.*"

Cai let out his breath. Autumn thought he was going to argue more, but he just said simply, "I'll help however I can."

"Really?" Autumn's knees went weak with relief and amazement. "I— Thank you, sir."

"Don't call me that." A shadow passed over his face, but his voice was as polite as ever.

"Okay." If Cai wanted to pretend they were friends, not servant and master, she didn't care. She would go along with anything if he helped Winter.

"Why were you named Autumn and Winter?" Cai asked curiously.

"I was born first," Autumn said. "It was just before midnight on the last day of fall. Winter was born—well, in winter. Ten minutes later. Though there was little difference between the two, Gran always says." Autumn smiled as she remembered the familiar story. "Snow piled up against the house in drifts that were like another door when Gran tried to get outside in the morning. That day was just like Winter, she says. Still and quiet as new snow." Her throat grew tight.

Cai watched her. "I'm sorry. You must miss him."

Autumn didn't reply.

"I'll need to consult a few books in the library," Cai said after a moment's thought. He didn't look vacant anymore, but calm and decisive. "Meet me there after dinner tomorrow, as soon as you can get away."

Cai reached out his hand, and Autumn hesitantly shook it. He looked every bit a proper magician standing there with his staff, stardust glinting about him like dust motes in a sunbeam, and Autumn felt her hope swell to bursting. Cai smiled and vanished into the darkness.

6

In Which Autumn
Visits the Skybrary

Autumn watched Cai go, her feet itching. She wanted more than anything to follow him to the castle. But if she went back now, she would have to explain everything to Gran, and Autumn was simply too used to being disbelieved to try. She knew Gran worried that she had never cried for Winter—she'd overheard her telling Sir Emerick. Autumn didn't see the point in crying—it wouldn't help her find Winter any faster, but try saying that to Gran. For a long time now, she'd accepted as truth that she was Winter's only hope.

Autumn thought of the look Cai had given her—coming from a less kind person, it could have been called pity. She wasn't at all certain that Cai had believed her any more than Gran did, and if a magician couldn't believe the impossible, what hope did she have of convincing anybody else?

She would sneak back to the window first thing, and as often as she could after.

She hurried back to the cottage and hopped silently up the front steps, avoiding the creaky one at the top.

"Never thought I'd entertain a famous magician at my table," came Gran's voice from the shadowy porch.

Autumn froze with her hand on the door. Had Gran heard what she'd said to Cai? If so, would she try to stop Autumn from seeing him?

"Cai wants me to teach him about the dragons in the menagerie," she said slowly. "About how they think. He says it will make him better at fighting them. Is that all right?"

This wasn't exactly how Cai had put it, but it also wasn't a lie. All in all, Autumn was pleased with her quick thinking. Gran puffed on her pipe and leaned back in her rickety rocking chair. "It's all one to me. Nice of him to come and ask, I suppose. He only had to tell the headmaster what he wanted, and we'd be ordered to give it to him."

Autumn hadn't thought of that. But Cai was probably embarrassed about needing help from a servant.

"He's not what I expected," Gran said.

"No," Autumn agreed.

"Ah well, most of them aren't," Gran said in a musing tone. "Them great ones that folks write prophecies about." She gave Autumn a sharp look. "Do you know the prophecy?"

Autumn frowned. Everyone knew the prophecy. "Cai's going to kill the Hollow Dragon."

Gran took another puff on her pipe. "The same dragon that

ate three of the king's best knights for lunch just last week."

"You mean you don't believe it?"

"Oh, I believe in prophecies all right," Gran said. "Been around long enough to watch a fair few come true. But I also know that when it comes to prophecies—when it comes to a lot of things in life—we often hear what we want to hear. Why, most folks don't even know how that prophecy goes, yet they're all perfectly happy to believe that beast will be done and dusted by some slip of a boy."

Autumn mulled this over. It would make sense if the prophecy was wrong in some way—if it was actually about a different boy, for instance. True, the seer who had made the prophecy had been none other than Taliesin, renowned as much for his wisdom as for his eccentric habit of sleeping on mountaintops with no clothes on in order to become one with nature. And it was also true that Taliesin had delivered the prophecy at Cai's bedside when Cai was barely a month old, a marvel witnessed not only by the family but by several servants. But perhaps the old seer had gotten the address wrong.

"Do *you* know how the prophecy goes, Gran?"

Gran released a great cloud of smoke. For a moment, Autumn didn't think she was going to speak. When she did, her gaze didn't stray from the forest.

The lightest winds wander far,
The quietest hunters draw blood.

The lowest may walk among stars,
In some hearts a forest will bud.

No blade or enchantment will slow
The empty song in the wilds.
Ere his thirteenth winter's snow,
The beast will fall to the stars' child.

Gran's voice faded into the night. Autumn felt the words wash over her, tingly and cool—there was magic in them, she was certain.

"What does it mean?" she asked.

"Well, the first bit's about Cai. The second's about the Hollow Dragon."

"The empty song?" Autumn thought it over. There were a number of singing monsters, though none of them were dragons, which added to the Hollow Dragon's strangeness. Monsters used music to lull, but also to frighten. And there was nothing more frightening than the tales of the Hollow Dragon's song, which was said to be an omen of death. Knights who fought the dragon reported that their fallen comrades had spoken of the beauty of his song before they died—a song heard by none who lived.

"But there's still no sense to it," Autumn said. "For one thing, there's nothing *low* about Cai. He's the most famous magician in Eryree."

"You should ask him about that one," Gran said in an

unreadable voice. "You know what the Gentlewood is, don't you, child?"

Autumn frowned. The question had the air of a riddle, like the prophecy.

"It's more alive than other forests," Gran went on. "It lives in the monsters, you see, as much as they live in it. They're not the same, but they're connected, like mushrooms growing on a log." She let out a stream of smoke. "They feed each other. The Hollow Dragon is all cruelty and malice, and he's *strong*. Ever since he came down from the north, the forest's been darker. Angrier. He's changing it, bit by bit."

"I know," Autumn said. She was well aware that the Gentlewood grew more ferocious with each new season—she felt it whenever she stepped beneath the boughs. The paths were more slippery, the trees more inclined to close in on you just when you needed to run away. Poison berries crowded out all the edible ones. "What does that have to do with Cai?"

Gran snorted. "What doesn't it have to with Cai? He's supposed to slay the Hollow Dragon, which is all well and good. But when he does, he won't just be fighting a dragon—he'll be fighting the forest itself."

Autumn fell silent, overwhelmed by the enormity of it all. She felt a stab of pity for Cai—poor silly, blushing boy that he was. He was going to get *flattened*. There wouldn't be anything left of him at all, not even a Cai-shaped scorch mark on the forest floor.

"Away with you, child," Gran said gruffly. "I've a mind to

have a few moments' peace from both monsters and munchkins."

Gran went back to her pipe. Autumn hastened into the light and warmth of the cottage, glad to leave the prophecy to the shadows.

Autumn tossed and turned all night and rose an hour before dawn, before even Gran was up. She climbed up to the castle in a sleepy half-daze, pretending she had another housekeeping errand.

Winter wasn't in the window. She tried shouting his name, tried pounding on the thick glass until the cracks spread like ripples. She even searched the other windows in the hallway, as well as you could search a window. When she went back to the cottage, her throat ached with disappointment.

She clung to Cai's promise. She would see him tonight. Surely if anyone could rescue Winter from the enchantment he'd fallen into, it was Cai Morrigan.

The rain picked up that morning, entangling the mountain in ribbons of drifting mist. But neither sun nor rain had any effect on the jobs that needed doing, and so after breakfast Autumn ventured out into the weather. She and Kyffin were in for it that day, for it was time to wash the menagerie with seawater again. The fisherfolk from Yr Aurymor were waiting down on the road at the base of the mountain, their cart laden with buckets.

As Autumn hauled seawater up the mountain path, her head bent to keep her hood from blowing back, Cai and their pact felt like a dream. Had he really stood there in Gran's cabbages, glittering with magic? She would have doubted her sanity if Emys hadn't spent the better part of the morning bemoaning the scarcity of leftovers, which he blamed on Cai.

"What's afoot, Malog girl?" called one of the fisherfolk, an old salt named Anurin.

Autumn lifted another bucket from the cart, dashing rain from her eyes. "Same as always."

"That so, that so?" the man crowed. "What's that on your hands?"

Autumn looked down. Her hands were a little muddy, which was hardly unusual.

"You're gleaming, girl," Anurin said. "Like fresh snow, like candy apples. Like trout under the waves . . ."

His voice trailed off into muttering. Anurin was a nice man, but quite mad. Autumn exchanged a look with his daughter, Seren, who smiled.

"He's been so good today," she said with a sigh, and took something out of her pack. "Here we are. Thought you kids might like a break from that awful black stuff your gran bakes."

She handed Autumn a package wrapped in paper, and Autumn caught the scent of Seren's seabread, soft as foam and sprinkled with the rough salt the fisherfolk pulled from the tide. Her stomach gave a rumble. Seren often brought treats for the Malogs when she visited, and her seabread was legendary.

Seren leaned down and whispered, "Put half in your pocket and tell Emys I gave it to the chickens. Else you won't get a bite."

Autumn smiled. She liked Seren and Anurin. Yr Aurymor was a poor, ramshackle village set on a bay like a jagged mouth. It was also nearly surrounded by the Gentlewood, apart from a narrow sliver that gave passage to the southern road. Gran said the forest would swallow it one day, and often told Seren to move to one of the southern fishing towns. Autumn hoped she would listen.

Autumn turned, but Anurin's hand darted out and caught her wrist. "They're not like us," he said.

Autumn blinked. "What?"

"We're the earth, and they're the mountains. You get yourself tangled up in their world, you may never get *un*tangled."

"I—I don't know what you mean," Autumn said.

"I can see it," he murmured. There was no madness in his gaze, only an odd intensity. "Magic. Not just the magic, but the trail it leaves, where it brushes the rest of us. It's on you like dew. People say I'm raving, but I'm not—not about this, at least."

Autumn shivered. She thought of her pact with Cai—surely the old man couldn't know about that. She looked down at her hands, as if she might catch a glimmer there among the mud and calluses.

"Da, leave the poor girl be," Seren said. "I'm sorry, love."

Autumn shook her head, smiling. As she walked away, the old man called, "We're the earth, girl! Mud's not meant to gleam."

It took most of the morning to get all the buckets lined up in the menagerie, and then there was the business of dousing the stalls. Monsters had to be moved, straw replaced, blankets washed in the river and hung optimistically from a clothesline. The Malogs cleaned the stalls weekly, but seawater was only applied once a month, spread in thin layers so it could soak into the stones. The Hounds of Arawn howled and Amfidzel fretted over her pressed flowers, which she kept lined up on a shelf. Autumn had to move the flowers herself, one by one, while Amfidzel hovered like a hawk over its fledglings.

Autumn's method of cleaning the stalls was haphazard but, in her view, effective. She liked to line up several buckets and then hurl their contents across the floor, after which she would slide and splash over the stones with her mop, spreading all the seawater out. Her brothers, on the other hand, would dip their mops into the buckets and then rub the seawater into the flagstones—tidier, it was true, but Autumn didn't hold with tidiness if it got in the way of efficiency. By the afternoon, Autumn had covered everyone with seawater at least once, even managing to get it up Emys's nose (or so he claimed). The two of them ended the day in a raging argument. Their bickering rose to such a volume that Amfidzel tucked her head under her wings.

"Gah!" Emys said finally, tossing his mop aside. "It's like arguing with a thunderstorm wearing boots. Do what you want, Autumn. Just keep my nose out of it next time."

Full of thwarted fury, Autumn turned to Jack for support, but he only unplugged his ears and got back to mopping.

At the end of the day, Autumn was soaked from head to foot, her fingers as wrinkled as an old woman's and blistered from the metal bucket handles. After dinner, she washed up as well as she could. She didn't have the energy to heat water, so she took a bar of soap to the wooden tub of cold rainwater out back by the privy.

Shivering, she changed into clean clothes, combed her wet hair back, and hoped for the best. She was gazing up at Inglenook, trying to settle her stomach, when a pair of arms wrapped around her.

Autumn gave Jack a shove. "What's that for?"

"Nothing." He gave her one of his vague smiles. "Only I could tell you were thinking about Winter today. I miss him, too."

Autumn was too surprised to answer. Gran had told the other Malogs not to talk about Winter when Autumn was around—she seemed to think Autumn would fall apart if they did, or maybe she was worried about starting an argument. Autumn supposed she meant well, but it just made her feel even lonelier. For the first time since she could remember, she thought about hugging Jack. It wasn't that she disliked the experience, but offering Jack a hug was like offering up your arm to a hungry mosquito—it was probably already on you before the thought occurred. Jack, though, just gave her another smile and disappeared back into the cottage.

Autumn marched up to the castle. She was nervous. She was excited. She was terrified. With the help of Cai Morrigan's magic and his experience with strange quests, she could have Winter back by morning. Or—

Or she would watch Cai shake his head sadly and tell her there was nothing he could do. And if the most famous magician in the kingdom couldn't help her, what hope did she have?

She felt as if she might throw up.

Autumn never visited the castle at night, and the other servants shot her odd looks. The corridors were warm with lanternlight and the smell of supper. Roast pork and scalloped potatoes, Autumn guessed. Apple pudding with hard sauce for dessert. Her mouth watered—it had been potato stew with barley for the Malogs that night, as it always was when Gran was trying to stretch the last of their wages.

She waited outside the library, nervously checking and rechecking her fingernails. She was wearing last year's cloak, and the sleeves didn't quite reach her wrists. A few students blinked at her as they passed. They couldn't have looked more befuddled if one of the dragons was there, slavering all over the carpet.

Autumn eyed a girl teetering under a stack of grimoires. The girl looked flustered, and Autumn stepped forward to help her. But another girl appeared and laughingly took a few books from her hands. They linked arms and hurried down the hall, cloaks billowing.

Autumn felt a familiar longing rap against her heart like

an unwelcome guest at the door. What she wouldn't give to be hurrying off to those cozy dormitories in the North Tower, every room lined with windows of stars. She'd helped Mrs. Hawes change the linens once—or, rather, she'd tangled the linens into knots and left behind stabby little pine needles, which must have been in her hair, then been banished to the corner while Mrs. Hawes struggled to undo her mess. The older students had their own rooms strewn with fur rugs and chests and lovely wardrobes carved with interlocking blue-bells, Inglenook's crest.

She wondered if Cai would ever show up. The library would be closing soon.

Autumn's hands clenched. If Cai had forgotten his promise, she'd *make* him remember. She'd shove him into the gorse the next time she saw him. She'd send the boggart to lurk under his bed and make growly dragon noises in the night. She'd—

The library doors swung open again, and Headmaster Neath emerged. Autumn shrank back as if from a wolf—she'd only ever seen the headmaster from a distance, during cere-monies or banquets.

Headmaster Neath was a large man, olive-skinned with a mane of graying golden hair and a craggy, handsome face. He was also a star magician, and like a star, he drew others into his orbit as he passed. Most of the students fell silent, while some of the braver ones called out greetings. The headmaster turned his warm smile upon them.

Autumn was so stunned by the headmaster's appearance

that at first she didn't notice Cai at his side. The two of them stopped a little distance away. Cai was speaking, and the headmaster listened, fixing Cai with the full weight of his bright gaze. Autumn was convinced she would melt under that sort of attention. Cai, though, didn't seem bothered. His gaze drifted away and found Autumn, and he gave her a small smile—as if he found conversation with the most powerful magician in the kingdom a bit dull. The headmaster touched his shoulder in goodbye, the gesture warm and familiar. The two of them looked as if they'd stepped out of an old ballad.

Autumn sank into a bow as the headmaster passed, but he spared her as little notice as the pattern in the carpet. She watched openmouthed as he strode away.

"There you are!" Cai said, and Autumn nearly leaped out of her boots.

She gestured weakly down the corridor. "Were you talking to the *headmaster*?"

It was a silly thing to say, but Cai didn't poke fun at her. "He wants my help with a spell he's working on. You know how crops can't grow in soil touched by dragonflame? The headmaster thinks starlight could draw the heat from the earth."

"He wants your help. The headmaster."

Cai didn't seem to notice Autumn's tone. He gave her an anxious look. "I'm sorry. I didn't realize you were out here. Why didn't you come in?"

"I'm not allowed." In addition to being a wuss, Cai was the most oblivious boy she'd ever met.

Cai's ears went pink. "Oh, right. Sorry."

Several students had stared at Autumn before. Now it seemed that everyone was. Cai took no notice whatsoever.

"Come on," he said, seizing her hand and drawing her through the doors, which swung open on their own. "You're with me, so it's all right."

Autumn only had a second to feel strange about Cai holding her hand before the sight of the library drove every thought from her head.

She first thought of a cathedral—not the tiny church many of the servants went to in Lumen Far, but a proper cathedral, like the kind they had in the big southern towns. The Main Library of Inglenook was near the size of Lumen Far itself. Pillars of marble reached into the shadows, and stained-glass windows took up the whole southern wall. Moonlight streamed through the intricate portrait of four magicians, each with a staff in their right hand and a raven in their left. A ghost tree loomed above them, ornamented with small dragons like Christmas baubles. The walls of the library were lined with shelves so high, she wondered if they had an end. Golden ladders leaned against them nonchalantly.

"Winter would faint," Autumn said, marveling. "He loves books. Taught himself to read—he's not too good at it, but he got through all the kids' books Gran gave him."

Cai stopped short. "You mean you can't read?"

"Nah." Autumn could sound out some of the words in Winter's books, but it took forever. Winter had made her try, though she hadn't bothered since he disappeared. Why should she, when beastkeepers didn't need to read? She told Cai as much.

Cai gave her a thoughtful look. "Is that what you want to be? A beastkeeper?"

Autumn narrowed her eyes. Was Cai teasing her? All servants kept the jobs they were born into. If your parents were cooks, well, so were you. "What I want doesn't enter into it. Though I wouldn't expect you to understand that."

Cai didn't seem offended. "I might be able to."

"Oh, no!" Autumn cried. Behind her was a trail of muddy footprints. She could have sworn her boots had been clean when she put them on. "Gran always says I draw mud like a lantern draws moths," she said mournfully.

One of the librarians had noticed Autumn's trail. She stood with her hand over her mouth like a witness at a grisly murder scene.

"Er—let's hurry." Cai pulled her deeper into the library. It was worse than being dragged into the Gentlewood—heads swiveled at every desk to gawp at her. Or, rather, at her and Cai. It was the *and*, Autumn understood, that was the true cause of the gawping.

"Where are we going?" she hissed.

Cai replied something over his shoulder that sounded like "skybrary." Autumn was certain she'd misheard. She *hoped* she'd misheard.

Unfortunately, they'd only gone a few steps when a voice called, "Cai!"

To Autumn's dismay, a girl was waving at Cai from one of the tables. Next to her, to Autumn's further dismay, was Gawain.

Cai made his way over, and Autumn trailed behind, not knowing what else to do.

"There you are," the girl said. She was the one Autumn had seen Cai with on the stairs. She playfully threw a crumpled piece of paper at him. "Come help me with this essay on reaving enchantments. It's a *nightmare.*"

"I would," Cai said. "But I have—ah, something to do."

"Oh, *something.*" The girl nodded. "It's nice that you're trying to be less mysterious, Cai."

Gawain was balancing his chair on its back legs. "Who's that?"

Autumn wasn't surprised he'd forgotten her. He seemed to forget her again the moment he looked back at Cai.

"This is Autumn Malog," Cai said. "Autumn, this is Winifred Greenfallow. And you know Gawain."

Autumn bowed. Winifred was one of those people who seemed more sharply drawn than everyone else. She was plump and auburn-haired, with a golden flush in her pale cheeks. A sun magician, without question.

She leaned forward conspiratorially. "He's not bothering you, is he?" she hissed at Autumn.

Autumn shook her head, tongue-tied. Winifred was joking, but she could tell the joke was meant for Cai—she wasn't really part of it. "Not at present, miss."

Winifred laughed. Even Gawain cracked a smile.

"What *are* you up to, Cai?" Winifred said. Autumn was relieved that she didn't point out that Autumn wasn't allowed there. She was still half-expecting to be hooked around the neck by a librarian's cane at any moment.

Cai blushed, fumbling for words. Autumn grew alarmed. Was Cai too polite to lie to his friends?

She stepped forward. "Begging your pardon, miss, but he's helping me with a project," she said. "You see, one of the dragons is sick. Master Morrigan found a book of dragon tonics. He offered to sign it out for me if I thought it of use to my gran."

Winifred's expression cleared and she gave Cai a teasing smile. "Of course he did. Doesn't Master Morrigan have enough homework of his own? Now he's helping the servants with theirs? Next he'll be out helping the hounds hunt rabbits."

Autumn forced herself to smile along, though her cheeks prickled.

"He's always got to be helping someone, you see," Gawain said. "It's a compulsion."

Autumn would have thought Gawain cruel if not for the warmth in his voice. He and Winifred clearly held this blushing, stammering, ridiculously polite boy in high regard. And Gawain knew about his fear of dragons! It was puzzling.

Cai said goodbye to Winifred and Gawain and led Autumn to the back of the library.

"Sorry about that," he muttered, scratching his face. Autumn observed with interest that he seemed to be breaking out in hives. Just from being put on the spot by his friends! What a strange boy he was. No wonder he was afraid of Amfidzel. Even the wisps could eat Cai for breakfast.

Autumn mulled over what Gawain had said. Cai was always having adventures at Inglenook. Why, when he was ten years old, he'd gone into the Gentlewood to rescue two apprentices and a master who had lost their way. It hadn't seemed strange to Cai's friends that he was helping Autumn, because that was what Cai did.

Was that what she was to Cai? Just another chapter in a book about his heroics, or a stanza in a ballad? It made Autumn feel strange. Small. She didn't think she wanted to be a stanza.

Don't be silly, Autumn thought. *You're barely a couplet. When's the last time you heard a bard sing about a servant girl with muddy boots?*

She remembered Anurin's words. *You get yourself tangled up in their world, you may never get un*tangled. But she wasn't tangled up in anything—Cai would help Winter, the way he helped everyone, and then they would go their separate ways.

You'll never believe this story when you hear it, Winter, she thought.

They came to a staircase with a librarian's desk guarding it. The librarian jumped at the sight of Cai, spilling his tea all over his book, which filled the librarian's face with such horror that at first Autumn thought he must have scalded himself. Cai stepped forward, and Autumn didn't see what he did, but a second later the book was dry. Now it looked as if the librarian was about to burst into tears. He nearly begged to help Cai find his books, so earnestly that you'd think Cai had rescued him from the maw of a dragon, not mopped up a tea stain. Cai brushed aside the librarian's exclamations with his usual politeness.

What a fuss! Autumn thought. The effect Cai had on other people was exhausting.

They climbed the staircase, which was so twisty Autumn felt dizzy. "Where are we going?" she called.

"I told you," Cai said over his shoulder. "The skybrary."

"What's a skybrary?"

Cai just smiled. "Come on."

Autumn and Cai huffed and puffed their way up the stairs. Autumn found herself losing track of how far they'd come and how long they'd been climbing. Was that magic?

Light flickered ahead, and a door appeared before them, slightly ajar. Through it came a cold wind and a sound like dry fingers rubbing together. Cai took her hand and pushed their way through.

Autumn's cry caught in her throat.

She stood on a round platform of white marble in the middle of nowhere. *Literally.* They were up in the sky, surrounded by thin clouds and an infinity of stars. The moon was enormous, a cold eye glaring down as if resenting their company.

"What—?" was all Autumn could get out.

"Don't worry," Cai said. "You won't fall." He reached out and tapped what looked like empty space, but his knuckles made a pinging sound. The platform was surrounded by the clearest, thinnest glass.

He led her to a row of stacks. Autumn went slowly, testing each step. Cloud tendrils swirled around her feet like ghostly fingers, and wind lifted her hair. The glass let in some of the night, or perhaps it was one-way glass: things could pass through from outside, but nothing that belonged in the library could leave it. Such as, to choose an example completely at random, a girl falling to her death.

Cai began pulling books off shelves. He tossed them onto a table topped with an ornate Inglenook lamp patterned with bluebells. The flame shone steadily through the wind.

"The librarians store all the oldest books in the skybrary," Cai explained. "The cold air preserves them."

Autumn looked around, being very, very careful not to look in any downward directions. "Why's it empty?"

"Most students aren't allowed here. You need special permission from the head librarian. Now, as far as maps go ... Ah, here."

He opened one of the books. Most of the pages were taken up by complicated drawings.

"These are old," Cai explained. "Drawn before the school was even built."

Autumn touched a page. It felt as fragile as a moth's wing.

"The thing is, we need more than a map of the school if we're going to work out where to look for Winter," Cai said, scratching his fading hives. "We need a map of enchantments."

"What?"

"The school is enchanted. I don't just mean the spells that created it. I mean all the spells that the masters—and probably a few students—have cast on it over the years. Spells to make rooms bigger or divide them in two, or to make them yellow. Spells that made a portal between one end of the castle and the other, because some magician wanted a shorter walk to his office."

"Right." The boggart had said something like this—spells overlaying spells. It made Autumn's head hurt.

"The thing is," Cai said, absently tapping one of the maps, "all magic has consequences. That's the first lesson you're taught at Inglenook. Summoning a spring could mean creating a drought several miles away. Let's say some magician decides to make two rooms into one. That spell might create a whole other room somewhere that nobody knows about. Or say she seals off the stairs leading to one of the towers. That might create a hidden staircase leading underground."

Autumn's head was pounding now. Hidden staircases? Disappearing rooms? "What a mess this place is!" she said. "Why haven't the masters tidied things up, instead of leaving spells lying around like old socks?"

"I guess they've never seen the need. And anyway, ancient

magic is hard to spot. It loses its glitter."

Autumn thought of the bay window overlooking the valley. Had some professor tried to add more windows somewhere and accidentally created a window-world, which Winter had fallen into? It seemed as likely as anything else.

"How are we supposed to find these hidden bits?" she said. "It sounds impossible."

"I've found a few over the years," Cai said. "It's tricky, but not impossible. I was thinking I could make a list of places to explore, and this Sunday we can—"

"Sunday?" Autumn stared at him. A heavy weight settled in her stomach, something like disappointment, but darker, and her fear came rushing back. Cai didn't believe her, and now he wanted to put her off. "What are you talking about? Why would we wait?"

Cai blinked. "Students aren't allowed to be wandering around the castle at night."

"You wander around all the time, Cai Morrigan," she said heatedly. "I've heard the stories, same as everyone else."

"Yes, but I've always known where I'm going beforehand."

Autumn stabbed her finger at the book, so roughly that the page tore. All she could see was Winter's face in the window. "What else are these dusty old maps for?" she demanded. "I thought you knew the school inside and out. Winter could be in *danger*. He could—"

Autumn realized that her voice had risen. *Button it, Autumn*, a little whisper said.

She stepped back, her cheeks heating. She felt like a shuttle on a loom, clanking back and forth between two versions of Cai: the hero of Eryree and the blushing scaredy-cat. "I'm sorry, sir. I mean, Cai—"

"It's all right." He looked down at the book, which was not only torn but scattered with bits of seaweed that must have fallen out of Autumn's sleeve. He reached up absently and pooled starlight in his palm. It glimmered like a handful of melted butter, and he smoothed it over the book, murmuring. The torn page knitted together.

"I think it's time you told me why you think Winter is trapped in the castle," Cai said. "And why you're in such a hurry when he's been missing since last year. Has something happened?"

Autumn didn't hear him at first. She was too busy staring at the book, which now had a faint shimmer. She'd never seen anyone cast a spell before—not up close, anyway. She wished he would do it again.

"I can see that you don't trust me." Cai's voice was mild. "But if you tell me what you know, it will be easier for me to help."

Autumn shuffled her feet. Cai was right, of course. Even if he didn't believe her, or only pretended to, she had to try to convince him. He was Winter's best hope.

So she told him everything. Not just about the window, but about her trips into the forest, the cloak, the boots. She stumbled through the story, wishing she was better at that sort of thing. She kept leaving out parts and having to go back, or not describing things as well as she wanted to.

But to her surprise, Cai listened carefully without interrupting. He asked questions: Which window had it been, and how long had Winter stayed there? Where had the boots been found? What exactly had the slumbering monsters in the Gentlewood said?

"The thing is," he said, tapping his chin with a pen after Autumn had finished, "the ones who saw Winter in the Gentlewood could have seen him anytime—years ago, even. Those old logs barely notice anything anymore. So your theory that it was a false trail could be right."

"Do you think I'm imagining things?"

"I don't know," Cai said. "It's possible. But it's also possible that you're right."

To Autumn's astonishment, she felt her eyes well with tears. She turned away from Cai quickly, pretending to examine another book. She didn't know why his words meant so much to her. Maybe because she was so used to people thinking she was just a silly girl, or half-mad with sorrow. Cai Morrigan was the only person who had ever taken her seriously. How perfectly ridiculous was that? She felt like pinching herself.

Fortunately, Cai either failed to notice her tears or politely pretended not to. He pressed his hand flat against the table, and starlight pooled beneath it, watery and undulating. It spread over the table and caught the books and papers in a tide, and they drifted into neat piles.

Autumn stared. "Isn't that a waste of magic?"

"It's a simple spell," Cai said, lifting the maps. Starlight dripped onto his boots. He caught sight of her expression, and his brow creased. "Are you all right?"

Autumn couldn't stop staring at the table. "How does it feel?"

"How does what feel?"

"To have magic. To have all that light inside you, ready to organize books or kill dragons or turn wood into gold."

Cai smiled. "Magicians can't turn things to gold." His gaze turned inward. "I'm not the best person to ask. I've always had magic, but I don't think it's the same for me. Other magicians talk about magic as if it's the sea. Something you can wade in, or fish in, or put in a bucket and carry around. But I can feel the magic inside me, all salty and cold, and it doesn't feel like it belongs there. Have you ever swallowed seawater?" He blinked. "I'm not making any sense, am I? You don't understand."

Autumn sighed quietly. "I wish I did."

Cai stood, his expression closed. The starlight was gone, and they were alone with the whistling wind and the cold. Autumn flushed, wondering if Cai thought her impertinent for asking such things. But he seemed to guess what she was thinking and smiled at her.

"I know you're scared," he said, "but I need time to think about all this, and I doubt one more day will hurt Winter. Let's meet again tomorrow night."

Autumn nodded, so relieved her legs wobbled. "You can come by the cottage for your first lesson in the morning."

He brightened. "Thanks."

She chewed her lip, watching him. "Why are you doing this?"

"What?"

The question had been too blunt, but Autumn pushed on anyway. "Why did you come to me for help?"

He slowly placed the books on a shelf. "The prophecy says I'm going to slay the Hollow Dragon. I can't very well do that when I'm—the way I am."

Autumn thought back to what Gran had said. "And you believe the prophecy?"

Cai gave her a blank look, and Autumn understood that to Cai, prophecies were not just things you heard people talk about, the way they spoke of magic or long-dead heroes. They were part of his world as much as air or rain. She looked down at her hands, suddenly feeling very small again. Much less than a couplet, less than a word.

Cai reached for a different book, opened it. "Look."

It was a map not just of Eryree, but the entire Island of Annan. There was the Gentlewood stretching east to the Asgorn Sea and north to the snowbound Boreal Wastes. There were the Southern Realms—tiny, perpetually squabbling kingdoms like Gormer Hills and Mittlebree. Autumn had never seen the Southern Realms, of course, but she knew the people who lived there were strange. They saw magicians as little more than craftspeople, and they didn't plant ghost trees outside their homes to gather the family memories. Some of them didn't even believe in monsters and thought the tales of Eryree carried to their ears by bards were nonsense.

Cai tapped the map. "The kings and queens in the Southern Realms are keeping an eye on Eryree. Some of their kingdoms are only a few miles wide, and they'd love to add our lands to theirs. They know that Eryree is weakening. They know we've been losing more and more of our villages to the Gentlewood, especially since the Hollow Dragon came down from the Boreal Wastes. He hates us, and his anger feeds the forest." Cai looked as if he'd half forgotten that Autumn was there. "If I don't kill the Hollow Dragon, it's not just the Gentlewood we'll have to worry about."

Autumn didn't know what to say. It was strange to hear a boy her age talk this way. Shouldn't the king and his knights be the ones worrying about the Southern Realms? But then, she reminded herself, he was Cai Morrigan, wasn't he? It probably wasn't strange at all.

She thought of all the stories of the Hollow Dragon. They were contradictory—some said he stood taller than the tallest tree; others that his whole body burned like a fire built dense and hot. But they all agreed on a few points: a towering beast little more than skin and bone, his terrible hunger a living thing inside him. She watched in wonderment as Cai calmly stuffed the remaining books into his bag.

She wrapped her trembling arms around herself. Cai didn't think she was mad. He hadn't shaken his head and told her there was nothing he could do. He was going to help her!

She could hear Winter's familiar laugh, feel his soft white hair against her cheek when he rested his head on her shoulder—hair that always smelled of grass and wool. She didn't dare to speak, in case Cai changed his mind.

Fortunately, Cai seemed lost in his own thoughts. He blew out the lantern, and the wind swallowed the curl of smoke. Then, to Autumn's relief, they left the skybrary behind.

Autumn had just tucked herself back into bed when she heard Gran's boots thudding up the front steps and the clank of the lantern being put back on its hook.

Having finished her rounds along the forest's edge, Gran did her rounds of the other Malogs, first looking in on the boys' room, from which arose a storm of snores, then thumping her way up the ladder to the attic.

"Still awake, are we?"

Autumn nodded, tucking her hands under her blankets. She thought of Anurin and wondered if Gran noticed any telltale glow upon her, if just talking to Cai had left smudges of light on her like ink. She was relieved that Gran had been out all evening—Autumn wouldn't have to explain her visit to the skybrary. Her stomach was still churning from the strangeness of it all.

"Waiting for a story, I suppose."

A smile broke across Autumn's face. A part of her thought she was too old for bedtime stories, but she didn't care.

"Which one?" Gran settled on the edge of her bed with a grunt. "Not—"

"The fox and the magician."

Gran groaned. "You could tell me that tale backward and sideways by now, girl."

Autumn only propped the pillow up behind her and settled into the bed with relish. This was just what she needed. And it wasn't as if she'd be able to fall asleep anytime soon.

Gran grumbled some and then began the tale, as Autumn had known she would. She lay back and let the story envelop her like a well-worn quilt.

"Now," Gran began, "there once was a fox living deep in the Gentlewood—"

"A fox with snow-white fur."

Gran rolled her eyes. "A fox with snow-white fur. And living nearby, all on her lonesome, was a powerful magician. See, this was back in the days when the Gentlewood was halfway to gentle, and many a magician made their home under those old boughs. One day, the magician gave birth to a lovely girl with hair like raven feathers. Not an hour later, the fox gave birth to a kit, with fur even whiter than his dam's—if snow had bones inside it, that's how pale he'd be. Now the magician and the fox were great friends, and so they made a pact between them to keep their children safe. They took the kit's heart, and they put it inside the magician's daughter, and they took the heart of the magician's daughter and put it inside the kit. Each child would carry the other's heart for as long as they lived.

"The fox's son and the magician's daughter grew to be great friends, too. One day, when they were about as old as you are now, they came upon a frozen lake. The girl promised the fox she wouldn't skate too far, but the fox knew her heart better than she did—it was beating in his chest, after all. He knew she wouldn't be able to resist the call of that lovely ice shining in the moonlight, and so he took the end of her braid between his teeth and held tight to it. And when the girl skated too far and fell through the thin place in the middle of the lake, he pulled her out.

"When they were older, and the girl was about to be married, the fox offered to bring her and her husband a beautiful wedding present. The girl didn't want him to go too far, because it was spring and the dragons were beginning to stir, so she asked only for a bucket of water from the hot spring to warm her feet. The fox pretended to agree, and brought her the bucket, but then he snuck away in secret. He traveled far, far to the north, where the dragons are all bones and teeth and hunger, and there are hot springs so deep they could fill a hundred buckets, enough to make a pond for the girl to bathe in. But the girl knew the fox's heart. She followed him with a basket of the rarest snow roses and used them to lure the dragons away. And so the fox filled up his buckets and returned home safely.

"A few years later, the girl was still young, with four pretty children, but the fox was very old, even for a fox. He knew his time was drawing near. The girl, now a powerful magician herself, spent all her time searching for spells to make him well again. She promised that she would be careful, but the fox knew her heart. He knew she would keep searching until she wore herself away to nothing. And so the fox went to speak to her mother, whose hair was now almost as white as his own fur, and they made a new pact between them.

"The girl's littlest child had been born too early, and it seemed like as not he wouldn't survive the winter. And so the old magician took her daughter's heart, which the fox had kept safe all those years, and gave it to her grandson. Straight away, the child sprang up out of bed, healthy as a spring lamb, and seeing that, the fox died happy. And as for the girl, she kept her dear fox's heart inside her until the end of her days. So you see, he never truly left her."

Autumn's eyes had drifted shut. She loved the story because it felt like it had been written about her and Winter. People called Winter her shadow sometimes, because he was quiet and as light-footed as the wind, and they were right, but not for those reasons. She'd always felt as if Winter was a part of her that lived outside her body—an important part, like her heart. Not because they each always knew where the other was without looking, or because sometimes it seemed like they shared the same thoughts. Because she simply knew, just as she knew that snow was cold.

"Think you can sleep now, child?"

"Mmm," Autumn said. She was already halfway there. Gran's voice near the end of the story had been like the gentle rumble of the sea. She felt Gran's rough hand brush her brow, and then all was quiet and dark.

7

In Which Winter Remembers His Name

– LAST SPRING –

For a long time, Winter thought he was a cloud.

He drifted here and there, not minding it, not minding anything. He had no eyes, no hands or feet. He sensed things—faces and shapes moving in the distance—and sometimes his attention caught on them, like a cloud caught on a jagged peak, but he always drifted free.

But at some point a familiar face floated into view. An old woman, her face a scowl, her shoulders broad and hunched. She didn't look at him as she went by, and an instant later, she was gone.

Gran, Winter thought.

And suddenly Winter knew who he was again—a boy, not a cloud. He was standing behind a sheet of glass. Beyond the glass was the grand foyer in Inglenook—there was the broad stone staircase, which fell from landing to landing like a tremendous waterfall. There were the tapestries of magicians and monsters, the stained-glass lanterns. There were the students in their glittering cloaks hastening to and fro.

Winter brushed his hand against the glass. He was looking out of a mirror—one of the big ones with gold frames that stood on either side of the staircase. Behind him, there was the same foyer, only with everything reversed. But it looked like the foyer the way a watercolor painting looks like the real thing.

He'd fallen into a mirror. But how?

You're not afraid, Winter told himself as the breath got stuck in his chest. *You'll wake up soon. It's a dream.*

But he knew it wasn't.

Autumn. The thought was like the lifting of a heavy weight. Autumn would find him soon. Autumn with her stompy boots and her loud voice. She would stomp up to him any minute, and everything would be all right.

He forced down the urge to run and run, screaming her name, the way he had when he was little and afraid for some reason and couldn't find her right away. He wasn't little anymore. He had to be brave.

Someone sniffled. Winter turned. A girl sat beneath the reflection of a grandfather clock, face buried in her hands.

Winter drifted toward her. "Excuse me. Where am I?"

The girl looked up. She was older than Winter by a few years. She wore a housekeeper's uniform, and her dark hair was woven into two braids that floated around her shoulders.

"What sort of question is that?" she spat.

Winter frowned. A moment ago, the issue of where he was had seemed important, but now it didn't.

"What's your name?"

"I—" The girl's eyes widened. "I don't remember. Oh no! That's how it always starts. They forget their names first. And then—and then—"

"It's all right." Winter made his quiet voice even quieter. It was a trick that always worked with . . . With what? He couldn't remember who or what he'd been before he came here.

A memory flashed through him like fish in a stream—there had once been a large yellow dog, panting in the sunlight. Had that been his dog? Why couldn't he remember if he'd had a dog? It was an important thing to know.

"Let's try guessing," he said. "I'll go through the alphabet. You tell me when a name sounds familiar."

He started with A, Abigail. His voice was growing hoarse by the time he got to M, Maddie, when the girl let out a squeal.

"That's it!" she cried. "Maddie. That's my name. I liked pomegranates—I used to spit the seeds out at Reese Jones, made him cry once. Serves him right for—for—" Her lip trembled. "I *had* it—just for a second. The memory, you know. But now it's just pomegranates."

"It's nice to meet you, Maddie," Winter said. "I'm Winter."

Maddie burst into tears.

It took her a long time to stop crying. Winter let her cry on his shoulder until she was done.

Maddie squinted. "Are you new here?"

Winter thought. He remembered drifting. He had drifted for a very long time. "I don't think so. I think I've been here awhile." He looked out at the castle. "But I think I used to be out there."

"We *all* did," Maddie said.

"There are others?"

She nodded.

"How did we end up here?"

Maddie's brow furrowed. "Dunno. Ask the Old One."

"Who's that?"

"The one who's been here the longest," she said, rolling her eyes. "He's fading away. We all fade away, eventually. He forgot his name."

Winter shivered. "I'm not going to forget."

Maddie regarded him with a faraway look in her eyes. "That's what I said."

Winter touched the glass. He tried to push at it, but it was as if his hands had turned back into clouds.

"Not like that." Maddie came to stand by his side. "Like this."

She pressed her hands and nose against the glass and pulled a hideous face. One of the Inglenook students gave a start and skittered sideways. He blinked at the mirror and seemed to shrug. He quickly checked his teeth, then hurried off. Maddie giggled.

Winter gazed at the glass. "Can you teach me how to do that?"

"Sure. You got someone you want to scare?"

Winter tried to remember. Yes, he wanted to scare someone. A moment ago, he had known who it was. A flash of white hair; a lopsided grin. Something about boots?

"Bye," Maddie said gloomily.

Bye? Was she going somewhere? Then Winter realized that *he* was going somewhere—he was drifting again, a wisp of fog in an invisible wind. He was only afraid for a moment, and then he felt nothing. He closed his eyes.

8

In Which Cai
Swallows Too Much Magic

The morning dawned gray and fickle as clouds soaked the mountains with rain, then parted in a spill of rainbows and wet sunlight. At the breakfast table, Autumn took her time stirring cream into her tea and scraping butter on her toast. The kitchen was filled with the sounds of eating; conversation had no place at the Malog table. Choo dozed by the fire. The boggart rustled around in the rafters in his unshape, hunting for spiders, his newest game. Every once in a while, one would drop onto Choo's head, and the dog would start awake at the tickly sensation. The spiders always beat a hasty exit, leaving Choo blinking in puzzlement. Quiet chuckling emanated from the ceiling.

"Gran?" Autumn said.

Her brothers looked up, startled, though their forks continued their uninterrupted journeys from plates to mouths. Gran raised a bushy eyebrow.

"Cai asked me to give him a lesson this morning," Autumn said. "So if it's all right with you, I won't be free to help with the Hounds' flea baths."

Kyffin regarded Autumn with a frown on his handsome face. Jack's eyes widened. Emys let out a bark of laughter.

"The fancy star kid's lost it," he said. "What are *you* going to teach him?"

Autumn gave him a brief glare. "Gran?"

"Hmph," Gran said, often her way of agreeing to things. "Jack, you'll help me with the Hounds. Kyffin, you're on your own with that fence repair. I want it finished by lunchtime, and no bellyaching about it."

"Easy," Kyffin said, flexing his biceps. He'd been doing that a lot lately. He'd also been given to taking his shirt off when he worked on the fence, particularly when the kitchen girls were down by the forest's edge gathering mushrooms. Autumn hoped he caught the world's worst cold, and serve him right for such silliness.

"You could teach him how *not* to clean a chimney," Emys said. He was in one of his sullen moods, and he was always mean when he was sullen. "Or how to come home covered in six kinds of mud, smelling like a swamp."

Autumn narrowed her eyes at her toast, affecting haughty indifference as she murmured a few words into the boggart's mind. A moment later, Emys gave a yelp and batted at his hair. A spider tumbled into his eggs.

"Can I help, Autumn?" Jack asked through a mouthful of

fried mushrooms. He hadn't looked pleased at his reassignment.

"Really?"

Jack seemed to mull it over. "Actually, I don't want to. I don't like Cai."

"Why not?"

Jack frowned. "He smells funny."

"Clean, you mean," Autumn said. "Some boys bathe, Jack."

"I bathe!"

"With soap?" Autumn raised a skeptical eyebrow. "In a tub?"

Stymied, Jack could only scowl at her.

A half hour later, Autumn was pacing in the shadow of the Gentlewood, watching the mountainside for Cai. Was he going to show up? It seemed unlikely, even after yesterday. But then, her entire acquaintance with Cai was unlikely. She tried to dispel her nervousness through vigorous stomping.

Behind her was a birdcage covered with a blanket. Within were half a dozen humming dragons—which were not, contrary to popular belief, named after humming*birds*, though they were about the same size. Gran kept half a dozen species of dragon in the menagerie, and Autumn had reasoned that if Cai was scared of dragons, it would be best to start small.

Not that humming dragons were particularly tame. In some ways, they were the worst dragons of all.

Autumn kept glancing up at Mythroor. The headmaster was up there on the rocky cliffs of Bawd Oer—she recognized his gleaming hair. With him were three senior apprentices weaving illusions, a magic that had always puzzled her. It seemed wasteful to paint the air with glittering vines and creeping roses, among other frippery. She guessed it was a sort of practice, like a musician going through scales, but what did she know? It wasn't as if magicians ever explained things to their servants.

The illusions broke apart in little mists of light, silver and opal and flame. Autumn let out her breath. The apprentices followed Headmaster Neath up the path, their lesson complete. Even from a distance, the headmaster seemed large. He had the sort of long, heavy stride that made you half expect him to lift his boot and kick the mountain out of his way, if it hadn't already given a polite cough and shuffled aside. Autumn was glad there was the usual amount of distance between them today. He unsettled her in a way she didn't fully understand.

But then, up until recently, hadn't she felt the same way about Cai? He was a different kind of large, as if his presence had more weight than other people's, likely from all the stories he dragged along with him like little moons.

We're the earth, and they're the mountains. She decided to follow Anurin's advice and turned her attention back to the muddy track she was wearing with her boots. Stomp, stomp, stomp.

The boggart circled above, flicking rapidly between shapes, a sure sign of temper. A cat became a dragon, a boy, a crow. Jack, it turned out, wasn't the only one who didn't like Cai.

The boggart hadn't been pleased to learn that Autumn was Cai's new sidekick. Not that she was *really* his sidekick. Cai was a proper hero, and proper heroes had proper sidekicks, not servants.

"Don't get your feathers twisted," Autumn said. "Cai and I have a deal. If I help him get over his fear, he'll help us find Winter. So I've got to keep my end of the bargain, else Cai might change his mind."

The boggart became a boy again, deep in a sulk. "I just don't know why we need help from some snooty magician."

"You don't know? We've been looking for almost a year, if you hadn't noticed! We have a clue now, a real clue, and we need Cai to figure out what it means. You haven't had any luck with that window, have you?"

"No." The boggart stared glumly at his feet. Autumn had assigned him to keep an eye on the bay window. He'd stayed all night, folded into the pane, but no boy had appeared in the glass.

Her hands clenched as she looked up at the castle. *Where are you?*

"Me and Cai are searching the school tonight," she said. "So you'd better not do anything to upset him. Now shut your trap—he's coming."

The boggart grumbled mutinously but disappeared into the trees as a squirrel. "And don't throw nuts," Autumn hissed over her shoulder. "Or spiders!"

"What?" Cai said. He looked as fresh as ever in the watery sunlight. He stepped neatly over the puddles Autumn had made with all her stomping.

"Nothing." Autumn leaned toward Cai and whispered in his ear, "You need to give the boggart a present."

"What?"

"He doesn't like you," she explained. "He's gotten used to it being just the two of us. If you give him a present, he'll warm up to you. He's real greedy."

Cai went pale. He didn't need to be told how dangerous it was to be on a boggart's bad side. "What kind of present?"

"Anything shiny," Autumn said. "He especially likes pocket watches. He thinks clocks are funny." She raised her voice. "Well, I guess we should get started."

"Right," Cai agreed, though he looked a lot less confident now. His gaze caught on the Gentlewood. They were near the forest's edge, where tiny saplings dotted the ground. Every year, the magicians burned the new growth, but it always came back. Bluebells nodded in the wind, spilling out from the trees like the train of a gown.

"Cai?"

His gaze drifted back to her. "Did you say something?"

Autumn frowned. "You have to keep your head around monsters. That's rule number one. You get distracted, and even the tame ones will take advantage—it's in their nature."

"Right, sorry. What's rule number two?"

Autumn paused. Gran had always said keeping your head was rule number one, but she'd never mentioned any others. "That's the only one," she said gruffly. "'Cause if you can't do that, you don't get to worry about anything else. Come over here."

Cai approached the cage with a jerky stride. He looked exactly like Jack had last spring when he'd watched Gran help a gwartheg give birth, right before he was violently sick.

"Well," she said, looking him up and down. "Maybe this is as close as you should get for now. We can always—"

"No." It came out sharp. He added with an apologetic grimace, "No. Let's keep going."

"But maybe if we took it slow—"

"Taking it slow isn't a good idea, Autumn."

"Why?"

He looked at her for a long moment, a look that seemed to measure and weigh her against something she couldn't see.

"Have you heard the prophecy?" he said. "About me?"

What prophecy? Autumn considered saying, but she decided it would be small of her to make fun of someone when their face was the color of porridge.

"Sure," she said. "Gran told me the whole thing." She could still remember all the words and recited them slowly. They felt cool and sharp, as if she'd taken a mouthful of starlight.

"I don't understand it all," she said. "What does 'his thirteenth winter's snow' mean?"

"I'm twelve now," Cai said. "So this will be my thirteenth winter. It means that I'm going to fight the Hollow Dragon before the first snow of the season."

Autumn's eyes widened. "But that's—that's soon."

Cai didn't answer. Autumn felt a dizziness wash over her. How long until the snows arrived? A month? Two at most? Her gaze drifted to the sky, though it was still the same messy tangle of sunshine and rainclouds.

She'd just assumed—like everybody else, probably—that if Cai was going to slay the Hollow Dragon, it would be when he was grown. Years and years from now. From that perspective, her helping him was of little importance—he would still have all sorts of time to find a better teacher, someone who could do a proper job. But now?

Now it felt as if her help—*hers*—was Cai's only chance.

"Right," she said, trying to keep the panic from her voice. She turned back to the humming dragons, desperate for a distraction, even one with claws and a nasty bite. "Right. Well, here goes." And she swept the blanket off the cage.

Humming dragons weren't like other dragons. It wasn't just their size, or their lack of fire.

Humming dragons, well, *hummed*.

Their song was close enough to a human voice to send a shiver down your back, but it was quiet and sweet as strawberries. It traveled through woods and marsh, over fields and hills, to reach children's ears and beckon them into the Gentlewood.

Humming dragons ate children—or, rather, ate their hearts. It made sense, then, that everything about them was made to tempt children closer. Their necks bore a lace-like frill, and they were covered in soft, downy feathers that shone in the sunlight. Framed against the forest dark, they looked like nothing more than tiny green jewels. To look at them was to want to trap them in your hands like fireflies, to carry them around in your pocket and nestle them against your pillow at night. They didn't *look* scary—which was why Autumn had chosen them for Cai—but their looks were a lie.

Hmm-hmm, hmm-hmm, hummed the dragons.

Shut it, Autumn commanded. One of the dragons fell silent. The other, the elder sister of the rest, kept humming. Autumn didn't have Gran's touch with monsters yet.

Autumn snapped her fingers in front of Cai's face—he was beginning to look dreamy. "Are you okay?"

He swallowed. "Did you—did you say something to them?"

Autumn nodded. She undid the locks on the cage door, blowing sharply on the dragons when they nipped at her fingers. They were so light that a good breath sent them soaring backward.

Cai was staring at her. "Then you're a Speaker?"

Autumn huffed. "No, I just mind my pleases and thank-yous, and the monsters do what I want."

"Sorry. I didn't realize. I knew your gran was one."

"We're all Speakers. My brothers aren't much good at it.

Kyffin's all right," Autumn amended grudgingly. "And doesn't he know it. Winter and I are better, though."

She felt a tug of longing at Winter's name, as if there was a hook in it pulling her back to Inglenook. She wanted to look for him *now*, to tear the castle apart stone by stone and window by window. But as she'd just told the boggart, she'd made a pact with Cai, and she needed him—she only wished she hadn't found out how much he needed *her.*

Cai's gaze drifted back to the cage, and he went white.

"Do you need a bucket?" Autumn said suspiciously.

"No."

"You better warn me if you do. I just washed my boots."

She undid the last lock and swung the cage door open. Cai took a step back. Autumn reached into the cage and, with a snap of her wrist, seized the smallest dragon by the scruff of its neck. The others hummed and growled—a deep, unsettling sound. The eldest clicked her jaws.

Don't even think about it, Autumn warned. Humming dragons had a poisonous bite. One nip, and you'd be paralyzed. That's when they'd eat you. And of course, given their size, the process took a while. At least regular-size dragons had the decency to bite your head off.

Hmm-hmm, hmm-hmm, hummed the eldest dragon, watching Autumn with her tiny black eyes.

Autumn shut the cage door firmly. "All right. Now, as you can see, if you hold him like this, he—"

She looked up and found that Cai was yards away.

"What are you doing?"

"Panicking?" Cai held up his shaking hands.

"Come on," Autumn said. "You won't get over your fear like that."

She marched over and grabbed Cai's hand. She pinched his fingers around the dragon's neck so that it couldn't bite, then stepped back.

Hmm-hmm, hmm-hmm, the caged dragon sang.

"There!" she said. "How do you feel?"

Cai looked stunned. He stared at the dragon writhing ineffectively in his palm. "It's—it's not that bad."

"What did I tell you?" Autumn grinned triumphantly. "You just have to face your fear. Now give him back to me— carefully. Keep your fingers on his neck, right?"

Cai didn't move.

"Cai?" Autumn didn't like the look in his eyes. "Stop listening to the song."

"It's not that," he said in a faint voice. "It's—I—"

He slumped to the grass.

"Cai!" Autumn shouted. The second Cai's grip loosened, the humming dragon sank its fangs into his thumb.

Autumn knelt at his side. As the dragon fluttered free, she spat, *Don't move an inch, you rotter.*

But at that moment, the dragons hummed a lovely quick melody that rolled over her like a wave. And though she was used to their song, Autumn's head spun briefly. The dragon

– 110 –

that had bitten Cai nudged its maw against the door, and out it swung.

The dragons soared free. The eldest came first, her wings snapping with delight.

Stop, Autumn shouted. *Get back in there!*

But their song was so loud that Autumn could barely hear herself. And then the dragons had her surrounded.

Hmm-hmm, hmm-hmm, they sang. The sound was like a violin played on the shore of a gentle brook, like birdsong in the treetops. It was a song meant for lazy days, for napping in summer shade. They churned around Autumn, wind woven with emeralds.

Back! she cried as a dragon swooped down, teeth bared. *Back! You're not getting his heart.*

"My heart?" Cai murmured.

Autumn froze. She hadn't said that out loud. She *hadn't*. So how had Cai heard her?

Cai? she said in the Speech.

"Here," Cai said fuzzily.

Autumn didn't have time to puzzle over mysteries. She drew a breath and hollered, *"Gran!"*

Her voice echoed down the mountain. Where was Gran? She could be in the cottage, or up in the castle helping one of the masters. She could be deep in the Gentlewood, where the trees were like stone walls. Autumn felt dizzy—and, for the first time, afraid.

"Gran!"

A light glowed at the corner of her eye. Cai had propped himself up on one elbow, despite the poison spreading through his body. Sweat trickled down his brow, and the whole left side of him was stiff as a plank. His skin shone like a curious mixture of silver and pearls—*starlight*. It was as if there was a lamp in his stomach, cool and flickering.

Autumn froze. Was this how magicians died, by turning into stars and drifting away? Had she killed Cai Morrigan? "What's happening?" she demanded.

"It's all right." Cai's voice was barely there. "I drank from the river this morning, before the stars went away. I thought I might need it."

He began to murmur an incantation. The light grew brighter and brighter. Even the humming dragons seemed transfixed— they hovered silently, malevolent eyes fixed on Cai.

Cai lifted his hand, and the light exploded.

It was like a globe of lightning, silent and swift. And yet it wasn't blinding—it was starlight, after all, and had no heat.

The dragons fell to the ground. Autumn couldn't tell if they were alive or dead and didn't bother to check. She scooped them up and thrust them into the cage in a pile. Then she grabbed Cai and wrenched him half-upright.

"Cai." She shook him. *"Cai."*

He didn't move. She couldn't tell if he was breathing. The stiffness had spread to the right side of his body. Would it stop his heart? Autumn didn't know. She'd never seen anyone bitten by a humming dragon. What should she do?

"What's all this yelling, child?" It was Gran, limping out of the forest with a net slung over her shoulder. Autumn let out a cry of desperate relief.

"He got bit," she sobbed. "He got bit, and then he zapped them, then he just collapsed—"

Gran's face shuttered as she felt Cai's pulse, and Autumn knew it was bad. "The river," Gran said. "Cold's the only thing that can push the poison out, if it hasn't spread too far."

She hoisted Cai onto her shoulder as if he weighed no more than a lamb, and then she was running.

Autumn ran after her. The Afon Morrel loomed ahead. Gran raced across the bank, paying no heed to the slimy deadfall. Two gwarthegs were drinking on the opposite shore, their bells tinkling.

Gran waded through the uneven shallows until she reached the first deep channel, then thrust Cai in.

Autumn followed. The river washed over the tops of her boots, but she barely noticed its bite. Some of the stiffness left Cai, but he didn't open his eyes.

"Fool child," Gran was muttering. "What have you done to yourself? This should fix an ordinary boy, but you? Who's to know?"

"He cast a spell," Autumn choked out. "He had starlight inside him, from the river."

"He did, did he?" Gran peered at Cai's face. "Well, that's what's done for him, then. Not just the poison. You can't swallow all that magic and then spit it out all at once without spitting out part of yourself. He should know that, being a magician and all."

"He did it to save us," Autumn said. "They would have gotten me, too, if he hadn't."

"I never heard of such nonsense," Gran said. "What were you thinking, playing games with those ill-tempered gnats?"

Tears slid down Autumn's face. This was all her fault. She had known Cai was terrified of dragons, and what had she done? Handed him one of the most dangerous dragons in the world! Humming dragons might look harmless, but Autumn knew better. She *knew better*, and still she'd made a mess of things, as she so often did.

The gwarthegs, tasting her fear on the wind, took a thoughtful step toward her. *No*, Autumn shouted, and there was such force behind it that they twitched and shrank back. Autumn had only seen them do that with Gran.

The sun peeked out from the clouds. The river brightened, while the shadows under the willows grew thick and foreboding. Among the darkness, something gleamed.

"Gran, look!" Autumn cried.

"What?"

Autumn didn't bother to reply. Ignoring Gran's shouts, she dragged Cai over to the willows. She slipped on a particularly slimy stone and banged her knee, almost losing her hold. She swallowed the pain and pushed on.

The willow boughs caught at her hair. She squinted in the darkness. She was certain she had seen it—a flash of light that had been less a flash than a cold and distant glow.

There it was! She drew Cai deeper into the shadows, where there was a pool gleaming with starlight. The current must have pulled it there before the sun could burn it away.

Autumn scooped up handfuls of the starry water and dashed it in Cai's face. He mumbled something, an encouraging sign, but didn't open his eyes.

"That won't do it, child," said Gran, who'd come up silently behind her.

Autumn took a breath. She didn't want Cai to choke, but he'd freeze to death if they kept him in the river much longer. His limbs moved more easily now, undulating in the current, but his skin felt like hardening wax.

Autumn scooped up another handful of water. The starlight floated on top like a film of oil. She opened Cai's mouth and poured it down his throat.

He jerked up in a fit of coughing. Autumn let out a sob of relief. She rolled him onto his side, keeping a tight grip on his shoulder, for the current was strong.

"Give him over." Gran lifted Cai and waded out of the river. She deposited him on the bank and wrapped her cloak around him.

"Cai!" Autumn knelt at his side. "Are you all right?"

"Yes," he said, but he was shivering so badly that Autumn didn't believe him for a second.

Nor did Gran. "The cottage," she said shortly. She lifted Cai again, and they took off at a run.

9

In Which Cai
Is Something

Cai's politeness made a full recovery before he did. After five minutes in front of the roaring fire, he was apologizing for the trouble he'd caused, for the escaped dragons, for interrupting Gran's duties. Autumn thought he would have started apologizing for the weather next, but Gran managed to shut him up with a plate of flatcakes (made by Jack, the only Malog who could bake) and tea topped with a layer of thick cream.

Next Gran dosed him with a big spoonful of her cure-all. Autumn watched in sympathy. The Malog children were subjected to Gran's cure-all whenever they fell ill, ensuring that when they did feel poorly, they hid it as long as possible. Gran refused to divulge the ingredients, but it smelled like a combination of cod-liver oil, raw garlic, and the moonshine whiskey she made in the cellar. It was difficult to imagine anything worse than that smell—until you tasted it.

"I'm sorry, Autumn," Cai said when they were alone, Gran having tramped outside to check on the humming dragons.

"Shut up," Autumn said. "I'm the one who should be apologizing. And if you argue, I'll dunk your head in the river again," she promised as Cai opened his mouth.

He sighed. The starlight was fading from his cheeks. "I'm still sorry."

"Fine. Be sorry quietly." She handed him another mug of tea. "I'm so stupid. I should have started you out with Amfidzel or one of the other babies. I just didn't think you'd actually faint. Next time will be different, promise."

Cai didn't say anything. He stared into the fire, his eyes pinched at the corners. "I guess you're wondering what happened."

"You got scared. I was there."

Cai set the mug aside. "Yes. But that's not all." He stared down at his hands. "Something happens to me when I'm around dragons. It's like—like there's a darkness all around me, full of shapes."

"Shapes," Autumn repeated. "What kind of shapes?"

"I don't know." Cai swiped his hand over his eyes. "I hear this sound, like something breathing. Something big. And then I hear fighting. I know it's fighting, even though I can't see in the dark. Someone's yelling, and there's this flash of light. And after it comes an awful *roar.*"

Autumn felt cold. "What kind of roar?"

"I don't know. I can't describe it."

"And that happens every time you're around a dragon?"

"Every time." His voice was very quiet. "I think it's a vision."

Autumn swallowed. "Of the Hollow Dragon?"

He gave her the faintest of smiles. "What else? That's who I am, isn't it? The boy who defeats the dragon and saves Eryree. That's what I'm meant for."

"You're not *meant* for anything," Autumn said, surprised by the heat in her voice. "You're just a boy. And you know what? You don't have to fight the Hollow Dragon if you don't want to. Who cares what some stupid prophecy says?"

Cai didn't reply. Troubled by the look in his eyes, Autumn went to let Choo in. The shiftless dog had been scratching at the door for the last half hour, though Autumn knew it would be all of ten minutes before he started scratching to go out again. As soon as the door opened, he bounded in, sneezing alarmingly. Oblivious to the tension, a phenomenon as incomprehensible to Choo as the rotation of the earth, he ran delighted circles around Cai's chair until he exhausted himself, whereupon he collapsed in a puddle of fur. The darkness in Cai's face faded, and he reached down to rub Choo's belly.

Autumn watched him thoughtfully. Cai had saved her life out there on the mountain. He'd done it even though he'd had to risk his own. She wondered if risking your life for someone else was what being a hero meant. By that measure, Choo was a great hero, given how he was always chasing after monsters. Of course, Choo didn't understand things like death or danger; to Choo, life was a game without stakes. No—a hero was someone who looked death in the face and took its measure. Autumn wondered if she could have done what Cai had.

"So, in this vision of yours, with the fighting and all," she said slowly. "Are you winning?"

Cai gazed into the dancing flames. He was quiet for so long that Autumn thought he wouldn't answer.

"I don't think so," he said.

Cai felt better within the hour, but he was still a bit wobbly in the knees when he stood up, so Autumn made them a hearty lunch—a better cure-all, in her opinion, than Gran's tonic. As far as cooking went, Autumn was all right in the sandwich department, and managed to toast a few pieces of Seren's seabread and fill them with tuna, cheese, and a handful of herbs from Gran's garden.

Cai was surprisingly good company when he wasn't falling all over himself to be polite. Autumn even discovered, to her astonishment, that he had a sense of humor. She was less successful with dessert—baked apple, something even Kyffin could usually manage. The apples were all golden and gooey with melted sugar up top, but the bottoms stuck to the pan like barnacles and burned.

"At least you didn't get seaweed on them," Cai said in such

a mild tone that it was unclear whether he was joking, until Autumn punched him in the arm and he grinned. She hadn't thought he'd noticed her mucking up his fancy old book in the skybrary. But apparently, polite, bashful Cai noticed more than he let on.

They ate the unburned halves of the apples and exchanged stories by the fire. Cai talked about his lessons, and though Autumn didn't understand half of what he told her about the principles of incantations and higher magics and balancing the realms, she found it fascinating. She'd never known, for instance, that star magicians had an affinity for healing enchantments, while sun and fire mages were best at blasting holes in things (monsters especially). She didn't feel as if she was any closer to understanding the world of magicians, but it was as if she could glimpse the edges of it now, like a coastline emerging from the fog.

She told Cai about her beastkeeper duties, which she didn't expect him to find very interesting. But there she was wrong—he asked question after question and seemed astonished by her answers.

"I had no idea it was so much work," he said after she told him about the gwartheg deworming process—not the safest of subjects for lunchtime.

Autumn raised her eyebrows. "You thought all those monsters looked after themselves?"

"I—" Cai blushed. "I guess I never really thought about it."

"Why should you?" Autumn said with a shrug, taking another bite of apple. But Cai looked bothered for some reason. He asked about her education, but there was little for her to tell. Servants at Inglenook weren't taught anything but their duties. What would they learn? Few servants could read. And it wasn't as if the cooks had any use for geography, or beast-keepers for mathematics.

Cai hesitated. "My parents can't read either."

Autumn didn't understand. "But all magicians can read."

"They're not magicians. They were servants here at Inglenook."

Autumn's jaw fell. *"Servants?"*

Cai nodded. "My dad was one of the cooks. My mom was a housekeeper. Your gran probably knew them. I wondered at dinner if she'd say something."

Autumn couldn't believe it. The prophecy said that Cai was of low birth, but she'd thought it meant his parents were merchants or something. Not servants! "Don't tell me they're still scrubbing floors somewhere."

"No. There aren't many magicians with nonmagician parents, but there are some. The king provides for them if they're poor. After I was born a magician, we moved to a manor house in Langorelle."

Autumn shook her head. It was like something out of a fairy tale, one where a goose girl became a queen or a wolf turned into a prince. She supposed it explained some of Cai's strangeness, though. He treated her differently than the other students did, as if he barely noticed she was a servant.

Some of his strangeness. Not all.

The sun began to move behind the mountain until only a sliver remained. The sunlight went slant and hung in the air like gossamer, clothing the treetops in white. Cai stared out the window, his eyes full of the forest.

Autumn watched him for a moment. "Why do you do that?"

He blinked. Autumn noted that his eyes were now the brown of the undersides of mushrooms. She found it interesting that they never changed dramatically. It was always small enough that most people wouldn't notice.

"What?" Cai said.

Autumn tapped her knee with her fingers. She felt like a detective, but she would have to be a careful one. She had her suspicions about Cai, but she didn't know how much he suspected about himself. It wouldn't be kind to scare him. "Why do you look at the forest like that?"

"Oh." Cai turned away. "You noticed."

"I notice a lot of things." Color-changing eyes, for instance. "What are you looking for?"

"It's not that I'm looking *for* something," Cai said. He wiped his palms against the knees of his trousers. He suddenly looked very nervous, and Autumn wondered if she should get the bucket.

"All right," he finally said. "I haven't been completely honest with you. There's a second reason why I came to you for help."

"Okay," Autumn said slowly.

"The forest—" He took a breath. "It pulls at me."

Autumn's brow furrowed. Was this magician-speak for something? "What does that mean?"

"It's like . . ." Cai seemed to search for words. "It's like I'm caught in a tide, and it's pulling me toward the Gentlewood. Always pulling. Whenever I'm near it, whenever I walk the paths, I want to go deeper. But no matter how deep I go, it's never enough. When I sleep, I can hear the leaves rustling." He stopped abruptly and looked down at his hands.

"You said there was another reason you wanted my help," Autumn said. "You should just say it."

"Right." Cai wiped his palms again. "You know a lot about monsters. I want you to tell me if I'm one."

His voice was quiet but steady. When he finally met her gaze, he blinked. "You're not surprised."

Autumn bit her lip. She tried to imagine what Winter would say—he always said the right thing, unlike her. She didn't want to hurt Cai—she realized that she cared if she hurt him now. She hadn't before.

"Like I said, I'm good at noticing things," she said. "Nobody looks at the forest the way you do. Nobody except, well, monsters. It's their home, see. They're part of it, and it's part of them. And you heard me down by the river, when I used the Speech. You could be a Speaker, I suppose. But—" She paused.

"You're different. I can't explain how I know that; I just do."

Cai leaned forward. His eyes were as bright as sunlit amber and full of longing. "What am I?"

"I don't know," she said. "That's the honest truth. You could be a shape-shifting monster that got stuck as a boy. Or maybe some magician caught you and made you look this way with a spell. Or you could be a changeling, left behind in the crib while some spriggan stole the real Cai. There are also stories of half-human monsters, though I've never met one. I don't know. I just know you're *something*."

Cai sagged back against his chair.

"I'm sorry," Autumn said. She really was. She couldn't imagine what it must be like, not knowing who you were. Not knowing *what* you were. "But I'll help you figure it out, Cai. I don't know how, but I'll try."

Cai gazed at his folded hands. "Sometimes at night, when I wake up from dreaming of forest paths and the smell of the pines, I think about just walking into the forest. Walking and walking, and never coming back. I've stopped myself a hundred times."

"Why do you?" Autumn said. "Stop yourself, I mean."

Cai made a helpless gesture. "I don't really belong there, any more than I belong here. When I go into the forest, it treats me like any other magician. The wisps lead me astray. Other monsters follow me or try to lull me asleep so they can eat my heart or bones or who knows what. I get cold at night."

He rubbed his head. "I don't really belong anywhere. Do you understand?" He frowned. "Of course you don't. I'm sorry. You have a home—you belong here."

"I suppose I belong here." She thought of Inglenook glittering up on the mountainside, the play of light from magicians' staffs. "But I would rather belong somewhere else. Even though I know it's impossible."

He gazed at her. "Then you do understand."

Autumn swallowed. They sat in silence.

"No one else knows," Cai said.

Autumn's mind boggled at that. Boggled at all of it. She shouldn't even be sitting there with Cai Morrigan. She shouldn't be sharing secrets with him, secrets so big they could tear a kingdom apart.

"You don't really want to fight the Hollow Dragon, do you?" she said. "Monsters don't usually fight other monsters."

"I have to fight him. I'm the only one who can stop him— that's what the prophecy says. It doesn't make a difference what I am. I can't just think about myself."

"Hmm," Autumn said. "Well, you're definitely not a boggart, then."

A smile tugged at Cai's mouth. "Your boggart might hear you."

Autumn snorted. "I hope he does!"

They talked for a while about Cai's parents and their home in Langorelle, where he had lived until he was eight, the customary age for magicians to enroll at Inglenook. There were no clues there—Cai's childhood had been disappointingly ordinary, apart from his constant yearning for the forest. His parents were ordinary; he had an ordinary sister named Bluebell; and they lived with two ordinary cats, Sir Purrsival and Catastrophe.

"You're not afraid of me, are you?" Cai said suddenly. He looked so worried that Autumn almost burst out laughing. She imagined the wyverns or the Hounds of Arawn sitting in their stalls picking their teeth and worrying about whether they were *too* scary.

"No," she said, slurping her tea contentedly. "You're all right."

It was the truth. If Cai *was* a monster—like Amfidzel, or her dear boggart—Autumn wouldn't like him any less. In fact, she would probably like him more. She spent plenty of time with monsters and understood their ways. She couldn't say the same about magicians with grand destinies.

"I should go," Cai said eventually. He looked lighter, as if he'd set down a heavy weight. His eyes were a peaceful mud color. "I'll see you later. Meet me in the hallway behind the Jenkins Library at midnight. I think we should investigate all our clues one by one, starting with the very first sighting in the kitchens."

Autumn nodded, not looking at him. Cai didn't seem well enough for another adventure. But what was she to say? Winter needed her. She'd risk her life to rescue him and not think twice—but risking someone else's was a harder matter.

Cai looked like he knew what she was thinking. "I'm going to help you find your brother," he said in a voice that Autumn couldn't imagine arguing with. It gave her a glimpse of the Cai Morrigan the stories talked about.

Autumn walked him to the door, Choo whining at their heels. There was nothing the dog disliked more than a guest rude enough to leave.

"Wait." Cai paused thoughtfully on the porch. "How will you get into the castle? They lock it up at night with magic. I have a secret door that I use, but you can't see it unless you're a magician. Why don't you come by after supper, and I'll hide you somewhere?"

"No, I don't want Gran wondering where I am," Autumn said. "I'll sneak out after she goes to bed. Don't worry. I've got it all figured out. Just tell me where to meet you."

10

In Which Winter
Wakes the Boggart

– LAST SUMMER –

The next time Winter stopped being a cloud, he found himself in the Inglenook kitchens. Or, rather, looking out at them from a grimy mirror above one of the sinks.

The kitchens were a hot, dark, steamy place. But they were also surprisingly cozy, nestled deep beneath the school. There a small army of men and women labored day and night—for the bread had to be started at three in the morning—to feed several hundred students and masters. Not just feed, but feed *well*, as only the best would do for magicians, Eryree's protectors. Every year, the cooks churned out thousands of braised hams, delicately flaky salmon rolls, gooey cheese sausages, mussels with cream sauce, vats of custard and treacle, and more tea cakes and marzipan drops and seaweed crisps than there were stars in the sky.

Winter had visited the kitchens a handful of times when he lived on the other side of the glass, when he and Autumn would try to cadge leftovers from a feast. Whenever the head cook proved unsympathetic, Autumn created a distraction—unsurprisingly, she had a knack for them—while Winter crept around on stealthy feet and shoved whatever he could reach into his pockets.

Autumn.

Just like before, the memories rushed back. Of course—Autumn would get him out of there, wherever he was. She was probably already looking for him.

Winter clung to the memory of his twin, her apple-red cheeks and light step, the way she snorted when she laughed. Thinking of her was like stepping into a patch of sunlight in a dank forest. He wouldn't forget her again. But how would he find her?

Something stirred under the table where the bakers stood in an intricate assembly line, preparing scads of blueberry flat-cakes. Winter leaned forward so that his forehead brushed the steamed glass. There it was again—the gleam of dark, sharp claws in an empty pocket of air that was far from empty, that seemed to vibrate with contained power.

Winter drew in his breath. "Boggart!" he shouted with all his might.

The boggart didn't stir. He was folded up small in a bread-basket beneath the table, dozing. Every few seconds, Winter caught the gleam of his black eyes, as if the boggart was waiting for something. No doubt that something was an opportunity for an unpleasant prank, perhaps related to the enormous birthday cake the head baker was frosting on the table.

Winter's breath quickened. The mirror-world of the kitchens was dark and indistinct, for the glass was too corroded and spackled with grease to reflect the world truly. It was like being trapped in a nightmare.

He pressed himself against the glass and shouted in the Speech, *Boggart!*

This time, the boggart started. *Winter?* His voice was sleepy and confused.

Boggart! Winter cried. *I'm here!*

The boggart uncoiled from the breadbasket and circled the long table. He turned himself into an astonishing replica of the tabby cat whose mouse-hunting grounds included the kitchens and sniffed the corners.

I'm here. Winter tried to shout, but he couldn't summon the energy anymore—it was as if all his strength had been funneled into that first cry. *Tell Autumn I'm here.*

The boggart sniffed everywhere. When he was finished, he turned himself back into a boggart—in other words, disembodied himself—and Winter couldn't track him anymore. He still caught flashes of his eyes sometimes as the boggart circled the pantry or nosed into cupboards. Winter kept calling, both aloud and in the Speech, but the boggart didn't reply again.

"Gosh, you're a noisy one." It was Maddie. Her black braids wavered behind her like branches in the wind. "Who are you yelling at?"

Winter was too sick with disappointment to answer. Nobody

had ever called him noisy before—that was Autumn. He was more likely to be called her shadow, which had always made him happy. Autumn's shadow was a comfortable place to be. He missed her so much.

"Can you tell me my name again?" Maddie said. "I've forgotten."

It took Winter a moment to remember. "Maddie."

She smiled. Her grayish body seemed to come into sharper focus. "That's right. And you're Winter."

Hearing his name made him feel better. "I need to talk to someone on the other side of the glass."

Maddie gave him a puzzled look. "You can't. Them outsiders can't even see us properly." She drifted closer. "Do you know any stories? Will you tell me one? It's been so long since I heard a story."

"What about that other person you mentioned?" Winter pressed. "The one who's been here for a long time. Would he know how to talk to the outside?"

Maddie's face fell. "The Old One," she murmured. "I forgot about him. He's gone."

"Gone?"

"The Dark got him." She shook her head slowly. "It gets everyone in the end."

"What do you mean? What's the Dark?" Winter froze. "Is there some sort of monster in here with us?"

But Maddie only shook her head again and wouldn't answer.

"Why don't you ever try to get out?" Winter asked, frustrated.

Maddie wrinkled her brow. "Where would I go?"

"Out there, of course! Where we belong!"

"With them?" Maddie shuddered. "I was always afraid of ghosts. I wouldn't want to haunt anyone."

Winter froze. "But we're not ghosts."

She stared at him. "Course we are. What else could we be?"

"I don't know," Winter said. "But I know I'm not dead. I don't feel dead."

Maddie snorted. "Oh, and you know what dead feels like, do you? You only die once. So how can you be sure of the difference?"

Panic rose in Winter's throat. He didn't want to talk about this anymore. He wasn't dead. They were trapped somewhere, somewhere bad, but they could still get out. Autumn would find him. It was going to be all right.

"Is there anyone else I can talk to?" Winter said.

She shrugged. "Sure. Take your pick."

Winter blinked. "What do you mean?"

"Can't you see them?"

Maddie gestured. She didn't seem to be gesturing at anything. But then, abruptly, Winter saw.

There were others there. Perhaps six, maybe as many as ten. Some were like wisps of fog with hands and feet. Others were recognizable as men or women or children, but they were all so gray, so faded, like charcoal sketches left out in the rain. One was little more than a smudge.

Winter's knees trembled. "What happened to them?"

"Same thing that happens to everyone." Maddie looked down at her grayish body. She was grayer than the last time he'd seen her. "They forgot their names. That's the beginning of the end in here." She motioned to the pale smudge. "Look at her, poor little ghostie. The Dark'll get her soon enough."

"No, it won't." Winter's voice was as quiet as ever, but there was a granite-like quality about it that made Maddie stare. "Whatever this Dark is, we should protect her from it. *I'll* protect her."

Maddie made a disbelieving sound. "You can't even protect yourself. Look at you!"

Winter looked. At first he didn't know what Maddie was talking about. But then he did, and his breath snagged in his throat. He was *blurring*. Not all of him, just the edges and angles, as if he were a mountain smoothed by a curtain of rain. He hadn't looked like that before.

He looked at Maddie, at the others. Whatever was changing them, wearing them away piece by piece, was changing him, too. How long did he have until he looked like Maddie? Like the little smudge of a girl?

"Winter," he murmured. "I'm Winter." Terror scattered little black dots across his eyes. He turned toward the kitchens, where the boggart was still scouring every nook and corner, looking for him. Looking, but not seeing.

Autumn, where are you?

11

In Which Cai
Hunts for Spellprints

It was almost midnight by the time Gran's snores filled the cottage. Stealthy as the wind, Autumn crept out to the old beastkeepers' hut and woke the boggart.

The boggart wasn't easy to wake. Autumn found him nestled inside the caved-in fireplace where he stored his favorite trinkets. Her lantern caught a flash of claws and a gleam of black eyes, the only hints of boggart that remained when he was bodiless.

Autumn rapped on the wall above the fireplace, and then, when the boggart only groaned and went back to sleep, she reached in and scooped him out. But he was a bodiless monster, which aren't very scoopable—the boggart simply drifted through her fingers and went back into the fireplace.

"Boggart!" Autumn's voice caught. She needed the boggart tonight—not only his ferocity, which wasn't exactly on display at the moment, but his ability to sniff out enchantments. "Boggart!"

WHAT, the boggart said.

"We have to search the castle tonight, remember?"

I thought that was tomorrow.

"Yesterday it was tomorrow. Today it's today."

The boggart sighed.

"And you have to be nice to Cai," Autumn said. "No pranks. No tricks."

The boggart didn't reply, but mild puzzlement emanated from his direction. Telling a boggart not to play tricks was like telling Choo not to chase rabbits.

"All right, look," Autumn said. "Be nice to Cai, and you can play hide-the-boots with Emys for a week."

The boggart laughed. Hide-the-boots was one of his favorite games. It was exactly what it sounded like—choosing an imaginative hiding place for a pair of boots every morning. Once he'd hidden Jack's in a fish trap at the bottom of the Afon Morrel. Autumn had forbidden him from playing the game after that, which meant she'd surely receive part of the blame when Emys's boots wandered off to the henhouse or slipped inside an intact pumpkin.

What Autumn had never told anyone was that Winter had come up with hide-the-boots. For someone who never forgot to bring Gran her favorite flowers from the forest or to steal extra treats from the kitchens for their brothers (who rarely, if ever, deserved them), Winter was unexpectedly good at pranks. It was, of course, the boggart's favorite thing about him, but it was one of Autumn's too. Kind people were all well and good, but you simply *had* to respect a kind person with a hidden well of wickedness inside him. Better still, some of Winter's pranks were so wonderfully disgusting that Autumn could only shake her head in awe, like pine-needle pie with snot sauce. Autumn had fallen out of her chair laughing after Emys had taken a bite of what he thought was Jack's famous green-apple tart, while Winter had sat there with a perfectly confused expression. He'd felt guilty afterward, as he always did, and Emys had found a little sack of mints on his bed the next day, which he had at first refused to eat.

Autumn's hands clenched on her knees. The boggart flitted around her, petting her hair, then settled on her shoulder like a warm ghost and filled the hut with the smell of sweet peas and shortbread.

"I'm all right," she said, hoping that by saying it, it would become a little more true. "Do we have a deal?"

The boggart thought it over. *Can I put leeches in his bed, too?*

"Fine," Autumn said with a sigh. She told herself that if she was going to get in trouble, she might as well get some entertainment out of it.

Autumn didn't have to sneak into the castle. She simply went to the servants' entrance and knocked four times—two slow and two quick.

The door swung open. "Hurry," Ceredwen's voice whispered.

Autumn and the boggart slipped inside. From the house-keepers' lounge down the hall came a distant murmur of voices. One of the pipes had burst in the masters' bathroom, and the floor was now three inches deep in water. Consequently, half the housekeepers had been roused from their beds to deal with it before morning came and a horde of cranky magicians con-verged on the showers.

Autumn stripped off her clothes. Ceredwen helped her into one of her old uniforms—a blue shift, white apron, and sen-sible black lace-ups. It was all a little snug, but nothing too noticeable. Lastly, Autumn wrapped her conspicuous hair in the flannel kerchief the housekeepers wore for really messy jobs.

She adjusted her buttons, fingers trembling with nervous-ness and excitement. "Did anyone suspect anything?"

"Nope," Ceredwen said, beaming. She'd unscrewed the plumbing in the masters' bathroom herself, then alerted the other housekeepers about a "burst pipe." If a master or servant stumbled across Autumn that night, wandering the school, she would have been in trouble, but nobody would bat an eye at a housekeeper responding to a housekeeping crisis.

Autumn stowed her clothes in a shadowy alcove beneath the stairs. Ceredwen handed her a mop, and they set off.

The castle at night was full of phantoms: lanterns dangling from carven hooks cast a fitful light, and the very shadows seemed to creak and groan. Such sounds were probably just the doors settling or windows shivering in the mountain wind.

Probably. Heavy tapestries kept out the worst drafts, but a few found their way through, trailing chill fingers along Autumn's cheek. Occasionally, she'd catch a glimmer from something that shouldn't be glimmering out of the corner of her eye, but for the most part, the magic of the castle was too old to sparkle anymore. Autumn pictured all the spells holding the stones together stretched across the corridor like invisible spiderwebs.

"I made up another verse in your ballad, Autumn."

"That's nice, Ceri."

"Do you want to hear it?"

"You know, I would," Autumn said, "but we have to be quiet now. Stealthy."

"Right," Ceredwen said. She was blessedly silent for a few seconds. Then, "What color would you say your hair is, Autumn? Would you say it's like snow, or like ivory? I like ivory better, but more things rhyme with snow."

"I don't know, Ceri," Autumn said through her teeth. "I never thought about it."

"I'm going to make up another stanza about your boots."

"My *boots*?"

"Yeah. About how you're always stomping around," Ceri said. "How just the sound of your footsteps makes the monsters quake in their beds. Oh, isn't that good? Only I couldn't remember what color your boots were. Would you say they're black as night? That means I could rhyme with *fright, height, might* . . . Have you ever flown a kite?"

Autumn was spared from replying by the appearance of

another housekeeper. Ceredwen smiled and brandished her mop and pail. The servant, dripping wet and sullen-faced, barely glanced at them. Then Autumn was forced to listen to the first ten stanzas of "The Ballad of Autumn Malog," until finally they came to the narrow corridor behind the Jenkins Library.

Cai was there, peering anxiously into the shadows. He blended into the darkness so well that Autumn wondered if it was one of the enchantments woven into his cloak. Only his staff, glowing with gentle starlight, gave him away. Ceredwen let out a shriek—she'd almost walked into him.

Cheeks flaming, she sank into a deep curtsy. "Master Morrigan! I'm s-so sorry, sir, I didn't see you."

"That's all right," he said, his own face reddening. "I'm sorry, I should have—"

"Good grief!" Autumn said. "We're on an important mission. We can't stand around apologizing to each other all night."

Ceredwen turned round eyes on Autumn. "You're on a mission with *Cai Morrigan?*"

"Yes, and you'd better keep quiet about it."

"Oh, I will," Ceredwen said earnestly. "I swear on my life, Autumn. I swear—"

"You don't need to swear on anyone's life, Ceri," Autumn said.

Cai looked even more embarrassed. He seemed to be breaking out in hives again.

"Right." Ceredwen gazed into the distance, and Autumn

guessed, with an inward groan, that she was already dreaming up new verses for her ballad. "Well, good luck, Autumn." She bowed to Cai and dashed off, humming to herself.

"What was she singing before?" Cai said.

"Nothing," Autumn said in a severe voice.

"Really?" Cai scratched his neck. "She mentioned a thunderstorm, so I thought maybe it was about you."

Autumn shoved him. Cai laughed. At that moment, there came a scratching sound from the shadows, and then a dragon's growl. Cai whirled.

"Don't worry," Autumn said. "That's just the boggart. He's being mean, but he's going to *stop*, or else I won't speak to him for a week."

The growling and scratching ceased. The boggart stepped out of the darkness in his boy shape, glaring at Cai.

Cai didn't look reassured by the boggart's appearance. "Hello," he said tentatively, which Autumn thought brave of him. How strange it was that Cai would faint at the sight of pocket-size dragons, but not a vastly powerful monster like the boggart.

The boggart cocked his head, examining Cai. His glare faded, replaced by puzzlement. "Which one are you?"

"I'm Cai," Cai said uncertainly.

"He knows," Autumn said, annoyed. "Stop playing games, boggart."

The boggart laughed. He laughed and laughed, then he melted into his unshape and said to Autumn, *He doesn't know who he is, this one. He doesn't know what he can do.*

Autumn froze. "Do you know what Cai is, boggart? Do you know where he came from?"

From the forest, the boggart said slyly.

"Can you hear him?" Autumn asked Cai. Cai shook his head.

I'm not speaking to him, the boggart said. *And I won't.*

Autumn threw her hands up. "Can't you be polite for once in your life?"

No.

"Is he a monster?" Autumn said. "Like you?"

No one is like me, the boggart said. *Not even boggarts. That's a human word—humans like naming things they don't understand. The Folk don't bother with that sort of nonsense.*

"He says the Folk—monsters, I mean—don't use words like *boggart,*" Autumn told Cai. "Maybe he doesn't know what you're called."

"Can you ask him how I can get back?" Cai said. Autumn could almost see the forest filling up his thoughts. "To wherever I came from?"

The boggart only laughed again.

"You're not going to get anything out of him," Autumn said. Boggarts hoarded mysteries like gold.

The boggart, naturally, was delighted by their confusion. He flitted around Cai, tugging at his hair.

Fortunately, Cai had remembered the boggart's present, a beautiful golden pocket watch. The case was carved in a pattern of holly leaves, inlaid with tiny rubies for berries. It was clearly enchanted, for it shimmered lightly in the darkness. Cai showed the boggart how the pocket watch grew or shrank to fit its wearer.

Blecch, the boggart said. *Why do magicians have to foul up a perfectly good watch with their enchantments?*

"He likes it," Autumn said as the watch disappeared with a flash of claws. "How do we get to the kitchens from here? I'm all turned around."

"Door on your left. Leads to a stairway the servants never use—too roundabout. First things first, though." From his pocket Cai produced a notebook, which was crammed with neat, tiny writing. "The way I see it, we have six clues."

"Six?"

"Yes. Three clues suggest we should look for Winter in the castle. Winter's right boot was found in a corridor, the boggart heard him in the kitchens, and you saw him in the window upstairs. The other three clues suggest we should continue your search in the forest. The masters found Winter's left boot at the edge of the forest, you found his cloak *in* the forest, and the sleeping monsters said they saw him and the Hollow Dragon at around the same time."

Autumn thought it through. "Okay. But you said those monsters couldn't be trusted."

"Right. And also, seeing and hearing Winter is stronger evidence than finding a cloak or a boot. Besides, if the Hollow Dragon did carry him off, there isn't—" He broke off, flushing.

"There isn't much point in looking for him," Autumn finished quietly. "I know. Go on."

Cai's blush deepened. "So we'll search the kitchens first. Then we'll move on to the other two clues—the boot and the window."

Autumn nodded, her heart thudding. There was something about having everything written down in a book in a tidy magician's hand that filled her with new hope. And Cai's logic was good—better than hers, she had to admit. She'd never been much for planning—easier to plow right into things and ask questions later.

She followed Cai down the winding stairs. Déjà vu brushed against her like a ghost as she remembered all the times she'd snuck down to the kitchens with Winter. But the boy in front of her was dark-haired, his cloak a shadow billowing smartly behind him. She swallowed against the sticky weight at the back of her throat.

The kitchens were warm and smelled of yeast. A dozen loaves sat rising on the counter, waiting to be popped into the ovens. Cai lit the cavernous room with flecks of starlight.

"When did you hear him?" Cai asked the boggart, who was a boy again.

The boggart shrugged. "The cooks were making raspberry preserves."

"It was July," Autumn clarified.

"No windows. But there's this." Cai wandered over to a mirror above the sink. He stared at it for a long moment. "Interesting."

"What?" In her excitement, Autumn leaned so far over his shoulder that she almost knocked him into the wall.

"Look."

Autumn was so close her breath fogged the glass, which was pocked and grimy with oil stains. She saw only their muddy reflections.

"Sorry." Cai glanced at her. "I forgot. There's a spellprint—only magicians can see those."

"A what?"

In answer, he murmured to his staff. Something resembling a smear of grease appeared on the glass. It wavered and drifted through the mirror.

"Oh!" Autumn exclaimed. "It's enchanted!"

"No," Cai said thoughtfully. "But an enchantment touched this mirror. Only the most powerful enchantments leave spellprints behind. They're like the fingerprints of magic."

Autumn ached as she gazed at her blurry reflection. Had Winter stood there, looking for her? She touched her own fingers to the glass.

"Let's examine the window next," Cai said. He looked around. "Where'd your boggart go?"

"Boggart?" Autumn called.

Heh heh heh, was the only response.

Autumn put her hands on her hips. "What are you doing?"

Nothing. Something rustled by the counter, and the lid on the sugar slammed shut. The boggart reappeared in his boy shape, grinning.

Autumn groaned. "Did you put salt in the sugar?"

"I didn't put salt in the sugar," he replied with such boggart-ish innocence that Autumn wasn't fooled for a second.

She popped open the lid and looked inside. "Well, what *did* you put in the sugar?"

The boggart's grin widened. "Lice."

"Urgh!" Autumn shoved the container away.

"We can't leave it," Cai said. "The servants don't deserve that."

Autumn raised an eyebrow at him. If Cai interfered with the boggart's prank, the boggart wouldn't forgive him for a thousand pocket watches.

Cai chewed his lip, and then he smiled. He murmured to his staff, and the buggy sugar rose into the air. At the same time, another sugar container sitting on a tray opened, and the sugar billowed out. The two white clouds, one wriggling, drifted into each other's containers.

"What did you do?" Autumn said.

Cai motioned to the second sugar container. "That's the tray that goes up to the masters' lounge in the morning."

The boggart burst into laughter that could only fairly be described as cackling, and Cai looked alarmed. But Autumn was laughing too, and after a moment, Cai smiled. The boggart became a black cat and rubbed his face against Cai's ankle.

Look, Autumn said. *He's not so bad.*

We'll see, the boggart said thoughtfully. There was a cruel amusement in his voice, but as there often was, Autumn chose to ignore it.

Autumn led Cai through the tangle of staircases and corridors to the bay window. He stood very still and ran his hand over the glass.

"Is there a spellthing here?" Autumn demanded.

"Yes." He seemed lost in thought. He roamed down the corridor, looking in the other windows. "Nothing. Interesting . . ."

Autumn let him mutter to himself for a few minutes before she couldn't stand it any longer. "Well?"

"I don't know if I'm right," he began slowly, "but all this reminds me of something. It's an old magic—so old nobody knows the enchantment anymore. The ancient mages used to trap people in mirrors."

Autumn froze. "*Trap* them?"

"Part of them, anyway," Cai said. "Their souls. A lot of the ancient magicians were vain. It was a way to punish their enemies. The magicians would force them to pay them compliments all the time, or else they wouldn't let them out. Sometimes they'd put one of their servants in a mirror and give it away as a gift. A person could have a mirror that told them they were beautiful every single day."

"That's horrible."

"A lot of the ancient magicians *were* horrible," Cai said. "Not that we're much better these days. The magicians at Inglenook barely looked for your brother. But when one of the students— her name was Gwendolyn, I think—disappeared in the forest three years ago, they went all the way to Carrack Falls searching for her."

Autumn puzzled over Cai's anger. It had never made her angry that the magicians hadn't searched for Winter, any more than she was angry at the river for flooding after the spring rains. She and Winter were important to each other, but why would any of the Malogs be important to magicians, who were practically royalty?

"It doesn't make sense," she said. "Why would some magician shut Winter away in a window?"

Cai shook his head. "Let me try a few spells."

He murmured something, and a gentle glow rolled over the glass. The stars shone through, and Cai seemed to be gathering their light, too, weaving it into the pattern with his staff. Despite the knots in her stomach, Autumn was enthralled. She settled herself against the wall with her knees up as ripples of starlight played across her face.

After a few minutes, Cai paused and leaned heavily against the wall.

"You're tired." Autumn felt a stab of guilt.

"I'm all right." Cai's hand shook, though, as he brushed his hair back. "I feel better than I did this morning."

"Gran said it takes a few days to get over humming dragon poison," Autumn said. "D'you want another dose of cure-all? Gran has bottles of the stuff."

"Thank you, but I think a good sleep is all I need. I'd like to try again tomorrow, if that's all right."

Autumn started. "So soon?"

Cai's hand tightened briefly on his staff, and for a moment

he seemed to gaze at something Autumn couldn't see.

"Sorry," she said before he could answer. "I keep forgetting that the prophecy—that there isn't much—" The words got all tangled up. Cai was still gazing at nothing with that gray expression, as if he was half there and half elsewhere. "I know you probably never forget."

"That's all right." He blinked and gave her a brief smile. "I wish I could, sometimes."

He went back to his enchantments. As the light drifted, he said, "It must be nice. Living with your family, I mean. Seeing them every day."

Autumn was happy to talk about something else. "Do you miss your family?"

"Usually I'm too busy to think about it. But whenever I'm not—" He stopped. "The first year was the worst. I was only eight. I wrote my parents every day, begging to come home."

Autumn asked Cai about his family's home in Langorelle. He seemed to like talking about it, and she had always wondered what a magician's house looked like. However, although Cai's house was grand, he and his sister, Blue-bell, had spent most of their time playing in the little wood that backed onto the garden, which reminded him of the Gentlewood. Langorelle was miles from the Gentlewood, but sometimes birds carried seeds there. One of the trees in Cai's wood was a Gentlewood tree, a great mossy thing that grew faster than anything else and muttered to itself in the wind. Cai had fallen asleep in its shade one fall day and awoken to find himself tucked under a layer of bright leaves like a blanket. Another time, the tree had covered him with spring blossoms. The flowers gave anyone else who touched them a nasty rash, but they didn't bother Cai.

He also told Autumn about his cats. Of the two, it was clear that Catastrophe was his favorite.

"She's black and white, with a big black patch around one eye, like a pirate," he said, moving his hands through the light, which dripped down the window like rain. "My parents got her before I was born. She used to sleep with me every night and lick my head. She still does when I visit."

Autumn laughed in surprise. "I didn't know cats did that. I only ever had Choo. Well, we used to have a dog called Jester, but I don't remember her much. She died a long time ago."

"Tassy's pretty old," Cai said. "She sleeps a lot these days. Sometimes I worry that I won't be there when . . ."

"Sure you will," Autumn said softly.

He absently murmured something to the light. "When I was little, Tassy got sick. We thought she was going to die, but an animal healer came and fixed her up. I used to think that's what I'd like to be."

"A healer?" Autumn was astonished. Healers weren't much higher than servants, particularly animal healers. Most of them traveled around Eryree with all their belongings on their backs and made barely enough money to keep shoes on their feet.

"Sure. I'd have a cottage in the Gentlewood, and people

would bring their animals to me to fix up. I could listen to the leaves rustling every night and live there like a witch in a story." He blinked, and added quickly, "I know better now, of course. I'm a magician. Magicians protect Eryree."

"S'pose so," Autumn said. When Cai put it like that, being a magician didn't sound so great. What good was magic if it stopped you from having what you wanted?

Clouds rolled in, covering the stars. Cai seemed more tired after that, as if the starlight had given him strength as well as magic. He kept leaning against the wall.

"I don't think anything's happening," she said as Cai rubbed his eyes. The window was as empty as ever.

"No," he said. "I'm sorry."

Disappointment settled inside her like cold ashes. "It's not your fault."

"There's still the boot," Cai said quietly. "The third clue."

Autumn nodded. Her disappointment was a weight heavy enough to root her to the spot. She'd hoped that Cai would take one look at the window and know just what to do. But it would be unfair to say it, with him worn down to the bone.

"We can keep looking tomorrow," she managed.

She picked up Cai's staff, which had a ghostly sort of warmth, the warmth of stars. With an effort so great it hurt, she turned her back on the window. Then she helped Cai down the hall.

12

In Which the Boggart Scorches the Sky

Autumn came down to breakfast the next morning to find Sir Emerick seated at the table, devouring a plate of fried eggs and mushrooms. Autumn had known he was there, of course. She'd heard him and Gran roaring at each other by the fire all night.

Sir Emerick greeted Autumn with the sort of hello you give somebody you see every day, though she hadn't seen him in months, and handed her a small sack filled with caramels. Autumn tried to be appreciative, despite the disappointment clinging to her like a shadow. She thought Sir Emerick looked a little worse for wear, but as he was so very worn to start with, it was a hard thing to judge. His clothes were so patched that the patches had patches, and he usually didn't smell very good. But his eyes were quick and bright, and while you could never be certain whether he was joking, the answer was usually yes.

Most knights were part of the king's army, but those found ill-suited for the job were turned out eventually. Some of them didn't know what else to do with themselves, so they wandered around the kingdom, fighting monsters too insignificant for the king to bother with in exchange for whatever reward the villagers could scrape together.

"Help out an old man, will you, Autumn?" he said. "I'm trying to convince Bea—that is, your gran—to go for a couple days' ramble in the forest with me, like we did when we were young."

"And what would I come back to?" Gran said, giving Sir Emerick a sour look as she dropped a raw egg yolk into some tomato juice. "A menagerie on fire and at least one headless grandchild, bet your boots."

"They make knights out of boys younger than your eldest," Sir Emerick said. "They'll be fine."

Autumn thought he was probably right. Gran, though, only let out a snort.

Sir Emerick started rambling about his travels up and down the coast of Eryree. He'd sailed all the way to the tiny islands of Inis Wen and Inis Dawl in a summer storm and been washed overboard. Fortunately, he'd been close enough to swim to shore, following the little light of his ship. Emys, who'd always loved Sir Emerick's stories, listened with his mouth half-open until Gran thumped her hand against the table.

"Don't you go getting any ideas about running off to the Outer Isles," she said. "Lonesome, hardscrabble places they are. And the sea dragons they have to deal with!"

"Didn't say I was," Emys muttered, scowling at his toast. "Be nice to see *somewhere* else, though, besides these nasty old woods."

"Just like your dad," Gran said, shaking her head, but Sir Emerick gave a snort of laughter before the tension could brew into an argument.

"Least the boy wants something in life," he said, folding his hands over his round belly. "No harm in that, Bea, my girl. Keeps the blood pumping." He leaned forward. "Don't let anyone beat the wanting out of you, boy. At least *want* to want something, even if you don't know what it is. You don't want to end up like this one, do you?" He stabbed a thumb in Gran's direction.

Gran threw a roll at his head.

Autumn found her thoughts drifting back to Sir Emerick's words as she mucked around the afanc pond with a shovel, digging out the bank to give the beast more room to wash his horns. She didn't quite understand what Sir Emerick meant by wanting to want something, but it made her think of Cai, who wanted all kinds of things. The forest. Catastrophe. Home, whatever that meant to him. She'd never wanted anything in that way—or at least, she'd never let herself. What would be the point? Her life was the menagerie and her chores, just as her parents' had been, and Gran's was, not to mention all those other Malogs who had faded into the past with only the boggart to remember them.

The afanc grumbled from the middle of the pond. Afancs looked like beavers, if beavers were the size of horses and had an appetite for human flesh. Autumn grumbled back at him, and he subsided.

Her boot sank ankle-deep in the mud with a wet *smuck*, and she paused to wrestle it out. Her gaze drifted over the mountainside, copper green in the sunlight. Sparrows flitted among the tall grasses. She knew every nook and burrow, and had counted all the spindly little nests they'd abandoned in the summer. She watched the shadow of Mythroor brushing the edge of Lumen Far—she could tell time by it like a sundial.

In her whole life, she'd never been beyond the places that shadow touched. Did she want that? She didn't know. The idea was a little frightening.

She shook her head, tossing another shovelful of muck over her shoulder. The boggart would kill himself laughing. *Afraid of villages the ravens fly over with one flap, but not a ravenous monster?* he'd say. *That's just like you.*

All thoughts of Sir Emerick disappeared as Autumn snuck out of the cottage again after Gran fell asleep. The knight had wandered off, saying something about an old, lone Hound that periodically strayed into a farmer's barn and ate all her cheeses before collapsing from indigestion, after which Sir Emerick would have to lure it, moaning, back into the forest.

This time, Ceredwen had not only flooded the bathroom,

but half the second floor. This struck Autumn as overdoing it somewhat, but Ceredwen seemed delighted. Autumn wondered if all housekeepers secretly fantasized about making enormous messes. Ceredwen was too intimidated by Cai to say hello, and left Autumn when they reached the corridor below the Silver Tower. Autumn kept going, the boggart invisibly in tow.

At that hour, the corridor was deserted and a little spooky. Of course, the Silver Tower was usually deserted. Sometimes visitors stayed there—for example, during festivals, when students' families were invited to join the celebrations. But for most of the year, the rooms sat empty, visited only occasionally by housekeepers sent to freshen them.

The third clue, Autumn thought. She imagined Winter's boot lying there among the shadows, a small thing, easy to miss. What would they find here? Autumn had searched the tower before, and so had the boggart. It was a clue leading to a dead end.

She found Cai seated at the bottom of the stairs, his staff leaning against the wall and his head buried in papers. He blended into the shadows better than the other students ever did, so well that, for the first time, he struck Autumn as a little monstrous. The effect was shattered when he jumped at the sound of her approach.

"I was looking through the maps again last night," he said. "I found something interesting."

He passed one to Autumn. It showed the seven towers of Inglenook—the Silver Tower, the South Tower, the Windfarer Tower, the West Tower, the North Tower, the Northmost Tower, and the Dawn Tower, which Autumn now knew held the skybrary. The towers were strangely named because of the castle's piecemeal construction by a dozen different magicians, each with their own opinion on where to put things and what to call them. Magicians hated teamwork.

"Look," Cai said. He was so intent on the map, his magician's brain so clearly humming along at lightning speed, that Autumn felt a shiver of hope. "This map is so old it uses the ancient name for the Gentlewood—Fairyland. Sounds nice, doesn't it? Back then, the forest wasn't as much of a menace."

Autumn nodded slowly. Gran called the forest that on occasion, when she was in one of her storytelling moods—Fairyland was what her own grandparents had called it.

She traced the dark line of the forest. It had been much farther from Inglenook back then—only the edge was visible, a green wrinkle at the corner of the map. Long-lost villages dotted the hills between the school and the trees.

"Have you heard of the cloud towers?" Cai said.

"Oh no," Autumn groaned.

Cai smiled. "You've already been in one—the Dawn Tower—and nothing terrible happened. Nobody calls it a cloud tower anymore, of course. People say there used to be three; they say the others went even higher than the skybrary, so high you could see all of Eryree from the top of the turrets. I thought it was just a story, but look here. The mapmaker drew the Silver Tower up to the sky."

Autumn squinted. "So some magician lopped the top off, then?"

"No. They took the easier path and hid the upper levels with a spell. But the magic's so old now that if I can find the seams, I might be able to find a way in."

"Where's the other one? You said there were three."

Cai tapped the map. Specks of light wafted off the paper like sparks. "I think it was enchanted off the map. Someone didn't even want the third tower to exist in a drawing."

Autumn shook her head. "Why would magicians have gone to all that trouble to hide two perfectly good towers?"

"I don't know. I could only find one reference to them."

Cai pulled out another map, which had tiny black lettering around the edges. He read: "'And in the third year of Queen Alys's reign, Inglenook's tallest towers were given back to the sky. To build them was folly, and their existence is best forgotten. Headmaster Lewelyn herself cast the final enchantment. We pray that they will never find their way in again.'"

"'They'?" Autumn repeated. A finger of cold trailed down her back. "Who's *they?*"

Cai shook his head.

"Poor castle," Autumn said, looking at the map. "You're not even a proper castle. You're a bunch of castle bits stuck together and rearranged a dozen times. How would Winter have found his way into one of these cloud towers if they're hidden with all kinds of magic?"

"Sometimes old spells start coming apart on their own," Cai said. "I've seen it happen. Especially when you have lots of spells stitched together. When magic starts to decay, it sort of . . . flickers. A door might open in a spell at midnight on the last day of summer, or at twilight on the twentieth anniversary of its casting, and then vanish for another ten years. Winter might've stumbled through a door and been trapped."

Autumn's heart thudded. She thought about what Cai had said about ancient magicians locking people up in mirrors. "Or fell through an old mirror?"

"Maybe. Maybe that's what we'll find up there—the place where he fell through. If so, maybe I can pull him out again. Or maybe we'll find *him*—maybe he's trapped in that hidden tower, half there and half not, and somehow he's using mirrors to communicate with us." Cai shook his head. "Sometimes magic is like pulling a thread in a tapestry. You never know how it will unravel."

"Boggart?" Autumn said.

Yes? The edge of the carpet, which had been arranging itself into a tripping hazard for an unwary foot, slid back into place.

"Did you hear that?" Autumn said. "We're looking for a way to the hidden cloud tower."

Cloud tower? the boggart repeated. *You don't want to go there.*

"Why not?"

The boggart seemed to consider. His invisible fingers played with the lanterns, making the flames dance. *The cloud towers are bad places.*

"Why?"

I don't remember. It was a long time ago.

"You'll be there. You can protect us."

Of course. A sly note entered the boggart's voice. *I'll protect you, Autumn.*

"No," Autumn said. "You'll protect *us*."

Isn't that what I said? Cai let out a sharp breath and clapped his hand to his ear, as if someone had pulled on it.

Okay, the boggart continued, all innocence, *I'll look for a door. But I've searched the Silver Tower lots of times. I didn't smell Winter anywhere.*

Autumn didn't find the boggart's answer reassuring, but she *had* told him not to harm Cai. She was reasonably certain he would listen.

Reasonably. But because you could never entirely predict a boggart, even her boggart, she told Cai what the boggart had said as they climbed the tower staircase. The boggart darted ahead with a flash of claws and was lost in the shadows.

"How old is he, anyway?" Cai said quietly.

"I don't know. He says he lost count after a thousand years."

Cai's eyes widened.

"He spent a lot of them asleep," Autumn added.

"And has he always been with your family?"

"As far back as Gran knows," Autumn said. "He tells stories about my great-grandparents sometimes, or their great-grandparents. He always has a favorite in every generation of Malogs."

"And you're his favorite now, I guess?"

Autumn nodded, her cheeks prickling with pride. After all, boggarts chose their friends carefully. "Though he likes Winter, too. He always says that when I'm grown and we get married, Winter can live with us if he wants to."

Cai stared. "When you *what?*"

"Oh, it's just something he says. He talks about building me a castle in the forest out of silver and lilies, a castle with a hundred windows, and stealing the Mynach Falls and putting them next to my bedroom, and other nonsense. It's all boasting. I don't think he even knows what it means to be married." She didn't tell Cai that she didn't know what it meant either. "What's the big deal?"

"The big deal? You're twelve. And he's, what, twelve thousand?"

"Well, it's not as if I'm going to marry him *now*."

"You could marry him when you're a hundred and it would still be weird."

"Oh, and you know all about weird, do you?" Autumn's temper rose. Cai didn't know what he was talking about. He hadn't known the boggart since he was a baby—someone who protected you when you were scared, who brought you bright flowers from the depths of the forest and let you cry into his shoulder when you missed the parents you couldn't even remember. "The hero who's also a monster."

Cai was quiet. Autumn felt a stab of guilt, but Cai didn't look mad, only wary.

"You should be careful, Autumn."

"You sound like Gran."

"Your gran's been around monsters a long time," Cai said. "Gosh, if I had a boggart following me around, threatening to marry me, I wouldn't get a wink of sleep."

"You don't understand, Cai. He's my friend."

Cai looked dubious.

"He's helping us, isn't he?"

"I guess so. Although if he shoves one of your *other* friends off a very high tower, you might want to think twice about him."

"Who said you were my friend?" Autumn gave Cai's staff a nudge. It tangled in his feet and tripped him.

"Whoops!" she called over her shoulder as Cai chased her, laughing, up the stairs. "Guess all that magic isn't enough to make you graceful, is it?"

They reached a landing and shoved through the door. There they found what could have been a cozy sitting room, its fireplace cold and empty. Then there was a corridor lined with rooms, two beds in each. They'd all been stripped and covered in white cloth.

"So much space," Autumn said, gazing through the window

at the moon bundled up in clouds. She'd never felt more like Cai's sidekick. It was an impossible, intoxicating feeling, even if it wasn't true. She wished Winter was there to be part of it.

She peeked into one of the rooms. There was something about the place that made her want to march back down the stairs. It was a *loneliness*, so heavy it hung in the air like fog. Why had the magicians bothered to build the Silver Tower just to leave it empty?

Cai was gazing out the window, his eyes on the scudding clouds. He had that elsewhere look on his face, and Autumn thought she could guess what he was thinking.

"Late frost this year, Gran says," she said lightly. "Might not even snow at all, except up on the peaks. Wouldn't that seer be red in the face?"

Cai looked amused, which was an improvement. "I doubt he got the forecast wrong."

"Never know," Autumn said. "Sure, he's a seer, but he's a man too. Gran says they're wrong all the time."

Cai and Autumn went to the not-top floor of the tower, which did a very good impression of the top floor of a tower. There was no mysterious staircase leading to nothing, and when Autumn stood on the balcony, she could see the crenellated roof above them. Did the tower really keep going? Was Winter really here somewhere, trapped up in the sky, or were they wasting their time? This was the last clue to investigate—or at least, the last clue in the castle.

Autumn swallowed her fear and closed her eyes and *looked*. There was Winter's presence, flickering as it sometimes did, but was he closer now or farther away? She couldn't tell.

Cai tapped his staff against the wall, murmuring incantations. Sometimes he just stood with his eyes closed, listening. When he did this, he began to glow lightly.

Autumn chewed her lip, watching him. She had to admit, she was still terribly curious about what sort of monster Cai was—or if he even *was* a monster, for she found herself doubting her certainty on that score with him pacing about all noble and hero-like, and bathed in starlight to boot.

Cai? she said in the Speech.

He started. "What?"

"Just checking your hearing."

He looked uneasy. "You don't have to do that."

"You don't like it?"

"No. It feels like—I don't know. Like you're sticking a hook in my ear or something."

"Most monsters don't like it," Autumn said. "Speakers can talk to monsters, but we can also order them around, if we're strong enough."

Cai looked thoughtful. "So you could order me to do something?"

"Maybe I could, but I wouldn't," Autumn said. "That's not fair."

Cai leaned his staff against the wall and faced her. "Try it."

Autumn's brow furrowed. "Really?"

"I want to know what I am." Cai looked pale but determined. "Maybe this will help."

Despite herself, Autumn felt a little shiver of anticipation. Well, she thought, who could blame her? The chance to order Cai Morrigan around didn't come up every day.

"Okay," she said. "Relax. Don't try to fight me, all right? Let's just see if this works."

Cai nodded.

Raise your left hand, Autumn said in the Speech.

Cai's hand jerked up. He blinked at it in surprise.

Autumn tapped her foot, thinking. *Now, try giving me some of your magic. Just a tiny bit.* She held her hand out in the shape of a bowl.

Moving like a sleepwalker, Cai placed his hand over Autumn's. Light gleamed in the cracks between their fingers, and Autumn felt something lighter than water and softer than wool fill her palm. When Cai drew back, she was cupping a handful of starlight.

She gasped with delight. The starlight trickled through her fingers and splashed against the floor, where it went out.

"Let's see how strong you are," she said. "This time, try to stop me."

Cai nodded.

Raise your left hand, Autumn said.

It was like walking into a stone wall. Autumn stumbled back a step, gasping.

– 164 –

"Are you all right?" Cai demanded. Autumn nodded. "What happened?"

"Nothing," she said. Cai looked so pale and worried that she couldn't tell him the truth.

Because the truth was that she'd never encountered a monster with a will stronger than Cai's—apart from the boggart. Usually, when a monster resisted her commands, she felt it struggle at least a little, like a person walking into a strong headwind.

What *was* Cai?

"Let's just say I'm glad you don't have a taste for hearts," Autumn said lightly, to cover her amazement.

Cai looked as if he didn't want to hear any more than that. He turned away. "I'm sorry."

"For what?" Autumn handed him his staff. She still wasn't afraid of him, and he must have seen that in her face. He managed a faint smile.

"Well?" she prompted. "Do you sense any old spells?"

Cai looked relieved by the change of subject. He touched the wall and glowed brighter than ever. "No. There's just the ordinary magic holding the walls together."

Autumn kicked at a chair. "Has anyone ever told you that you'd make a very nice lantern? Gran could stick a hook in your collar and carry you around the Gentlewood."

Cai blinked. "Do you always say whatever goes through your mind?"

Autumn sighed. "Pretty much. Winter used to say I was

born with one foot in my mouth."

Cai smiled. "I wish more people were like you. Most of them just say what they think I want to hear."

"Well, they want to impress you." She was glad it was too dark for Cai to see her blushing. "I don't."

"I wouldn't want to see you try to impress someone. I'd fear for their life."

Autumn tripped him again.

The walls of the tower were lined with tapestries so dusty that great clouds billowed out when Autumn shook them. The scenes were strange—there were no magicians, who were always recognizable by their glowing staffs. Women and men walked alongside monsters or held out their hands as if offering gifts. Autumn saw dragons of all varieties, fat and happy in luxurious gardens, as well as afancs and gwarthegs, and some beasts she didn't recognize. There was even a shadowy window edged with claws, from which gazed a pair of disembodied eyes that looked decidedly boggartish.

"I wonder if this is where the hedgewitches lived," Cai murmured.

"What?"

He shot her a look. When he spoke again, he seemed to choose his words carefully. "It's something I read in one of those old books in the skybrary. There used to be two kinds of magic folk in Eryree. Magicians and hedgewitches."

"Hedgewitches?" Autumn repeated. She'd heard the word

witch before—they appeared in old legends as a sort of magician gone bad, who lived alone in forests and got up to all kinds of wickedness. Servants also used it as an insult for magicians they didn't like. She didn't know there was another meaning.

"Hedgewitches were magical," Cai said. "But it was a different kind of magic. They could speak to monsters and beasts, brew healing potions, weave talismans from branches to ward off enemies, that sort of thing. But even though their power was just as useful as magicians', some people thought it was unimportant. Hedgewitches didn't use staffs or incantations or do flashy stuff like summoning castles from the ground." He waved a hand at the room. "Magicians called it 'low' magic, the opposite of their 'high' magics. Two hundred years ago, one of the old headmasters decided Inglenook wasn't going to teach hedgewitches anymore. Since then, their kind of magic has been mostly forgotten in Eryree, while the influence of magicians has grown and grown. Which was probably the point."

Autumn's mouth was dry. "What happened to them?"

"Nothing. They're still around. Only now they're just called Speakers—people forget that they can do more than just speak to monsters."

"That's ridiculous," Autumn said with a huff. "Us Malogs are Speakers, but we can't make healing potions or any of that other rubbish."

"Bet you could, if someone taught you," Cai said. "What about your gran?"

"Well, she has her cure-all," Autumn said. "But that's swill, that is."

"I won't argue with that, but I don't think it matters what it tastes like."

Autumn felt flustered, torn between fascination and dismissal. What Cai was saying was nonsense—wasn't it?

She thought of Gran's cure-all. Yes, it was foul, but Autumn had to admit that it usually worked. And then she thought about Gran's yearly tradition of placing a doll woven from river reeds above the door to ward off winter coughs and sniffles. Gran always shrugged and said it was just what her parents had done, giving Autumn the impression that even she believed it silly superstition. Yet when was the last time any of the Malogs had caught a cold? And them being outdoors in all weather.

It was ridiculous. Of course it was. Even more ridiculous was the seedling of hope that sprouted inside her, tiny leaves twisting in search of light.

Autumn gazed at the tapestries. The hedgewitches—if hedgewitches they were—wore simple cloaks and carried baskets of leaves and herbs. They were, in many ways, the opposite of magicians, who were usually shown blazing with light or posing atop a pile of dragon heads. Also, they seemed to be *talking* to the monsters. Negotiating. Magicians didn't talk to monsters. They killed them.

"So," she said hesitantly, "you think I'm a hedgewitch?"

"No," Cai said. He looked determined and a little nervous,

as if he was giving a speech he'd already worked out in his head. "I *know* you are. And I think what's ridiculous is the fact that you haven't been taught anything about your powers. I'm going to speak to Headmaster Neath about it."

Autumn's confusion turned to horror. "Oh, Cai, no! You can't. What if he sacks Gran?"

Cai looked astonished. "Why would he sack her?"

"Gosh, I don't know." Autumn threw up her hands. "Maybe because he'll think we've been filling your head with nonsense about us being magic. If that's not acting above your station, I don't know what is."

"I'll tell him it was all my idea, Autumn. Promise. I'll tell him—"

"And if he doesn't believe you?" Autumn spun Cai around and grabbed him by the shoulders. "Cai, I know you're just being nice and all, but you don't get it. Me and Gran and my brothers, we're beastkeepers, all right? That's it. And if we start going around telling people we're something else, either they won't believe us, or they'll get mad."

"I do understand." Cai's face was red. "My parents were servants, remember? If I didn't have magic, I'd be just like you."

"But you're *not* like me, Cai." Autumn released him. Suddenly she felt very tired. "And I bet your parents tell you to keep quiet about them, don't they? I bet when they have visitors at that fancy manor house of theirs, they pretend they've always been there, drinking their tea from nice china. Right?"

Cai's face fell.

"*Please* don't say anything," Autumn said. "Look, there isn't a lot of work out there for beastkeepers. There's a few in Langorelle, working for the king's magicians, but that's it. If we lose our position at Inglenook, we're in trouble. We'll lose our home. We'll lose *everything*. Do you get it?"

"Yes," Cai said, though Autumn wasn't sure she believed him. Cai's worries were all about magic and heroism and grand quests. He'd never known what it felt like that winter when a wyvern escaped from the menagerie and attacked one of the students, and the parents had written angry letters to the headmaster about Gran. That dark cloud that had settled over the cottage, all of them worrying where they would go if Inglenook turned them out. The headmaster had stood by Gran, but he hadn't *had* to. Autumn's place at Inglenook wasn't guaranteed the way Cai's was. Her home was a twiggy, fragile thing.

"Anyway," Autumn said into the silence. "I don't care about magic."

She said it loudly, as if that would make it true. She *wished* it was true. She wished she didn't dream of a cozy dormitory of her own at Inglenook, or a cloak woven with so many spells it glittered when the wind brushed it. But dreams were only that—dreams. And even if she was a hedgewitch, she still wouldn't belong there.

"I won't say anything," Cai said. "But after we find Winter, if he's here to be found, I'm going to help you learn about your magic. The way you're helping me."

Autumn was too relieved to argue. Truthfully, she felt a little shiver of excitement. The seedling of hope sprouted new leaves. What if she really *was* magic?

She looked at the old-fashioned tables and chairs. Had students once sat here, talking and laughing, students like her? The loneliness of the Silver Tower seeped into her like a damp chill, and Cai's tale of hedgewitches made her feel strange.

Winter, she thought.

Cai paused by the fireplace. "I haven't seen your boggart in a while."

"Boggart?" Autumn called.

The boggart appeared an inch from Cai, who leaped backward in surprise.

"Don't go in there," the boggart said.

"Where?" Autumn said. "The *fireplace?*"

"I thought there was something strange about it," Cai said.

"Boggart," Autumn said slowly, "is there a door there?"

"Possibly."

"Boggart."

He crossed his arms. "That's all I know. It's a *possible* door. It smells like the sky in there, but if it's a door, I can't see where it opens. There's too much magic in the way."

"Why didn't you tell me about this before?"

"Because you shouldn't be here," the boggart said. "Let's look for Winter somewhere else."

Autumn turned to Cai. "Well?"

He nodded. "There are loose threads here. The fireplace is a seam in some sort of enchantment, a big one. It's old and frayed."

"What is it?"

"It could be anything," Cai said. "Maybe the fireplace was enchanted larger. If I pull at the threads, maybe it will only shrink to its original size. That's the trouble with enchantments— you never know what you'll find beneath them."

Autumn took the boggart's hand and drew him away from the fireplace. He didn't stop glowering at Cai.

Cai tapped his staff against the fireplace. He didn't murmur any enchantments, but his fingertips began to glow. He put his hands inside the fireplace and moved them as if he were stroking an enormous cat.

"There!" he said. "Found it. Give me your hand."

"I won't be able to feel anything," Autumn said. And yet she wanted to try. She wanted to so much.

"Let's see."

Autumn stuck her hand inside. The fireplace was large enough for both her and Cai to fit inside. She felt nothing at first, and then—

Something brushed her skin. It was cool, like Cai's starlight, and tickled horribly. Autumn choked on a giggle.

"Oh!" she marveled. "Is that it? The hole in the enchantment?"

"Yes." Cai's gaze was distant. "Stand back. I'm going to rip it."

Autumn and the boggart backed away. Cai thrust his glowing staff into the fireplace, and there was a sharp flash of light.

"There," Cai said.

Autumn opened her eyes. The fireplace was still there, but it had grown. The mouth of it nearly stretched up to the ceiling, and a chill breeze wafted out. It smelled like fog and mountaintops.

"Autumn," the boggart warned. He sounded much older suddenly, and his voice had claws. The room grew so cold that the damp in the air froze into ice crystals, which sprinkled the floor.

"Stop it," Autumn said. "I'm going. Are you coming or not?"

The boggart's face darkened. He disappeared, spinning round and round the room. The windows shattered one after another, and the wind rushed in, tugging Autumn's white hair free of the kerchief. Cai threw his arms over his head.

Fine, the boggart said. Now that he'd had his tantrum, he didn't sound angry anymore, just resentful. *But I'm going first.*

He darted into the fireplace.

Cai stood frozen, staring after the boggart with his mouth hanging open. Autumn, who was used to the boggart's temper, said, "Come on," and pulled him in.

It was like walking through fog, one of those ponderous fogs that rolled in from the sea in September, thick enough to drink from a spoon, as Gran liked to say. But unlike fog, the doorway in the enchantment was soft and gummy and sent shivers over her skin.

Then they were through and facing a spiral staircase. She and Cai were covered in a fine glitter. The tapestries and furniture were gone—entire chunks of the walls were gone. Autumn was afraid to step onto the staircase in case it gave way.

"Interesting," Cai murmured, brushing the wall. "They didn't change the tower's substance; they just folded it into the sky."

The wind moaned, and Autumn shivered in her thin house-keeper's uniform. "Plain words, please, not magician-speak."

"Sorry," he said. "I just mean that it's all still here."

"It isn't," Autumn said. "And you don't need magic to see that." She went to a gaping window. If she leaned out far enough, she could see some of the ruined tower above them, broken and haunted, before it disappeared into the clouds. The rest of the castle spread out below—they were no higher than the other towers, not yet. Dots of light glowed in one of the courtyards—magicians' staffs. She looked for the beastkeepers' cottage, but it was hidden in the folds of the mountain.

"Let's see how high it goes," Cai said. "Watch your step."

He held his staff before him, murmuring a word to brighten the starlight. They climbed slowly, minding the stairs that were cracked or broken.

Each floor was the same—an empty ruin with cloud rippling through it. The upper slopes of Mythroor ran parallel to the Silver Tower, and in places the steep mountainside was only a few yards away. Autumn thought she could jump to it with a running start. An ewe and her lamb stood nearby, calmly browsing the grass on a precarious ledge.

"Can they see us?" she said.

"No," Cai said. "We're inside the enchantment. There's no

door here. In fact, they could walk right through us."

"Oh." Autumn went faster after that. Being inside an invisible tower was one thing. Having a sheep walk through you was something else entirely.

The higher they climbed, the colder it got. Frost furred the steps, and some stones were icy. Cai seemed perfectly calm as the stairway took them up, up, up into the sky. Autumn supposed he'd had so many adventures at Inglenook that enchanted towers were all in a day's work. She wished she could be just as nonchalant. She had no experience with adventures, and her heart was beating like a rabbit's. Where was the boggart?

"What's that?" Autumn said as Cai's starlight gleaned off something pale. She knelt beside it, waving her hand to clear away the cloud.

It was a bone.

She couldn't tell what kind, for she backed away quickly. Cai drew in his breath—he'd found another bone beneath one of the windows. It was long and curved, like a rib. Autumn realized something else—the floor was covered with animal droppings.

"Birds, I guess," she said, as much to herself as to Cai. She didn't think birds usually roosted this far off the ground. But what else could it be?

The next floors were much the same, only with more bones. Some of the windowsills were scored with deep scratches. They were above the summit of Mythroor now. Below was a carpet of mist and mountaintops; above, a tapestry of stars and slow, lacy clouds.

"Where does it end?" Autumn asked. The wind was like ice and dried the sweat on her brow instantly. She was holding up better than Cai, who, as a pampered magician, was a little soft. The higher they went, the more he huffed and puffed and stopped to lean against the stairwell.

"I'm not sure." Cai looked up. "What was that?"

From the floor above there came a sharp, whispery sound. *Scritch-scratch, scritch-scratch.*

Autumn and Cai froze, staring at each other, neither daring to move another inch. The boggart appeared before them with as little warning as the last time. Cai yelped, but Autumn had never been so relieved to see anyone in her life. She threw her arms around the boggart's neck. He looked annoyed and pleased at the same time.

"I wish you'd listened to me," he groused, pulling free. His glossy black curls were unmoved by the wind. "You'd better keep your voices down, or they'll hear you."

Autumn's relief curdled inside her. "They? Who's they?"

"Oh, you mortals and your *names*," the boggart said. "They call themselves the Lords and Ladies of Above. They live in the cloud tops, mostly, and on high mountains. They like to lure mountain children from their homes and onto slippery crags." The boggart rolled his eyes, as if he disapproved of this solely from an entertainment perspective.

Autumn swallowed. "Are you talking about gwyllions?"

Cai let out his breath. "There are *gwyllions* here?"

The boggart looked pleased by their reaction. "I remember

what happened now. The magicians who made the castle built its towers too high, and the Lords and Ladies found them. They killed a great many students." He wrinkled his nose. "It was messy."

Autumn leaned against the wall. Gwyllions. There were *gwyllions* up here. Not even Gran had ever encountered a gwyllion. They kept to the highest places and weren't social monsters like boggarts or wisps. But they were the reason mountain dwellers in Eryree kept their children close. Few knew exactly what they looked like, though mountain folk likened them to man-size ravens who lurked in shadow and mist, ready to snatch children up with their talons.

"If you keep quiet and don't touch anything, you should be all right," the boggart said. "But if you get into trouble, I won't be able to help you."

"Touch what?" Autumn said. The tower was an empty ruin. "And why can't you help us?"

"There are rules. You know that. This is their territory, not mine."

Autumn swallowed. Creatures like the boggart—higher-order monsters who could think and reason and plot—couldn't interfere with each other in the lands they claimed as theirs.

"Go back, Autumn." There was a pleading note in the boggart's voice that Autumn had never heard before.

Autumn wavered. She looked up the dark stairs. What was she doing? She should be home in bed, ready to be up early to attend to her duties, not mixed up in dangerous adventures.

"Autumn," Cai said. "You can go. I'll carry on and look for Winter."

He said it firmly, as if he couldn't imagine her arguing with him. She supposed most people didn't—they just let him march off and do stupid, brave things all by himself. Something rose inside her, closer to annoyance than courage, but it was fortifying nevertheless.

"No you don't, Cai Morrigan." She lifted her chin. "We'll do this together, or not at all."

She set off without another word. Fortunately, Cai was right behind her, lighting the stairs. The boggart flitted ahead, muttering furiously.

The next floor was empty, but the one after that? The breath left Autumn's body.

The round floor was clustered with tables piled with all manner of treasures. There were spyglasses and telescopes; tiny glass horses and even tinier glass soldiers; porcelain dolls with gleaming black hair and layers of silk skirts. There were marbles and brightly painted playing cards, silver jumping jacks and music boxes that murmured when the wind brushed them, a rocking horse so lifelike that Autumn could feel the muscles bunching in its leather hide.

It was like stepping into an enchanted toy shop.

"Where?" Cai murmured. "How?"

"I think I know how the gwyllions lure mountain children from their homes," Autumn said.

Her hands trembled. She'd seen such toys before, in the

Inglenook dormitories, carelessly scattered on the floor or jumbled up in chests. She only had one toy to her name, a doll that had been her mother's, its dress a faded gray. She was too old for dolls now, and yet her heart ached for the chestnut-haired one peeping out at her from a wicker basket, its eyes like jewels and its feet shod in petal-pink slippers.

"Winter would have loved that book," Autumn murmured. The book was pocket-size, as children's books often were, with a fine leather cover engraved with a picture of a boy and a dog framed against a snowy cabin.

Cai was staring at a music box with a forest and a dancing wolf inside it. "The boggart said not to touch anything," she reminded him.

Cai swallowed and stepped back. Autumn tried to see only the jagged remnants of the tower, the clouds billowing about them. She turned her back on the gleaming treasures and pulled Cai after her.

Unfortunately, the next floor was just like the last, as was the one after that. If anything, the toys became more elaborate. There were ships in bottles that rocked against real waves and cups-and-balls that crackled like lightning. The dollhouses could more accurately be called dollcastles, each a confection of turrets and staircases and shining windows.

Cai gripped her shoulder. "Autumn."

His voice was strange. Autumn turned and found that one of the windows had darkened.

Something crouched there. Something shaped like a bird

as large as a wolf. Its talons went *tap-tap, tappity-tap* against the windowsill.

Cai murmured a word, and a mote of starlight floated off his staff. Before it went out, Autumn saw two vast black wings, an eyeless head that held only an enormous curved beak, and far, far too many filthy talons. Though it had no eyes, she knew the creature was staring at her.

Autumn croaked and staggered back into Cai.

Two thieves, sirs and madams, the gwyllion murmured with obvious delight. *Two thieves. Trespassing where they don't belong, taking what isn't theirs. No respect!*

Autumn turned slowly to Cai. "You didn't take anything, did you?"

"No!" But Cai's hand crept to his pocket. "No . . ."

He reached inside and withdrew a book. He and Autumn stared at it in horror.

"I—I barely remember picking it up," Cai whispered. "All I remember is you saying that Winter would have liked it and wishing that you could have it."

"Oh, Cai," Autumn said. She took the book with shaking fingers. *We're sorry. Here, we'll give it back.*

She'll give it back! The gwyllion hopped back and forth. *The Lords and Ladies of Above don't care, do they? The Lords and Ladies are too busy for time-wasting children.*

To Autumn's horror, the book began to transform in her hand. It became a stack of crumbly leaves glued together with spidersilk. A worm poked its head out of a hole. The toys on the tables changed too, crumbling to leaves and grass blades and twigs and bits of string and other things often carried on the wind.

The Lords and Ladies don't care, another voice agreed. A second gwyllion appeared in the window behind them. *For the Lords and Ladies own the sky and everything in it. Trespassers!*

Nobody owns the sky, Autumn said.

She regretted it immediately. The gwyllions froze, staring down their beaks at Autumn and Cai. Feathers rustled, and suddenly there were gwyllions clustering along all the windowsills and wheeling through the sky beyond.

This Lord proposes that the thieves be eaten alive, one of the gwyllions said.

No! another exclaimed. *Such a mess! This Lady objects to messes. Uncivilized.*

This Lord apologizes to Her Ladyship, the gwyllion said, bowing his beak. *The thieves will be killed and then eaten. The eating will be done in an orderly manner, and all shall mind their table manners.*

The second gwyllion nodded. *His Lordship is wise.*

The other gwyllions also nodded. Nodded, and sharpened their beaks against the stones.

"Cai?" Autumn whispered. Her knees wobbled. "There's—uh—a lot of them."

"Yes," Cai said. His voice was very calm. "Run!"

Autumn ran. But a flock of gwyllions exploded from the stairwell before they could reach it, beaks clacking with a sound like enormous gardening shears. Their way down was cut off. Cai grabbed Autumn's hand and dragged her up the stairs.

"What are you doing?" Autumn yelped. "We can't go *up*! Up is bad!"

"It's the only direction that doesn't have gwyllions!" Cai yelled back.

They raced on, feet thundering like panicked heartbeats. The next floor was empty of anything but a swirl of leaves and debris, and a glassy-eyed doll slowly crumbling into sand. A gwyllion lunged through the window.

Back! Autumn shouted in the Speech. The gwyllion jerked back with a furious scream.

Cai shouted an enchantment, and a net of starlight wrapped around the gwyllion, pulling it to the ground. They ran up and up. Cai blasted the stairway behind them with a bolt of starlight. It speared two gwyllions, but it also punched a hole in the tower.

The tower shuddered and began to list.

Autumn shrieked and fell against Cai. He steadied her, and they ran on.

"Here!" he said as they burst onto another floor. This one had fewer windows, and several still had glass, though Autumn doubted that would hinder the gwyllions for long. Cai hurled another bolt down the stairs, then gathered a net of starlight and threw it out the window. A gwyllion that Autumn hadn't even seen screamed and fell.

Back! she yelled again and again. *Back! Back!*

Cai's staff pulsed, and the entire stairwell collapsed in a heap of rubble, starlight leaking out of it. At least a dozen gwyllions were crushed. Black feathers filled the air.

"Cai, no!" Autumn shouted. "You trapped us up here!"

"You know, Autumn," Cai said through gritted teeth, his brow furrowed in concentration, "you really need to worry about one thing at a time."

A gwyllion soared toward them, scythe-beak gaping, but a coil of starlight wrapped around it and hurled it back. Cai was chanting spells so fast that the incantations ran together into a stream. He shone in the darkness like moonlight on water. It would have been dazzling if they hadn't been about to die.

"Watch out!" Cai yelled as the tower let out a terrible groan. His spells had destabilized it—stones and dust rained down on them. Autumn tried not to think of that long, long drop through clouds and more clouds to the ground below.

That was when she felt it.

Not it. Him.

Winter.

Autumn whipped around. It was as if a map had unfurled before her eyes, the map that had shown Winter's whereabouts before he went somewhere she couldn't follow. Winter was *close*.

"Cai, Winter's up here!" Autumn cried.

Cai turned to stare at her. "What?"

A gwyllion lunged out of the darkness, its beak aimed at Cai's throat.

Back! Autumn screamed with everything in her. The

gwyllion crumpled to the ground. Unfortunately, Autumn hadn't aimed the command but thrown it wide, and Cai fell over too.

"No, no, no!" Autumn cried. "Cai! I didn't mean it!" *Cai!* she yelled in the Speech.

Then— ·

THUD.

Autumn was knocked off her feet by an impact that rolled through the tower. Light poured across the sky, and the gwyllions screamed in chorus. Feathers wafted into the tower, singed and smelling of an unpleasant sort of roast chicken.

Autumn ran to the window.

"Boggart!" she screamed.

The creature that hung in the sky, painting the night clouds with jets of flame, looked nothing like the boggart. It was a dragon the size of a castle, possibly even the size of Inglenook, so large that one of its fangs could have skewered Autumn vertically if you wanted to think of it that way, which she didn't, but couldn't stop herself from doing. And yet there was something in the flash of its black eyes that Autumn knew very well.

The gwyllions were screaming. They wheeled around the boggart, screaming, *Rude! Insolent! Lack of respect!* They slashed at him with their talons, but it was like watching moths try to take down a tiger—admirable, but entirely pointless. The boggart released plume after plume of flame, so vast and hot that the clouds dissolved and fell to the earth as steaming rain. The heat beat against Autumn's face, forcing her back from the window.

She realized she was shaking. She'd never seen the boggart do anything like this—she hadn't known he *could*. She didn't know any creature that could set the sky on fire like this. Was this really her dear boggart?

Come on! the boggart snapped, and her fear vanished at the sound of his familiar voice, which held an equally familiar petulance not at all suited to such a situation. He was hovering outside the window, which couldn't contain even one of his vast eyes. *That tower's going to fall on you, and if your head gets crushed, I can't put it back together again!*

More stone rained down. Autumn wrapped her arm around Cai and helped him to his feet, and together they raced back to the window.

"Oh no," she said when she realized what they had to do. "Oh no, I can't, oh no—"

Fortunately, Cai had plenty of practice with stupid heroics. He didn't even hesitate. He grabbed her around the waist and leaped out the tower window.

Autumn screamed. They fell for barely three seconds through cloud and nothingness before they landed on the boggart's vast, scaled back, but those three seconds felt like three hours. She didn't realize she was still screaming until Cai, who had landed smoothly behind her, clamped his hand over her mouth.

"Sorry," he said. "My ears."

I TOLD you, the boggart raged. *I told you not to keep going. I knew that useless magician wouldn't be able to protect you, but would you listen to me? Nooo—*

Autumn wanted to tell the boggart to shut up, because she could barely breathe with all the steam and feathers hanging in the air, let alone argue, but she also wanted to throw her arms around her boggart and sob with relief. But he was too big to hug just then, and soon she couldn't focus on anything other than the feeling of her stomach leaping clear out of her body as they careened through the night toward the mountain. Then she was tumbling off the boggart's back and rolling over grass and stone and hawkweed, and coming to a stop in a heap on the cold bank of a stream.

13

In Which Autumn
Is Entangled

Everything was hazy after that. Autumn remembered Cai leaning over her, chanting something, and suddenly her head stopped spinning. Then they staggered over the mountain for a while, eyes streaming from the lash of the night wind.

Autumn woke slowly, covered in blankets and very muddled. Her stomach was inside out, and she ached all over. Had she been sick?

A familiar voice said, "Autumn?"

"What time is it, Winter?" she murmured. But Winter didn't reply.

Then Autumn opened her eyes and found herself in a tower in Inglenook.

That shocked her awake, and the memories of last night rushed back. She knew right away she was in Inglenook, not her cozy attic bedroom. Sunlight poured through a circular column of windows that overlooked the Mythroor col and the green darkness of the Gentlewood. And it *smelled* like Inglenook—of well-banked fires; of old, damp limestone; of the mint and lavender sprigs the housekeepers rubbed into the tapestries to freshen them.

Autumn sat up. She was in a beautiful oak bed canopied in sky-blue velveteen. The bed was big enough to fit three girls and looked more like a cake than anything, with its layers of creamy silks and soft furs. She glanced across the room, and there was Cai, reposing with a book atop an equally ornate bed.

"You're awake." His expression was strange—had she been talking in her sleep? She couldn't remember. "How do you feel?"

Autumn blinked. "What am I doing here?"

"I didn't know where else to go," Cai said. "I didn't think it would be a good idea to take you home all cut up and dirty. Especially when your grandmother didn't know you were out. I managed to sneak us into the castle through one of my short-cuts without anyone seeing."

Autumn lifted her hands. Her palms were bandaged. Dimly, she remembered taking a tumble down a steep slope in the mountainside, a tumble halted by a prickly gorse bush.

"I sent a message to your grandmother." Cai looked guilty. "I said you were helping me with another essay. She thinks you left before sunrise."

"Good thinking." Autumn rubbed her head and felt an

acorn-size lump. "What time is it? Won't you be late for your morning classes?"

"I have a few minutes." Cai sounded so unconcerned about the prospect of lateness that Autumn's mind boggled. "Are you hungry? I had the servants bring breakfast. I met them at the door so they wouldn't see you."

He gestured to the table by her bed, where a tray of toast and marmalade and soft-boiled eggs sat next to a pot of tea. The teapot was wrapped in a thick flannel cozy and the tea was still hot. Autumn *was* hungry, but she could only pick at the food. Alongside the cup was a square of fresh honeycomb, an extravagance beyond her imagining. She popped it into her tea and watched it dissolve, then slurped up the remnants before she could stop herself. The honeycomb crunched wetly when she bit down, oozing summer sweetness.

Autumn felt dizzy. She was in the students' tower in Inglenook, eating honeycomb brought for her by servants. She felt like a bedraggled duck who had accidentally wandered into a peacock aviary. She focused on the only thing that mattered.

"Cai, I felt Winter in that tower," she said. "We have to go back."

She expected him to argue, to say it was too dangerous, but then she remembered that he was Cai Morrigan, hero of a dozen stories. He drummed his fingers on his knee thoughtfully. He looked well, if a little pale, his hair combed and his clothes clean. Not at all like a boy who'd climbed up into the clouds and fended off a horde of gwyllions. Autumn had only to look at the pillow her head had just vacated—scattered with soil and tufts of gorse—to know she was nowhere near as presentable.

"Well?" she said as he just sat there, thinking. Her voice rose. "You believe me, don't you? I *know* he's up there. I don't know where exactly, or how, but we *have* to go back, Cai—"

"I believe you," he said simply, and Autumn heaved a sigh. "We go back as soon as I can replenish my magic—a day or two should do it."

They went over their plans, and Autumn felt herself relax a bit, despite the strangeness of her surroundings. Talking to Cai was so easy. Apart from Winter, he was the only person she'd met who didn't find her loud or annoying or simply *too much*. She supposed that was what having a friend felt like. She'd never had one of those before, apart from Ceredwen. And really, Ceredwen had always been more of a fan than a friend.

Someone tapped on the door, and Autumn started like a thief with her hand in a jewelry box. A tall girl with dark skin and black hair drawn back in an elegantly messy bun poked her head in.

"Can I grab my books, Cai?"

"Of course," Cai said, looking embarrassed. "Bryony, you didn't need to—"

"That's all right." The girl grabbed a stack of books off

the floor, giving Autumn a quick, blank stare. After she left, Autumn rounded on Cai.

"Is this her bed?" she demanded.

"I was going to sleep on the floor," Cai said. "But Bryony insisted. You were in rough shape."

"And your roommate didn't think it was strange, you stumbling into the tower in the middle of the night with one of the servants, all covered in mud and magic?" Autumn fell back against the pillow and found she could answer her own question. "No. Of course she didn't."

"It's not the first time I've snuck out at night," Cai said, almost apologetically. "Bryony's used to it by now. She'll tell everyone the same story I told your gran, that you're helping me with an essay."

"Will people believe that?"

Cai made a shrugging face. "People believe what they want to."

Autumn supposed that was true, especially where Cai was concerned. She was trying not to be impressed by it all—how the entire world seemed to orient itself around Cai, even roommates, who jumped at the chance to give up their beds to strange, dirty servants just because they were in Cai's company. By now, she was used to seeing Cai as Just Cai—not Cai Morrigan, Hero of Eryree—and she didn't want that to change.

She finished her tea and carefully washed off the worst of the dirt and blood in the bathroom. The taps were gold and the sink had been carved into intricate ridges like a scallop shell, and she didn't want to touch anything. Her hair was a bird's nest that would require some serious elbow grease to sort out, so she just stuffed it back under her housekeeper's kerchief.

She gazed into the mirror and imagined Winter looking back at her. Determination burned inside her like embers.

"I know where you are now," she whispered. "And I'm going to bring you back."

When she got out, Cai had his cloak on, and they left the dormitory together. Near the bottom of the tower was a study overlooking the vegetable garden. The study was large but cozy, the fire crackling in the hearth and armchairs arranged haphazardly around tables.

Autumn saw all that, but what really drew her eye were the small things. The salted chocolates lying under a chair, perhaps fallen unnoticed from a satchel because the owner had never bothered to ration them. The hats and gloves and scarves, all in leather or the finest angora and gleaming with magic, strewn about the floor with no thought given to the risk of stains or tears. The flashes of gold competing with the faint background shimmer of enchantment—cuff links and pocket watches; bracelets and rings. Little luxuries that made Autumn so aware of the holes in her old boots that she almost felt them boring into her toes.

Every head in the study—and there were quite a few heads

in attendance—swiveled toward them. Cai didn't seem to notice. His friends greeted him as he passed, and he answered calmly. Autumn, on the other hand, was oddly conscious of her every step, and probably looked like a marionette. Even more alarming than the stares were the whispers that followed in her wake.

"Is that her?"

"One of the beastkeepers, I think—"

"No, she's a housekeeper. I saw her changing the linens once."

"—heard she's not human, she's part monster or something—"

"Cai's helping her break in a new dragon, Gawain said."

"What's he doing helping a servant?"

"I always said there was something off about him—"

Few of the stares were friendly. One of the older boys muttered something to his friends as she passed, and they sniggered. Then she and Cai were through the study and descending the last staircase. Autumn nearly sprinted toward the first servants' hallway she saw, but Cai grabbed her hand.

"Are you all right?" He was frowning. "I'm sorry about all that. Students always gossip. They think I had something to do with the dragon last night, so they're guessing you did, too."

"What? They saw the boggart?"

Cai raised his eyebrows. "With all that flame? Plus, he was as big as a mountain. He was a little hard to miss."

Autumn wished she could tell Cai how strange she felt, as if she were wearing someone else's skin, but Cai would never understand. How could he? He'd been attracting stares and gossip since he could crawl.

She thought of Anurin. *Mud's not meant to gleam.* What had she gotten herself tangled up in?

"Cai!" Winifred was beckoning to him from down the hall, standing with two other friends of Cai's whose names Autumn didn't know, all three of them alight with magic with their glowing staffs and glittering cloaks. As Cai was, and as Autumn decidedly was not. Her feeling of strangeness deepened.

"I'm going to be late," she said, and she fled toward the familiarity of the beastkeepers' cottage, and her familiar invisibility.

14

In Which the Dark
Comes for Winter

– LAST MONTH –

Maddie taught Winter how to move between the mirrors in Inglenook, and how to catch the attention of the
outsiders. Usually, he could only show himself for a second or
two, but sometimes he managed to mouth a few words at them.
The outsiders would look confused, and some would touch the
mirror briefly. But then they always turned away.

Autumn. He needed *Autumn* to see him. Somehow, he had
to find her.

It was hard to practice as often as he wanted to because he
kept losing himself. There would be hours, possibly days or
weeks—for time had no meaning in the mirror world—where
he would simply drift. It was as if a tide, cold and gray, was
pulling him out to sea. It grew stronger and stronger, that gray
tide, though Winter fought it as hard as he could.

Each time, when he came back to himself, it was a little

harder to remember his name. And each time, he looked a little grayer, a little blurrier.

These weren't easy times. But Winter never lost hope, for he knew Autumn would find him. He knew because she was Autumn, and Autumn would never let him go.

He came to know several of the other mirror-folk—who, to Winter's dismay, all referred to themselves as ghosts, and would only sigh and shake their gray heads when he argued.

"Poor thing," they said. "You were too young when you went."

"But I didn't," he always replied. How could he make them listen? They weren't dead. They weren't dead for the simple reason that Autumn was going to rescue them. It made perfect sense to him.

Among them was Tom, who had owned a cat and worried whether anybody was feeding her; Daw, whose only memory was of a red wheelbarrow; and Gwendolyn, who had been a senior apprentice at Inglenook and spent all her time trying to remember her incantations. They called her the Old One sometimes, for she had been there longest of all of them, and only Winter seemed to remember that there had been someone else who had been called that before.

Winter helped them remember their names the same way he had with Maddie. Some, though, were beyond remembering, including the smudged figure who drifted at the edge of their little group. She eventually disappeared, and Winter was sad at first, but then, like the others, he forgot her.

"What's my name?" Tom asked Winter one day. Tom asked whenever they saw each other, whenever they both stopped drifting.

Winter wrinkled his brow. "Tom," he said finally, and the man's gray face brightened.

Though Winter sometimes forgot his own name, he didn't ask the others. They never remembered. He carried all their names around with him as best he could, jostling inside him like keys in a pocket, though he knew it made it harder for him to remember his own. As time passed, Winter began to feel thin. He clung to the few memories he had, but they kept slipping away. How much longer could he hold on to them?

Then one day, when he was drifting through the mirrors on the fourth floor, he saw her.

She was pacing up and down a deserted corridor, muttering to herself. Her hair was white and tangled, twigs sticking out here and there, and her boots were muddy up to the calves. *Clomp, clomp, clomp,* they went. She held a lantern in one hand and was lifting up the tapestries one by one. It was clear she was looking for something.

Or someone.

Every once in a while, the girl muttered orders at things, or kicked them. "Move it," she hissed at a tapestry that wouldn't come free of the wall. "Why, you old rotter."

She wrenched at it as if it had given her a grievous insult, and the bolts gave way. The girl wore an expression Winter knew well—brows lowered over narrowed eyes, mouth flattened, as if she were marching into battle.

Winter felt a rush of desperate joy. He was in a window just then—for windows worked like mirrors at certain times of day. He pressed himself against it and shouted with all his might:

Autumn!

And she turned, and she saw him. She rushed at the window, her face red, her mouth forming words he couldn't hear. *Winter!* she shouted into his mind.

Autumn, I'm stuck, Winter shouted back. *I'm still here. There are others with me—we can't get out of the mirrors!*

He didn't know how much she heard. He could no longer hear her voice in his thoughts. She seemed to be pounding on the glass, but he couldn't hear that either. Could she still see him? He pressed his hands against the glass the way Maddie had taught him and *focused.*

Something moved at the edge of his sight.

Winter turned, and his stomach plummeted. To his left, everything was shadow. The shadow had no shape or form—it was simply an absence. In that direction, there was no mirror, no Inglenook. And yet Winter knew that the shadow was watching him. It crept closer, swallowing the reflection of the corridor.

It was the Dark.

Winter ran. He darted from mirror to window to mirror. The other mirror-folk had warned him about the Dark. It followed them, too, and the more you forgot, the more often you saw it. The folk who vanished, the ones who were now forgotten except as *the folk who vanished*, had complained, shortly before they disappeared, that the Dark never left them alone.

Winter was always able to escape the Dark, and this time was no exception. By the time he reached the kitchen mirror deep beneath the school, he had shaken it.

He went back to the window. The corridor beyond was full of shadows now. How long had he been running from the Dark?

Too long. Autumn was gone. She had left him.

Winter rested his head against the glass. He tried to tell himself that Autumn couldn't have known where he'd gone, or if he would come back, but he was sweaty and sick, and so cold. A strange cold that nestled deep inside him. He'd escaped the Dark, but for how long? For the first time, despair crept into his heart.

He slumped to the ground. When the gray tide pulled at him again, he let it carry him away.

15

In Which Autumn's Plan
Has Holes

Cai kept his promise. The next night, they went back to the Silver Tower.

This time, the boggart wasn't with them. When Autumn had gone to the old beastkeepers' hut, he hadn't been there. It was strange. The boggart was always easy to find—all boggarts were easy to find, given their homebody natures. He was clearly still angry at her.

When they stepped through the fireplace, they found a gaping hole in the side of the tower. The first staircase had completely collapsed, and the tower had a distinct lean. Clouds clung to the soggy mountainside, swollen with rain. The wind that billowed through the enchanted tower was wet and cold, and Autumn was soon shivering. Cai shifted stones and rubble with tiny shovels made of starlight while Autumn wore a groove in the floor stomping back and forth, frustrated by her uselessness.

"It's no use," he said at last. "It's not just wood and stone blocking the way, you see—it's magic. The spells are torn and tangled together. If I pull at one, the rest may come loose, and the tower will collapse. Or maybe I'll blast a hole in the sky or turn myself inside out. You can't predict these things."

Autumn didn't reply.

"I'm sorry," Cai said quietly.

He sat down beside her. Autumn brushed away tears, and he pretended not to notice.

"At least we know we're on the right track," Cai said. "You felt Winter up there above the school. That's something. I'll keep looking for the third cloud tower."

Autumn nodded. Cai was right—she couldn't forget that they had a trail now, and even a trail leading into the sky was better than no trail at all. It was equally clear that Cai was no longer humoring her. He believed her completely and had fully donned his hero guise now that he had somebody to rescue. But, if anything, the ache inside her only worsened. What had happened to Winter? Would he still be himself when they pulled him out of the enchantment he was tangled in?

And if they were closer to finding him, why did it feel like he was moving farther away?

"Where are you?" she whispered to the swirl of clouds and rain.

She took to visiting the bay window as often as she could. Sometimes she fell asleep there, head resting upon the cold glass. But he never appeared again, and though her determination never wavered, each time she left with her heart a little heavier.

She was glad for the distraction of Cai's lessons, but their progress there was just as discouraging. She tried introducing Cai to Amfidzel while the snowy dragon puttered around her garden, reasoning that there were quite a few things in the world more intimidating than a dragon with a spade in her mouth neatly digging up dandelions. Indeed, Amfidzel had never seemed less interested in disemboweling someone and had even taken a step back when she saw Cai, bleating worried queries about whether he'd come to practice dragon-killing spells on her. Cai had promptly eased her fears by keeling over backward, landing in a boneless sprawl in Amfidzel's strawberry patch. The dragon had been quite happy to see the back of them—or, at least, to see the back of Autumn as she dragged Cai from the garden.

Next Autumn introduced Cai to one of the wyverns, who were among the least dangerous dragons of all. Wyverns were two-legged, and only those who lived in the snowy reaches of the Boreal Wastes could breathe fire. Their most dangerous quality was their temper—a wyvern would claw you to death just for looking at them sideways. The menagerie's wyverns were both elderly, and while they remained every bit as peevish as their brethren, they had lost the motivation to do much about it beyond a few growls and clawing gestures. They spent most of their days asleep, tangled together in a pile of limbs and scales in their sunny corner of the menagerie or lazing about the overgrown garden at the forest's edge they had tended when they were young. Autumn had chained the eldest wyvern securely to a tree, which the dragon suffered only in exchange for a crab-apple sapling and the promise of two hours' weeding. After adjusting the chain beneath her wings, she had curled her serpentine body into a comma and gone to sleep.

This time Autumn had let Cai approach the dragon slowly. He started off well, even managing a watery smile at a distance of twenty paces. Things went sideways from there. At fifteen paces, Autumn could see the familiar symptoms setting in—shaking and sweating. At ten paces, Cai had started to sway. Autumn had gone to his side then, arriving just in time to catch him under the arms and lower him onto the heather. The wyvern didn't see Autumn drag the savior of Eryree from her presence, for she hadn't even woken up.

Autumn tried everything she could think of. She got Cai to clean Amfidzel's stall, hoping that getting used to the smell of dragons might help with the real thing. She brought him bits of shed scale and antler tips, which Sir Emerick said knights used as good luck charms against dragon attacks. She had the boggart dress up as different dragons, which they all thought a successful experiment at first, but it only turned out that the fearful part of Cai was able to recognize the boggart as the boggart, which she should have guessed after their misadventure in the cloud tower. She suggested that Cai shield himself with a protective spell before approaching Amfidzel, and he promptly summoned a sort of strange cocoon for himself made of shiny silver-blue threads. This had no effect at all, other than to cover him in an attractive glitter after he fainted and the spell collapsed on top of him.

Nothing worked.

As frustrating as Cai's lessons were, Autumn couldn't help being impressed by his determination. How many times would he topple over like a hare conked on the head by Gran's slingshot before he admitted defeat? A part of Autumn noted that Cai reminded her a little of Choo, who would affably greet the badger in his den every morning despite the growling and hissing this provoked. The rest of her was filled with a sense of dread, which worsened as the days grew shorter and the morning frost lingered into the afternoons.

How long did Cai have?

Another frustration was the boggart. Autumn had hoped he would help them dig out the cloud tower, but the boggart refused. He was acting quite unlike himself—he slept, but fitfully, waking when she made enough noise but often refusing to talk to her. Autumn was beginning to worry about him. As the trees put aside their October finery and wrapped themselves in November grays, she took to visiting him each morning before her chores.

One day, she found him rustling around in the oven like an old dog turning round and round in his bed, muttering dyspeptically to himself. Autumn tossed her shovel aside (she was on mucking-out duty that day) and knelt next to the oven.

"That's it," she announced. "What's wrong with you, boggart?"

Nothing.

"You're lying. I've never seen you like this. Did you hurt yourself in that tower?"

No.

Autumn drummed her fingers on her knee. She knew from experience that the boggart was a champion sulker. When he got in a snit, nothing and no one could shake him out of it, and the best thing to do was keep out of his way until he slept it off. But this seemed different. Usually, when the boggart was in a bad mood, he expressed it with a variety of cruel tricks— creeping into the castle at night to put worms in some poor student's birthday cake, for example.

I feel strange, the boggart said finally. *I wasn't supposed to rescue you. That was gwyllion territory. I broke the rules.*

Autumn felt a wave of guilt. "I'm sorry, boggart."

You should be.

Autumn blew out a breath. "Well, at least let me look at you."

She had no idea how to examine a boggart—after all, they had no bodies. But she was determined to try, and she was going to annoy the boggart until he let her. He seemed to guess as much, and only complained a little before drifting out of the fireplace.

"Hmm," Autumn said, poking him. There was little to be gained by poking an insubstantial being, but at least she could tell that he wasn't any *less* insubstantial. "Does it hurt anywhere?"

No. The boggart changed into his boy shape. "I can't sleep."

Autumn glanced around the decaying hut. The tumbledown stones were furred with frost. The spiders had gone back to wherever spiders went in winter, and their abandoned webs crunched when broken. "Gosh, it's cold out here," Autumn said. "Maybe you should come inside."

The boggart rolled his eyes. "That's ridiculous."

Autumn thought he was probably right. Boggarts didn't feel cold—still, it was worth a try. "Come on."

The boggart grudgingly followed her into the cottage— Gran and her brothers were already about their duties—and let her tuck him into Winter's bed. There he immediately fell into a deep sleep. He wouldn't wake even when Autumn prodded him.

The boggart slept all day and night and woke in much better spirits. He followed Autumn around as she fed the monsters, alternating between his cat shape and his boy shape. Autumn was relieved to see him acting like himself again, until she happened to glance down.

"Boggart," Autumn said slowly, "you're *touching the ground.*"

"Am not."

Autumn grabbed his arm. "Look!"

The boggart looked. His eyes widened. It was as Autumn had said: his feet were deep in the frosty grass. Behind them were two sets of footprints, and while the boggart's were much fainter than Autumn's, they were distinctly *there*.

"Are you—" She stared at him. "Are you *human* now?"

"Human?" The boggart said it in the tone Autumn used to describe Gran's cure-all. "No. But . . ." He looked puzzled—and, for the first time since Autumn had known him, afraid. "Maybe a little bit of me is."

"A bit of you? How can you be a *bit* human?" Autumn froze. "Do you mean that if you break any more monster laws, it'll make you all-the-way human? Is that how it works?"

"I don't know." The boggart's voice was small. "I've never broken a law before. It felt strange, like—like misplacing part of me, like a hand or something." He looked down at his clawed human hands.

Autumn didn't know what to say. It frightened her to see the boggart frightened. He wasn't supposed to be afraid of anything—he was the boggart, the thing everything else was afraid of. Autumn threw her arms around him.

"I'm sorry."

"It's not your fault."

Autumn didn't like the way he said *your*. "It's not Cai's fault, either."

The boggart didn't reply, but his face was dark. Autumn

thought about telling Cai to bring the boggart another present. Somehow, though, she didn't think that was going to work this time.

For that reason, Autumn left the boggart sleeping in Winter's bed two nights later when she snuck out to meet Cai for another one of his lessons. Instead she took Choo, waking him from his contented doze by the fire. The dog yipped in delight when he realized there was adventure afoot, and there came a brief pause in Gran's snores. Autumn froze, her hand on Choo's snout. Slowly but surely, Gran's snores sputtered back to life, and Autumn let out her breath.

Cai was waiting for her at the edge of the forest, gazing into the waving boughs. He knelt to greet Choo, who vibrated with joy before letting out a tremendous sneeze.

"Did you find the third tower?" she asked. Cai had unearthed another sheaf of old Inglenook maps in the skybrary the day before, tucked inside a boring book about sheep spells.

"Maybe," Cai said. "The maps are original plans, so they'll have all three towers on them, likely as not. But they're so old they need stitching back together with magic before I can read them. Gawain's working on it now—he's good at magical repairs."

"Gawain?"

Cai noticed her expression. "He's a good person. When it occurs to him. And he's a good friend—he'd help me with anything."

Autumn kept her mouth shut. Cai's friends, Gawain in particular, reminded her a little of Ceredwen. She supposed they liked him, but how much of that liking was for the hero of Eryree, and how much for the actual boy?

"Gawain thinks we can have it finished in a few days," Cai said.

"A few days," she repeated dully. She had that feeling again, the one that had started in the cloud tower, that Winter was moving farther away from her, or she from him.

It's taking too long. She knew it with a certainty that went down to her bones, though she couldn't have explained why.

She swallowed her sadness, which lately had been following her around like a cloud of midges, never leaving her in peace. They were going to find Winter—they *were.* They'd worked out where he was, thereabouts at least, and that couldn't have been for nothing. She wouldn't *let* it be for nothing. And besides, Cai had his own problem to solve, and she owed him her help.

"What's that?" she asked.

Cai shook out the bundle under his arm. It was an Inglenook cloak, a little worn but otherwise shipshape. "You can have this. It's one of mine—it will make it easier for you to hide. There's a good camouflage spell worked into the overlay."

Autumn had to stop herself from snatching the cloak from his hand. It was a little big when she slung it over her shoulders, but it was wonderfully warm and heavy, probably from the weight of all the spells.

"Are you sure?" She fingered the Inglenook crest wonderingly.

"Of course. It suits you." He smiled, though it faded before it reached his eyes. "Better than it does me, when you think about it."

Autumn spun around slowly, watching the cloak glitter. It was the best present she'd ever received, and she didn't know what to say.

"So what are we doing here?" Cai said as he gazed into the forest, politely letting her have a moment to herself. "What about our lesson?"

"It starts now." Autumn handed him a lantern. "We're going into the Gentlewood."

A frown tugged at Cai's mouth. His eyes had a shimmer of green in them tonight, and Autumn wondered whether it was because of the nearness of the forest. "Why?"

"I don't believe you're a coward," she said. "After all, you were plenty brave up in that cloud tower. I think maybe it's hard for you to be brave around Amfidzel and the rest because you don't *need* to be—they're not going to hurt you. I bet your fear will have a hard time getting the better of you when you're truly in danger."

"What about the humming dragons?"

"I thought about that. You didn't know how much danger you were in when you fainted—neither did I. Once you realized it was life or death, you got ahold of yourself and cast a spell." Autumn folded her arms, pleased with her faultless logic.

Cai didn't look as impressed as she'd imagined he'd be. "So we're going to go *looking* for a life-or-death situation?"

"Not exactly. But we're not going to play it safe anymore. There's a folded dragon who lives in the forest near the Briar Path where it crosses the stream. Gran knows him. She says he's old and cranky and just wants to be left alone, so they've agreed that as long as he stays put and doesn't roast anyone, she won't tell the headmaster there's a dragon living so close to the school."

Cai's eyes rounded. "A *folded* dragon? But they're enormous! How have the magicians never stumbled across him?"

Autumn snorted. "Size doesn't enter into it. You think a dragon can't hide from a few magicians when they come crashing through the underbrush, glittering away and yammering enchantments?"

"So what are we going to do? Knock on the dragon's door and ask if he'll have us in for tea?"

"We won't let him see us at all," Autumn said. "He'll be asleep. We'll get as close as we can, close enough for you to get a good look at him, then we'll run for it."

Cai looked queasy. His fear seemed to fade, though, as he gazed at the Gentlewood.

"Also," Autumn said, "the forest may help me figure out what sort of monster you are. You feel more yourself when you're in there, right?"

Cai nodded silently.

"Good. Maybe you'll feel so much like yourself that you'll turn back into whatever you really are."

"And if I turn into something that likes having children for dinner?"

"Then I'm sure I'll have plenty of time to make a run for it while you're apologizing."

"No offense, Autumn," Cai said, "but your plan seems to have a lot of holes."

"Holes or not, we don't have time to wait for a better one to come along. Do we?"

She wished she could call back the words as soon as they left her mouth. She and Cai usually avoided talking about the prophecy. Or the slow retreat of fall as it gave way to a sullen wet that never left the air, threaded with an ominous chill.

"You're right," Cai said quietly. "We should try everything. Just—be careful."

So Autumn led them into the forest. The boughs closed over their heads like a second layer of night. Autumn surreptitiously motioned for Choo to walk next to Cai, remembering how much he missed his cat.

"Is it safe for him to come with us?" Cai said as he rubbed Choo's head. The dog leaped up to lick his face, and he laughed.

"We're taking Choo because he'll know the way home if we get lost," Autumn said. "He's never fooled when the paths move. Dogs' noses are stronger than magic."

The path curved around a boggy patch of low-lying ground,

then wandered past one of the moss-covered trolls. So far the scenery was familiar—the path hadn't changed course as it sometimes did.

"That's right," she muttered, stamping a few times. "You mind your manners tonight and stay put."

Cai looked bemused. "What?"

Autumn shrugged. "Gran talks to the paths sometimes. Can't hurt, can it?"

They came to the place where the Briar Path met the stream, then forked into two separate paths, the Green Path and the Mushroom Path (all the paths had been named by Gran, who had no use for fancy titles or for imagination in general). The Green Path was usually all right, but the Mushroom Path was a real scoundrel—sometimes it led toward the Twyllaghast Mountains, other times it ran south; still other times it rambled into a boggy area and then disappeared just when you decided to turn around. Fortunately, or perhaps unfortunately, they wouldn't be using either path tonight.

"Ready?" Autumn said.

Cai nodded, gripping his staff tight, and they plunged into the forest.

At first the going was rough, for the forest pressed up against the paths in a dense tangle, saplings and ivies fighting to the death for the narrow sunbeams that fell through the breaks in the trees. But eventually the trees thickened and the underbrush cleared. Wisps hovered in midair, flickering softly. From a distance, they looked like lanterns held aloft by friendly fellow travelers, or the hearth-lit windows of a distant cottage. Bluebells glazed with ice carpeted the forest floor, heedless of the November cold burrowing into the soil.

"Don't pick any flowers," Autumn warned. "They're worse than wisps, they are. You'll gather up an armful, and then when you look up you'll see another patch deeper in the forest, too pretty not to pick. You can guess the rest. Before you know it, you'll have the nicest bouquet you ever saw, and you'll also be good and lost and on somebody's dinner menu."

Cai nodded. "I've never left the paths before. How do you know which way to go?"

"Gran told me," Autumn said blithely. In truth, she had only a fuzzy idea of where to find the folded dragon—she knew the spot Gran had described, because it was just past the swamp, but she'd never ventured that far herself. She wasn't worried— she went into the Gentlewood all the time. Besides, she had Cai with her.

She began to doubt her assurance, though, the deeper into the woods they went. The shadows were so thick you could almost feel them against your skin, smooth and clammy, and a cloak of silence shrouded the trees. It reminded Autumn of the hours after a snowfall, when the whole world seemed taken aback by the arrival of winter. Where were the owls, the mice, the foxes? The sounds of the nightly wars and toil that were part of every forest?

Something was watching them. Or listening, or sensing their

footfalls on the soft needles—Autumn didn't know which, but it made little difference. She'd never felt that sort of awareness from the Gentlewood before. She swallowed, remembering what Gran had said about the forest soaking in the Hollow Dragon's anger. Did it know Cai was there?

Cai seemed unbothered. He brushed his hands over mushroomy tree stumps and caught hold of pine boughs, letting them run through his fingers in a spill of needles. He touched the trunks of trees as he passed, as if they were old friends. After a while, his silence became too much. She filled the quiet with small talk, pointing out unusual flowers or misshapen trees. Cai murmured replies, but only after a pause, as if Autumn's voice had crossed a great distance to reach him.

"What?" she said finally. "You're not about to run off, are you?"

He scrunched up his eyes. "I'm not sure," he said finally.

"Oh, great," Autumn muttered.

"Here." Cai plucked a scrap of starlight off his staff, blew on it, and handed it to Autumn. "Use that if we get separated. It's a trick me and Gawain use whenever we go into the forest."

Autumn took it hesitantly. It looked like the wool left behind by sheep when they rubbed against a fence post, but it felt like nothing but cool air. She tucked it into her pocket.

Choo ran helter-skelter through the forest, scrounging around in this animal burrow or that, rolling in leaves or mud or—on one deeply unfortunate occasion—slug. Autumn had to wrestle several mushrooms and unidentifiable bones away from him—the dog would eat anything and seemed to have a special fondness for things that made him sick. To distract Choo from his self-destructive tendencies, Autumn played fetch with him as they walked, which lightened her mood. It was difficult to witness the pure delight the dog took in a moldy old stick and *not* feel easier about her own worries. The forest took on an almost sulky quality, as if it knew its ominous charms were being underappreciated.

Then, without warning, Autumn fell over.

"Are you all right?" Cai helped her up.

"Fine." There was a stick in her path, which had been hidden by a hollow in the ground. She picked it up, brushing away leaves and needles. She had thought it might be suitable for fetch, but no, it was too big. It had probably fallen off the hagberry tree looming over them. She was about to drop it, but something stopped her.

"Did hedgewitches have staffs?" Autumn tried to say it casually, as if the answer didn't matter one bit. As if the idea of hedgewitches hadn't been lurking constantly at the edge of her thoughts.

"I don't know." Cai's voice was distant. "But I remember reading that they used hagberry boughs to ward off harmful spells and curses."

"Hmm." Autumn examined the branch. It was the right size for a staff, with a nice smooth area right where her hand would go. Other than that, it looked very little like a magician's staff—certainly nothing like Cai's, gleaming like a fallen star. It was, in truth, a little creepy. Scaly moss clung to the bark and spiky twigs stuck off the tip at odd angles. A line of small red mushrooms curved along the wood just below her hand. And yet there was something about it that Autumn liked. It reminded her of the walking stick Gran sometimes carried when she went into the Gentlewood.

Cai wasn't looking at the stick. He wasn't looking at anything that Autumn could see. Up ahead was a wall of dark—that was all a forest was at night, after all, walls upon walls of dark— and a few drifting wisps.

"Cai?" Autumn said.

"I hear something," he murmured.

Choo whined. He was standing next to Cai, his highly pattable head within patting range, yet Cai was ignoring him. Something was wrong.

Cai took a hesitant step forward. Then he broke into a run.

"Cai!" Autumn yelled.

She ran after him, following that glowing staff. Unfortunately, the wisps were almost the same color as Cai's staff, and they rose out of the forest floor in great numbers as Autumn ran. She didn't realize she was running toward one until her boot sank into a boggy patch of earth.

She drew back, but now she had no idea which of the bobbing lights was Cai's. And his cloak, that fine Inglenook cloak enchanted with a dozen protective spells, would only make it harder for them to find each other.

Cai! she yelled in the Speech. *Cai, stop!*

Autumn kicked a tree in frustration. She couldn't believe Cai—was he being heroic, or responding to some wicked instinct? What a ridiculous boy, or monster, or whatever he was!

Then she remembered the lock of starlight and fumbled around in her pocket. Why hadn't she asked Cai how to use it? Was she supposed to throw it into the air? Speak a magic word? Cai had blown on it, so that's what she did.

The starlight wavered and went out.

"No!" Autumn cried.

Choo cocked his head at Autumn, puzzled. Why was she just standing there? He knew exactly where Cai had gone—his nose wasn't hoodwinked by wisps or magical cloaks. With a bark, Choo plunged back into the woods. Autumn sprinted after him, her mind full of images of Cai getting sucked into a bog or swarmed by wisps or roasted by the folded dragon.

Cai! she yelled. *Cai!* She had worked herself into such a panic that she didn't see Cai until she ran right into him.

She yelped. Cai yelped. He had been doubled over against a tree, his hands pressed to his ears, and barely caught himself on a branch.

"Ow," he said, rubbing his head. "How is it possible that you're just as loud when you're speaking silently?"

"You can't just take off like that!" Autumn cried.

"I thought you would follow me! I gave you that spell—"

"Which I didn't know how to use!" Autumn stamped her foot. "I'm not a magician, Cai! I'm not like one of those friends you drag around on your adventures. I'm not like you."

Choo gave a tremendous sneeze.

Cai looked sheepish. "I'm sorry. I should have—I mean—"

"It's all right." Autumn felt embarrassed, too. She realized that she had been enjoying herself in her Inglenook cloak with Cai at her side, playing his sidekick. She thought of the unfriendly stares in the Inglenook study. She didn't belong in Cai's world. If she ever forgot that, it would make it impossible to go back to her own.

Choo gave another, even more tremendous sneeze.

"What did you hear?" Autumn said.

"Something strange." Cai cocked his head, listening. "There it is again!" he murmured.

Autumn listened, but she heard only the rustle of the leaves, the soft trill of some distant stream.

Choo sneezed again, this time so forcefully he raised a cloud of dirt.

"Choo, will you *shush*—" Autumn's voice faltered.

Something was moving through the forest. Not toward them, but across their path. Autumn felt it before she saw it, for the creature was large enough to stir the breeze, and send it drifting through the forest, scented with brimstone.

It was the Hollow Dragon.

16

In Which Choo
Saves the Day

Autumn knew the creature was the Hollow Dragon because it couldn't be anything else. There was the flash of jagged claws, the quiver of a spiny back, the muffled glow of a throat filled with embers. And yet she was equally certain that it wasn't a dragon at all.

Weaving in and out of the shadows with a strange sing-song gait, the Hollow Dragon couldn't be *seen*, only glimpsed. But those glimpses told Autumn that something was very, very wrong. The dragon was taller than the beastkeepers' cottage—twice as tall, three times even. His skin flapped like the oilcloth of a tent, as if it held nothing but air. His eyes were empty sockets that seemed to stare at nothing and everything.

Choo woofed, his posture alert. Was this something he could chase, or something that would chase him? He liked both.

"Get back." Autumn took Cai's arm and drew them into

the deepest shadows, where their cloaks would hide them. Cai murmured a word, and the light in his staff went out.

The Hollow Dragon gave a long, undulating howl, and Autumn fell back against the tree, her hands pressed to her ears. The trees in the Gentlewood seemed to bend toward the dragon, and as they did, they darkened and grew wilder. The thorn tree's thorns sharpened; the rowan's roots twisted like snakes, ready to snare and tangle. To Autumn's horror, one of the neighboring trees gave a shiver, for it wasn't a tree at all, but a sleeping monster too gnarled and ancient to decipher, and it was waking.

The forest is answering, she thought numbly.

She turned to Cai and found that he'd collapsed in a patch of moonlight, his hands tangled in his hair. Choo sniffed him, whining.

"I've heard that before," he murmured. "It's what I hear in my visions. This is worse, Autumn. It's worse than any of the other times. I can't stop it—"

"Yes, you can," Autumn hissed. She grabbed his arm and pulled him back into the shadows. "Just do it over here. Choo, *quiet.*"

The dog understood the command and stopped panting. The smell of smoke grew stronger, and the wind lifted Autumn's hair from her brow. Had the Hollow Dragon sensed them? She lost sight of the monster as he passed through a dense copse of oak trees.

"That song," Cai murmured, so quietly that Autumn had to

lower her ear to his mouth. "It's beautiful."

Autumn went cold. She couldn't hear anything. She clamped her hands over his ears.

"Don't listen," she whispered. *"Don't listen."*

Cai's head fell back. His eyes were closed, his breathing shallow. *So much for my theory,* some distant part of Autumn noted. True, Cai hadn't fainted immediately. Perhaps she should count that as an improvement.

Autumn managed to drag him behind a fallen tree. She crouched next to Cai and drew the hood of her Inglenook cloak over her white hair, praying that it would conceal her.

"Useless hero," she muttered.

She arranged Cai's cloak so that it covered his legs and his face and gave his hand a quick squeeze. "Don't worry. I'll protect us."

She felt relieved, at least, that this couldn't be the prophecy coming about—Cai couldn't exactly fight the Hollow Dragon unconscious. She just hoped it wasn't some prologue to the prophecy that the seer hadn't bothered mentioning, one in which a nameless servant got herself roasted alive while Cai took a nap.

Autumn gripped her walking stick and peeked over the lip of the tree. Choo poked his nose over.

At first, she didn't see anything. The forest was dark and silent. Something gleamed among the boughs—a wisp, Autumn thought. But the gleam grew brighter, warmer. The shadows played tricks on her eyes, and she couldn't work it out.

Then the outline of the Hollow Dragon seeped out of the darkness like oil rising through water, and Autumn realized that he had been there all along. The glow came from the embers deep in his throat.

She froze.

What moved through the forest couldn't be alive—and yet it was. The stories said the Hollow Dragon was skin and bone, yet Autumn had never guessed how horribly accurate that would prove. Ribs poked through a hole in the dragon's hide, and his tail was a long curve of bone—hide and bone and fire were all the dragon *was*, as if everything else had been eaten away. Autumn had once seen the corpse of a dragon deep in the forest that had looked similar—dragon hide was tougher than leather and remained long after the soft parts had decayed.

She looked closer. The Hollow Dragon had two horns just behind his ears, though one was broken. His skin was covered in patchy fur the color of a winter forest. He looked like a boreal dragon—clearly a male, given the horns. Gran had kept a boreal dragon in the menagerie when Autumn was little, until it had grown too big, and she had released it. While large, dragons of that species were nearly harmless. They avoided people, keeping to their gardens of mushrooms and winter berries in their snowy northern fastness.

The boreal dragon gliding through the forest was clearly

dead. Yet monsters couldn't rise from the dead any more than people could. Autumn knew of only one explanation for what she saw.

Something's possessing that dragon.

Her stomach roiled. Gran had spoken once of monsters who could possess other living things. They were ancient monsters whose names had long since been lost to human memory. Some of the stories said they were bodiless, like boggarts; others that they had bodies, but abandoned them to drink the souls of other creatures. At some point, the monster inside the boreal dragon had taken over his body, and then the dragon had died—or perhaps he had already been dead. And the monster had been inside him ever since.

What *was* the Hollow Dragon? And could he even be fought?

The monster slid closer. He hadn't seen them. He would pass by.

Cai's body twitched, as if he was trapped in a nightmare. Autumn reached out a hand to still him.

Cai groaned.

The Hollow Dragon stopped. His head turned.

His empty eyes met Autumn's.

A terrible hiss sounded in his throat, like a cauldron boiling over. Steam billowed from his nostrils and clouded the trees. Leaves caught fire from the heat and tumbled to the ground, black and smoking. The Hollow Dragon drifted toward Autumn.

When he did that, Choo stood up. And, for the first time in his life, he growled.

Choo had no enemies. He was beloved by everyone he met, monsters included—who, after all, were just animals with more interesting smells. On the odd occasions he'd been swatted or charged by one of the creatures in the menagerie, he had accepted it as an amusing spot of roughhousing between friends. Yet although Choo knew himself to be universally cherished, some deep-buried part of him was aware that his family, the Malogs, were not so blessed. *They* had enemies. All two-legged creatures did, the poor lumbering things.

So when Choo saw the Hollow Dragon turn slowly to face the smallest member of his family, fire in his throat and rage in his empty eyes, Choo knew what he had to do.

"Choo, no!" Autumn cried. The dog wrenched free of her grip and charged at the Hollow Dragon's ankles. Barking madly, he dodged and wove and nipped at any bits of dragon he could reach.

The Hollow Dragon drifted backward. He appeared more confused than anything. Like the boggart, he didn't quite touch the ground. Also like the boggart, he was all quicksilver grace. One moment, he was in front of Choo; the next, behind him, fanged mouth stretched wide as fire bloomed in his chest.

Autumn leaped out from behind the tree. *Stop!*

She put everything she had into that command. The trees trembled, leaves spilling from their boughs. For a moment, the

Hollow Dragon seemed to tremble too. He looked at her, his decaying face empty and yet terribly intent.

He glided toward her.

Stop! Autumn cried again.

But the Hollow Dragon did not stop. Autumn wasn't Gran; she hadn't learned to command every monster. Autumn wasn't sure if even Gran would have power over this creature. But she knew that she had none.

Choo hadn't finished with the Hollow Dragon, though the monster had dismissed him as something akin to a fluffy insect. He latched on to the dragon's leg and pulled. The Hollow Dragon howled.

"Choo, come!" Autumn shouted. She lifted Cai and slung him over her shoulder. The first time she toppled over, but the second she managed to stand up. Then she was running.

Or, rather, limping. Autumn was stronger than most girls her age, but carrying an entire boy was no joke. The Hollow Dragon would have caught her in a heartbeat if not for Choo.

Choo. He was still back there. Was he all right? Autumn didn't dare look. Her legs shook with terror.

Help, she shouted in the Speech as she staggered and stumbled through the trees. *Help.*

She threw the word into the forest like a net, grabbing at any monsters she could reach. Wisps swarmed out of the trees, chittering in confusion. They were among the easiest monsters to command. Autumn glanced back. They had swarmed the Hollow Dragon, darting into its empty eye sockets and through its fleshless ribs. For a moment, it looked as if the creature wore a cloak filled with glowing bees.

The Hollow Dragon hissed. But Autumn knew the wisps wouldn't delay the beast, whatever it was, for long.

Help, she screamed.

Choo raced to Autumn's side, circled once, and ran ahead. He was leading them back home. She shoved her way through a dangling wreath of honeysuckle—the sticky flowers caught at her hair. What was honeysuckle doing in the Gentlewood?

She managed to pick herself up the first time she fell, though her shoulders screamed and her left arm was completely numb. The second time, though, she couldn't lift Cai again, no matter how hard she tried. Her legs simply wouldn't cooperate. They wobbled and shook like jelly. Choo circled the two of them, barking madly. He seized Cai's trouser leg and tried to drag him on. Burnt leaves drifted over them, along with something sickly sweet-smelling—rose petals? Autumn realized they were in a clearing, sitting on a neat bed of winter pansies, which tumbled down a tiered path. Where were they?

Autumn looked back.

The dark boughs rocked in a smoky wind. There among the darkest shadow was a gleam of light, like a campfire hovering in midair. Slowly, other things came into focus—the patchy fur of the Hollow Dragon's belly; the gleam of his teeth. The creature drew near, not bothering to hurry, until they were separated by a scant few paces. He opened his steaming jaws.

Autumn closed her eyes. She was still crying for help, but

now it was a whisper inside her. Choo was barking and growling, but the sound seemed far away. She gathered Cai in her arms and buried her head in his shoulder. She felt the little light flicker inside her, as if somewhere, wherever he was, Winter could sense her danger.

I'm sorry, she told the light. *I'm so sorry.*

Something gave a rumbling growl.

The Hollow Dragon's head whipped around. The growl came again, louder this time. Leaves rustled, as if a small animal—surely no larger than a bird—darted through the trees.

Two huge nostrils poked through the boughs. The nostrils were followed by a fanged snout, gleaming black eyes, and curving horns. Folds of skin gave the face a droopy appearance, like an old hound, but there was nothing hound-like about those glittering teeth, nor the plume of smoke wrapped about it like a scarf.

The folded dragon howled. He had been shaken out of a deep, satisfying sleep by Autumn's cry. Only the old woman who lived at the edge of the forest could shout like that, and so the dragon had come to investigate. He didn't like the old woman, but he respected her, and she would surely reward him if he helped her out of a bind. Perhaps another basket of daffodil bulbs?

But instead of the old woman, he had found an intruder. What was this strange counterfeit of a dragon doing in his garden? And was that *his* rosebush it had scorched, *his* honeysuckle it had mangled?

The folded dragon lunged at the intruder. But the Hollow Dragon faded back into the shadows and unleashed a geyser of flame at the folded dragon's side.

Suddenly the forest was on fire. The tree next to Autumn and Cai burst into flames. Autumn screamed: the light threw the Hollow Dragon into relief, illuminating every rotting tear and gash in his ancient hide. Her terror filled her with new strength. She managed to pick Cai up again and stagger on.

Choo raced at her side, barking encouragement. There was heat at her back and smoke clouding her vision, and her hair fell into her face tangled with ash. The hisses and howls of the dragons reverberated through the forest even after she could no longer smell smoke. Autumn ran and ran until she couldn't run anymore. She put Cai down and began slapping his face.

"Wake up," she chanted. "Wake up, wake up, *wake up.*"

She poked him with her walking stick. Cai groaned.

"Finally!" Autumn dragged Cai to his feet. "You missed a lot. Come on, sleepyhead."

Cai mumbled something. To Autumn's relief, he began moving his legs. With Cai's arm slung around her shoulders, Autumn stumbled on through the woods, following Choo's bouncing yellow tail.

She began to recognize the forest as they ran on—there was the twisted old yew; there the mushroom ring beside the old stump. Autumn summoned the last of her strength and yelled, *Boggart!*

Was he still asleep? If so, she doubted she could wake him by shouting. To her immense relief, though, within a few seconds there came a ripple of pure movement among the brambleberries. A familiar voice demanded, *What happened?*

"Help me with Cai," Autumn said. Distaste lashed through her mind, but then the boggart turned himself into a black pony and let Autumn help Cai onto his back.

"We have to hurry," Autumn said. "I don't know if the Hollow Dragon is following us."

What? Autumn was taken aback by the fury in the boggart's voice. *The magician made you fight that thing with him?*

"Not exactly," Autumn said. "We stumbled across him, is all."

Oh, well, if you stumbled across him, that's just fine. The boggart was trotting as though he had fleas, jolting Cai with every step. *What were you doing going into the forest without me? Did Cai—*

"Calm down," Autumn said. "It was my idea. That's why it turned into a shambles, all right? I thought I could just attack Cai's problem, and it ended up attacking us." Autumn felt like kicking herself. "Oh, why do I always make a mess of everything? We barely got away from the Hollow Dragon."

Where is he? The boggart turned his pony head around. *I'll teach him not to scare you.*

"Could you?" Autumn said curiously. "He's like you, boggart—he has no body. Do you think he's another boggart?"

No, the boggart said.

"Why not? The way he moved, it was like—"

It wasn't like.

"Fine!" Autumn was exhausted, and singed, and her hair was sticky with honeysuckle and rose petals, as if she'd stuck her head in a bowl of potpourri. She didn't have the energy to pry information out of the boggart when he was in one of his moods. "But I don't want you fighting him. You might break another law, and I already feel bad enough about the last time."

What she didn't say was that she wasn't at all confident in the boggart's ability to defeat the Hollow Dragon. The creature she and Cai had met in the woods, which wasn't really a dragon at all, didn't seem like something anybody could fight.

It was better before he *came*, the boggart muttered. Autumn knew he didn't mean the Hollow Dragon.

When they finally emerged from the forest, it was like the lifting of a heavy weight. Autumn hadn't realized how oppressive the forest had become, as if the Hollow Dragon's fury had enveloped them as they ran.

Cai tumbled off the boggart's back. Autumn and Choo were at his side in an instant, while the boggart became a cat, no doubt to project as much disdain as possible.

"Are you all right?" Autumn demanded.

"Yes," Cai murmured. His eyes were open, but he looked wrung out and limp, like wet laundry.

"No, you aren't." She felt his forehead. She only did that because she'd seen Gran do it—it felt like a regular forehead. "Should we go to the healers?"

"No." Cai sat up. "I'm all right. I'm just—I'm sorry."

He *did* sound sorry, so sorry that he looked ready to collapse beneath the weight of it, and Autumn was alarmed. "We got out all right." She squinted. "Did you have another vision? What did you see?"

It was clear he'd seen something. His brow was furrowed, his gaze focused on the near distance, as if he was reading a grim book.

"I saw it happen," he said. "I was floating outside myself. The Hollow Dragon was nearby—I couldn't see him, but I could hear him. I think he was dying." He swallowed. "But I think I was, too."

"Was I there?"

"No."

"Oh." Autumn shrugged. "Then it wasn't a true vision, Cai. Because when you fight the Hollow Dragon, I'll be with you."

Cai stared. "What?"

"Why are you so surprised?" Autumn worked her fingers through her hair, trying to dislodge the honeysuckle, but she just ended up getting her fingers stuck. "Of course I will."

"Autumn, this isn't a joke," Cai said.

"Really? I thought the Hollow Dragon was hilarious. I was laughing my head off back there while we were running for our lives."

"I'm serious." Cai gazed at her with his strange eyes. "You don't know what you're offering."

"Cai, listen to me." Autumn drew a deep breath and put her

hands on his shoulders. "You're *useless.*"

He blinked. "I'm useless."

"Completely, totally useless. You are the most unscary monster I've ever met. On top of that, you're literally the worst dragonslayer in Eryree. You're probably the worst dragonslayer in all the realms, even the ones that don't have dragons in them. What are you going to do the next time you see the Hollow Dragon? Faint more dramatically?"

"The prophecy—"

"I don't care about the prophecy," Autumn snapped. "Maybe the prophecy doesn't say anything about me, but it also doesn't say anything about you having to do this alone."

Cai was staring at her. "You're either the bravest person in the world or a complete lunatic."

"I'm not either of those. I'm just not a magician, which means I'm not too busy worrying over magical nonsense to see what's in front of my face. You can't fight the Hollow Dragon alone, Cai. You just can't."

Cai was quiet for a long moment. "Nobody has ever offered to help me."

Autumn thought that over. "Well, they should have."

Cai shook his head. "Autumn, I appreciate everything you've done," he said. "I can't even say how much. But I have to face the Hollow Dragon by myself. It's not what you think," he added quickly, seeing her expression. "I'm not trying to be heroic. It's that I—I don't want you to see it happen."

Autumn frowned. "What are you talking about?"

Cai paused. "There are two lines missing at the end of the prophecy. My parents asked Taliesin to keep those secret, because they didn't want to scare me. But I always knew the prophecy was incomplete—I don't know how. When Taliesin came to visit when I was six, I made him tell me the rest."

Cai recited the prophecy slowly, from the beginning. The air seemed to vibrate as he spoke, as if each word was a note on a harp.

The lightest winds wander far,
The quietest hunters draw blood.
The lowest may walk among stars,
In some hearts a forest may bud.

No blade or enchantment will slow
The empty song in the wilds.
Ere his thirteenth winter's snow,
The beast will fall to the stars' child,
Whose fate he will share with his foe,
From night he came, into night he'll go.

Cai fell silent. It took a moment for Autumn to shake off the magic of the words, which made her feel sleepy and still.

"No," she murmured. "It can't— There must be some other explanation."

"Maybe." He gave her a smile, which was awful. Because

Autumn knew he didn't actually mean it, that he was just doing it for her.

Cai thought he was going to die fighting the Hollow Dragon. He had for a long time.

"There must be a way around it," Autumn said. Her voice was too loud. "Maybe the seer meant something else. Maybe—"

"Now you know why I came to you." He let out his breath. "You see, I don't have much time left to figure this out."

Autumn felt numb. "And your parents know?"

He nodded. "They've always done their best to prepare me. I've had magic tutors since I could walk, and knights who trained me in swordsmanship."

Autumn shook her head. She thought of Cai growing up, knowing that he would never grow older than twelve. Knowing that his parents knew, that they accepted it. She thought of them sending him to expensive tutors, buying him fancy swords, all so that he would be strong enough to fight the Hollow Dragon and save Eryree.

And then die, like a proper hero.

"Oh, Cai," Autumn murmured. She could imagine him when he was little, facing his swordfighting tutors with the same expression, no matter how many times they knocked him down. She'd seen herself how stubborn he was. Choo rested his head on Cai's knee.

Autumn clenched her hands into fists. She wished there was something in front of her she could fight—a dragon, a pooka, anything. "How can you be so calm? Doesn't it make you angry?"

A shadow passed over Cai's face, but then it cleared. "I wish I could have kept it from you. But it's all right, Autumn. The Hollow Dragon has hurt so many people. It has to stop."

"And you're the one who has to stop it," Autumn said bitterly. "Not your parents. Not the king's magicians, or the headmaster with all his magic. All those grown-ups aren't even going to help you?"

Cai smiled faintly in a way that made him look older than twelve. "Grown-ups never help. They always leave the important things to us."

Autumn's fists clenched. "I don't believe that. Gran would help. Gran—"

"Autumn, the prophecy says—"

"The prophecy can pipe down," Autumn snapped, brandishing the walking stick. "I'll fight the prophecy too, along with the Hollow Dragon. You're not getting rid of me that easily, Cai Morrigan." Her voice trembled, but she was *not* going to cry. She didn't believe in prophecies. Cai wasn't going to die, because she wasn't going to let him.

"Autumn," he said, "you're the bravest person I've ever met." He hugged her.

Autumn didn't know what to do. People didn't hug her very often. Gran wasn't the hugging sort of grandmother—there wasn't much motherliness about her, when it came down to it—and if she were to hug one of her brothers, they'd probably fear for her health. Jack liked to hug, of course, but he'd hug a wyvern if it turned its back long enough.

From the shadows there came a terrible growl. It was the sort of growl that could only come from a very large mouth lined with a great many teeth.

"What was that?" Cai grabbed his staff.

"It was the boggart." Autumn would recognize her boggart's voice anywhere, no matter what shape he took. "Boggart?"

No reply. The trees rocked in the wind, and the gorse rustled its prickles.

"Boggart!" Autumn yelled.

"What's wrong with him?"

"He's upset with me." Autumn didn't see the need to tell Cai that he was the reason for the boggart's anger. "And he's not well. He had to break one of his laws when he rescued us from the gwyllions. It made him a little bit human."

Cai frowned. "That's not good."

"He's still the boggart," Autumn said defensively. "Anyway, what's wrong with him being a bit human?"

"I don't know." Cai looked into the shadows, the frown hovering around his eyes. "Maybe nothing. But Headmaster Neath always said that monsters are only more dangerous than humans because of their powers to beguile and mislead. That a human with the powers of a boggart would tear whole kingdoms apart. He said that even a monster hungry for hearts is only hungry for hearts. A monster's hunger is a thundercloud that frightens but can only hold so much rain, while human hunger is a bottomless well."

"You magicians like talking in riddles," Autumn said. But she felt the stirrings of unease. Surely there was no reason for it. The boggart's moods changed with the sky. He'd always forgiven Autumn when they quarreled—why would this time be any different?

"Are you all right?" she said. "You look . . . funny."

Cai *did* look funny, though she couldn't explain how. Something about him had sharpened. His eyes were too dark—no longer like pinecones or mushrooms, but morasses and tree hollows.

He touched his head. "I—I think so."

"Wore yourself out with all that fainting, I bet," Autumn said. She hid her worry and helped Cai to his feet. "You'd make an excellent maiden in a ballad, you would. Let's get you back to the castle."

She looked over her shoulder, hoping to catch the telltale glint of claws. But the shadows were empty. The boggart was gone.

17

In Which Autumn Has a Terrible Idea

The next day, Autumn took every opportunity to look for the boggart. He didn't return to the old beastkeepers' hut, nor did he come out when she stood at the edge of the Gentlewood and called to him in the Speech. Where else could he be?

The sky stayed low and gray, the clouds sagging under their burden of rain. It was one of those days when dawn brought with it only a watery version of night. And yet every splash of rain across her face, cold as it was, came as a relief. The weather was still coming from the sea, laced with salt and warmer than the storms that blew down from the north.

"That's right," Autumn muttered to the sky as she stomped across the mountainside. "You just wait. He's not ready for you yet."

She kept herself busy with her chores and, of course, with fretting over Winter. The day after their misadventure in the

Gentlewood, Cai sent Autumn a very strange gift. It was a beautiful gray-and-gold feathered mask with a long, wolfish snout. Attached to it was a note inviting her to the Hallowtide Masque in Cai's neat, clear handwriting. Cai thought the masque would be the perfect opportunity to look for the third cloud tower.

It took Autumn half an hour to read the short message, tracing each letter with her fingertip as she sounded them out. When she finally had it, her heart was pounding.

Hallowtide took place in mid-November and celebrated the coming of winter. It was a festival of games and pranks, the one time when rank disappeared and servants and commoners, magicians and nobility alike dressed in costumes and mingled together. Inglenook held the masque in the banquet hall—that night, the rest of the school would be empty.

Autumn set aside the note with shaking hands. Would they find Winter on Hallowtide? They'd failed to find the third tower before, and there was no particular reason why this time should be different.

But it *felt* different. Maybe it was because Hallowtide was a time when impossible things felt possible. Or maybe it was because Winter had disappeared soon after Hallowtide, and now the great wheel of the year was returning to the place where everything had gone wrong, and maybe Winter would return with it. Whatever the reason, Autumn clung to the new stirring of hope.

On the morning of the masque, Gran came upon Autumn

in the cellar, where she had been hoping to find the boggart nestled among the flour or preserves. Gran snorted when Autumn told her the boggart was missing.

"He's been ill," Autumn said defensively. "And he's upset with me. I have to talk to him."

"Never heard of a boggart being ill," Gran said. "He's upset, you say? What makes you think that's your problem? Monsters who've walked the earth since before we mortals could light fires or spin cloth don't get to be angry with children. Leave him to his moping and moaning."

"But he seems different, Gran." Autumn shook her head. "Did he ever get upset with your sister?"

Gran's sister had been the boggart's previous companion until her death, a year before Autumn was born. Usually, Gran didn't like talking about her sister—her shoulders would stiffen whenever her name came up, and she'd bustle off somewhere. Autumn wondered if she would answer.

"Not upset, exactly," Gran said after a long moment. "Though that one's always been given to tantrums when he doesn't get his way. No, the only time I saw him upset was when Jane got sick. Wouldn't leave her side either night or day, and woe betide any healer who suggested bloodletting or any such quackery—he'd throw them through the window. I was certain the old trickster was done for when she died. He didn't move for years—just stayed there under her headstone, curled up small. Some nights there'd come this wild wailing—even the students in their towers could hear it, they said. But, for the most part, you'd never know if he was still there, or if he'd simply faded away, like my Janie." Gran pressed her lips together. "Until you came along."

Autumn knew the rest of the story, though she didn't remember it herself. One day, she'd escaped from her nursemaid—the first of many successful escape attempts—and gone tottering and tumbling down the mountainside. She'd stumbled across the mossy gravestone and the boggart snoring gently beneath it. Delighted by the discovery of a snoring nothingness, she'd set about poking the boggart until he awoke. By that point, Autumn had torn her hands and knees falling into gorse bushes and had a painful lump at the back of her head. The boggart, seeing her pitiful state, had taken Autumn home. He hadn't returned to his little hollow beneath the headstone but had slept at the foot of Autumn's bed in the shape of a hare, or sometimes a cat, which infant Autumn had liked better, until she was healed. Eventually, he returned to his old sanctuary, the former beastkeepers' hut, where he'd lived with generations of Malogs.

"You'll have enough to keep you busy today without worrying about that malcontent," Gran said. "Come."

Puzzled, Autumn followed Gran to the menagerie. Choo trotted behind them, tail swinging, but Gran made him wait outside. He sat down smartly, delighted to be entrusted with the role of guard dog.

"Gran, what about the gwarthegs?" Autumn said. "I thought we were moving them to the eastern pasture today."

"That can wait. We've a few new guests, you see."

"Oh!" Autumn felt a shiver of excitement. New monsters! Had Gran found a clutch of dragon eggs?

Emys was waiting for them inside the menagerie. He had a bandaged hand and an especially sour look on his face.

"I stumbled across them last night on my rounds," Gran said. "They were down in the combe in a right state, moaning and hissing. Wouldn't tell me who they'd been fighting with, though they did have the energy to accuse me of thievery. Apparently they own the air."

Autumn's heart stopped, then restarted unevenly. Gran led them to the very back of the menagerie, past the grumbling Hounds and the brownies. She stopped before the last stall.

"I've patched them up," she said. "Two broken wings and a half dozen burns between them."

Curled up at the back of the stall was a dark shape. Autumn squinted. No—three dark shapes, piled together in a heap. They were feathered, but they were too big to be birds. A thin bath of seawater covered the tile floor, rippling faintly when the creatures breathed.

"Gwyllions," Autumn murmured. She took hold of one of the iron bars, for she felt suddenly unsteady.

"Find out what they eat," Gran said over her shoulder as she tromped away. "Some of the stories say mountain goats. Others say babies. Let's hope it's the first. Easier to come by, goats."

Autumn's head spun. The masque was tonight. Cai wanted to look for the third cloud tower, which could be a pathway to

Winter, who Autumn had sensed—impossibly—up in the sky.

And here were three monsters who would know exactly where that pathway was. The Lords and Ladies of Above, rulers of the sky itself.

Autumn felt a little shiver, fear or excitement or both. It was a feeling she'd had a lot since teaming up with Cai.

Emys gave her a dark look. "Stop that."

Autumn blinked. "Stop what?"

"You have that look. Like you're getting ideas."

"Sorry," Autumn said. "Didn't mean to make you jealous."

"I hope you're not thinking about skiving off for one of your mad jaunts through the Gentlewood. I don't want to be stuck with these things alone. Just the smell of them gives me the creeps."

"They're not *jaunts*," Autumn said. "I don't go into the Gentlewood to take in the scenery. I'm looking for Winter."

Emys rolled his eyes. Of all the Malogs, Emys had the least patience for Autumn's conviction. He'd told her a dozen times that Winter was dead and there was nothing to be done about it. Oddly, it was the thing Autumn liked best about Emys. He didn't treat her like some old mug with a crack down the middle, liable to come apart at the slightest jostling.

Chewing her lip, Autumn watched Emys. She could hardly believe what she was about to say. Of all the things she'd done in recent days, this was probably the most preposterous, the most likely to blow up in her face. Was she mad to even consider it?

Probably. But it had to be done.

For Winter.

"I need your help," she finally managed.

Emys looked at her as if she'd sprouted horns. "You what my what?"

"Need," Autumn said. "Help. I'll give you a moment."

Emys looked like he could use it. His shock was fading into astonished suspicion—not much better. "What are you plotting, Autumn?"

"Nothing that's going to get you into trouble," Autumn said. It was, of course, a bald-faced lie. "Cai's helping me find Winter. We think we know where he is, approximately. But we've run into a little hiccup—"

"Good grief," Emys said. "Why are you getting mixed up with that kid? Has he been filling your head with his hero nonsense? Millie says he's a weirdo." Millie was Emys's secret girlfriend.

"My head isn't particularly fillable," Autumn said. "And Millie's one to talk, isn't she? With that squint?"

"Squint!"

"She looks like she washes her face with lemons," Autumn said. Remembering her purpose, she hurried to add, "But apart from that, she sure is pretty, Emys. And I bet the way she walks around with her nose in the air like Choo sniffing out a fox is something you could definitely get used to eventually."

Emys looked sour. "This is some prank you've planned with

the boggart, isn't it? Well, I'm not falling for it. I still haven't found my boots."

"They're in the badger's den by the old willow," Autumn said. "I don't think you'll want them back. Emys, please. You know I wouldn't ask for your help if I didn't really need it. Really, *really* need it."

"Ugh, I'm going to regret this." Emys shook his head. "What do you want?"

Autumn blinked. She closed her mouth, swallowing all the arguments she had been marshaling. She felt as stunned by Emys's offer of help as he had been by her asking for it. She'd been certain he'd never give it willingly, not without some serious bribery, or blackmail, or a creative combination of both.

Autumn drew in her breath. "This is going to take a while to explain."

18

In Which There Is a Cloak
Full of Monsters

"It's not very convincing," Jack said, stepping back.

"Really?" Emys said. "I think the resemblance is uncanny."

Jack glared at him.

The gwyllion gazed back at them. "Gazed" was perhaps a strong word. It had no eyes that Autumn could see, apart from two pinprick-size spots of black on either side of its head. The gwyllion was actually three gwyllions standing atop each other, which they'd dressed in Jack's nicest cloak. He'd been planning to wear it to the Hallowtide Masque, but would likely never wear it again, given the gwyllion stink now woven into the fabric. To add to the ridiculousness of the picture, they'd tied an old mask from the Inglenook lost and found around the topmost gwyllion's head. This, together with the hood, hid most of the gwyllion's face while simultaneously attracting the eye, as masks patterned with roses and violently yellow bumblebees had a tendency to do.

The gwyllions were docile and sleepy surrounded by all that sea water, and they had followed Autumn's commands without resistance. Now, though, they were pacing slowly back and forth, muttering. A lot of monsters did that, the first time they came to the menagerie. The boots worn by the lowest gwyllion made an ominous wet dragging sound, for the thing didn't lift its feet when it walked.

The Lords and Ladies will have their vengeance, the gwyllions muttered as they paced. *Wretched children will bow to the Lords and Ladies . . .*

Amfidzel, in the next stall, gave a low hiss that Autumn had never heard from her before. *I don't like them*, she said. *Make them hush.*

I'm sorry, Autumn said, putting her hand against Amfidzel's stall. She could just see a sliver of the dragon's red eyes through the boards. *We'll try to keep it down.*

Amfidzel lowered her head back onto the straw. *Nobody likes their kind*, she added in a sulky voice. *Sky rats, dragons call them. They shouldn't be here.*

With any luck, they won't be staying long, Autumn told her.

"They just miss their home," Jack said. "Poor thing. Things, I mean." He petted the gwyllion's shoulder, or the most shoulder-like part.

The gwyllion slowly turned its head in the direction of Jack's hand.

"Jack, how many times has Gran told you not to pet the

monsters?" Autumn said, hastily drawing him back.

"This is a terrible idea," Emys said. His arms were folded, and his long face looked even longer. "This is actually the worst idea you've ever had, which is quite an accomplishment. Congratulations. Do you know how dangerous this is?"

"Of course."

"I don't think you do. If you did, you wouldn't have spent the last ten minutes choosing a pocket square."

"Everyone else at the masque will have a pocket square!" Autumn said. "It's an important accessory!"

"Of course," Emys said, nodding. "The key to sneaking monsters into balls: accessories. Remind me why we're doing this again?"

"I *need* them," Autumn said. "They'll know where that last tower is."

"We should give them names," Jack said.

Emys and Autumn exchanged looks.

"Horrible Sky Stinkers?" Emys suggested.

Jack frowned. "No. A proper name, one word. Something that suits them."

"Slither?" Emys said. "Squelch? Bogey?"

"We're not naming them, Jack," Autumn said. "Stop trying to make friends with them."

"You're friends with the boggart," Jack said sulkily.

"That's different." Not for the first time, Autumn mused that Jack should be the one to marry the boggart, since he loved monsters so much.

"Phlegm?" Emys said.

"I think this will do," Autumn said decisively. "With the hood up, it will hide the mask, which hides the gwyllion." It was close enough to a sensible plan that Autumn was satisfied.

"And after you get into the masque?" Emys said. "Do you really think these things will lead you to this cloud tower?"

Autumn had told Emys and Jack everything—well, almost everything. She hadn't told them Cai's secret, because that wasn't her secret to tell. Autumn hoped she didn't end up regretting it.

Emys looked the gwyllions up and down. "I mean, why would they help you? Out of the blackness of their hearts?" He laughed at his joke.

Autumn supposed she did regret it a little.

Autumn turned to the gwyllions. *Look at me*, she commanded.

The gwyllions paused. They were hunched over, and while their strange bulk was hidden by the cloak and the drawn-up hood, they did not resemble anyone you'd care to introduce yourself to at a party.

If you help me tonight, she said, *if you lead me and Cai to the other hidden tower, the boggart and I will fix yours. We'll put right everything that we broke.*

The wicked child thinks she can bargain with the Lords and Ladies. The gwyllion's voice was a scandalized hiss.

Do the Lords and Ladies bargain? the one in the stomach said.

No, they do not. They own. They have. The air is theirs, and all that breathes it.

Such disrespect! said the feet.

"That went well," Emys sighed.

Autumn glared at him.

She took a step forward, then gave a deep bow. *Lords and Ladies of Above,* she said, *I spoke wrongly before. I'm not asking for a bargain, but for a favor. I've heard that you are a very—er, generous folk.*

The gwyllions did not reply, but they fell to a startled muttering among themselves.

If you grant me this favor, Autumn went on, *I will give you a gift as a thank-you.*

Gift? the gwyllions murmured. *What gift does the child mean? The Lords and Ladies are rich beyond imagining, for they own the air.*

Autumn swallowed. *Me.*

"Have you lost your mind?" Emys hissed.

"Autumn, you can't," Jack said plaintively.

"I'm not going to," Autumn muttered, making a *be quiet* gesture. "There's only three of them. Me and Cai can handle three gwyllions."

Jack fell silent. The mention of Cai's name was enough to mollify him, Autumn knew, but Emys still looked furious.

"Is this what Winter would have wanted?" he said. "For you to risk your life for him?"

"I've already risked my life for Winter." Autumn drew

herself to her full height. "I'll do it as many times as I have to."

Emys rubbed his eyes. He seemed to be swearing under his breath.

The uppermost gwyllion said, *A sacrifice. Ah, how the Lords and Ladies enjoy those. Mountain folk used to leave babies on mountaintops to appease us. The Lords and Ladies miss those days, for babies are the tastiest of all, particularly their little toesies*

Is that a yes? Autumn said.

The Lords and Ladies will grant you one favor, the gwyllion said. *Then they will take what is theirs.*

There was a cruel cunning in its voice. Autumn's heart quickened. She knew better than to strike bargains with monsters—they almost never worked out in your favor, for monsters were far more skilled than humans at trickery. But why should she worry? She would have Cai with her.

Autumn glanced out the window. The November sky was darkening like a bruise. The masque would be starting soon.

We have a deal, she said.

19

In Which Winter
Drifts Too Far

– *TODAY* –

"Winter!"

Someone was yelling his name. They'd been yelling for a while, Winter realized.

"Autumn?" he murmured. And just like that, he was himself again.

"*There* you are," Maddie said. "I've been looking everywhere for you. The others forgot about you, but *I* remembered your name."

Winter rested his hand against the window. They were in one of the towers—the Windfarer Tower, he thought, but he wasn't sure. Beastkeepers spent most of their time outside, so though he was a servant of Inglenook, he didn't know it very well.

"If you keep that up, the Dark will get you," Maddie said. "I don't want to forget you."

"Keep what up?"

"Drifting. The more you do that, the harder it is to stay *you*."

Winter looked down at himself and found that he was even more colorless than usual. Maddie was right. Still, he found it hard to care. He felt as if the grayness of the mirrors had gotten inside him.

"Please try," Maddie said. Her lip shook a little. "I need you to help *me* remember. You're so good at it. I think I would have faded by now if it hadn't been for you."

Winter sighed. "I'll try."

She relaxed and smiled. The shadows deepened beyond the window as the sun ducked its head under the mountains. But one shadow loomed up above the others and twitched as if sniffing the air.

"Maddie!" Winter cried.

He grabbed her by the arm and pulled her away from the Dark. She came free slowly, as if the Dark was *sticky* somehow. They ran from the window and into the next one. Then they ran to the windows on the floor below, for all the windows in Inglenook were connected, and up and down was the same as left and right. But still the Dark followed.

Maddie looked behind her and screamed. She tore away from Winter and ran ahead, running too fast for him to keep up.

"Maddie!" he cried. "Wait!"

He stopped, panting. He *had* been drifting too long—it had made him slow. He could feel the other windows and mirrors—before, he had been able to leap between them, not just run from one to the next. But now it was like trying to jump to a stepping-stone yards away. No matter how hard he tried, he knew he couldn't make it.

He looked around. He was in the banquet hall—music played in the distance, muffled and twisted by the glass, and every surface was crowded with food and pumpkins and candles. It looked as if the hall had been decorated for Hallowtide. Winter couldn't believe it—if it was Hallowtide, that meant he had been trapped for nearly a year.

In the corner of his eye, something large and dark shifted position.

Horror rose inside him. Normally, he was able to outrun the Dark. It might follow him through a window or two, but he always shook it off. Always.

He ran to the next window, praying that this time, *this* time, the Dark wouldn't follow. But he had only stood there for a moment, panting, before a shadow began to seep across the glass.

A sob caught in his throat. He forced his weary legs to move, to feel for the edges of the next window, and pull himself into it. Was there an end to the mirrors? A place where he wouldn't be able to reach the next one? He didn't know. He didn't know how long he could keep running.

He only knew that he had to.

20

In Which the Gwyllions
Take What Is Theirs

Autumn, Emys, and the gwyllions made an unusual group as they climbed the mountain path to Inglenook. Emys, scowling magnificently; Autumn, wearing her only party dress under one of Gran's oversize cloaks (the only clean one she could find) and carrying the walking stick she had taken from the Gentlewood, which somehow looked more stick-like than ever; and the cloak full of gwyllions, which formed an ominously hunched and hooded figure with a crow-like strut.

Autumn's thoughts kept drifting to the boggart. It was most unlike a boggart to stray from his home, and Autumn was worried for him. She was also worried for herself and wished he was at her side.

Inglenook loomed ahead, an immense darkness glittering like a constellation. Smoke drifted from the chimneys, and even from a distance, Autumn could smell food. Her mouth watered despite her nervousness. She could make out the masked figures of several gardeners walking some yards ahead, and pointedly slowed so that they wouldn't catch up. There was no need for the gwyllions to be seen by more people than necessary.

The massive oak doors had been thrown open, and Autumn, Emys, and the gwyllions passed into the school without incident. The foyer was awash in candlelight. Masters, students, and servants mingled freely, in keeping with the spirit of Hallowtide, though it was also true that most people stuck to their own for the better part of the evening. Many students were wearing costumes—there were knights and dragons, ravens and Hounds of Arawn. Headmaster Neath, laughing at some joke with a knot of masters, seemed to be wearing a wolfskin for a cloak. Autumn even saw a girl wearing black claws and a rippling dress that could only be a boggart costume.

As they stepped into the banquet hall, Autumn drew in her breath. The hall was beautiful even on ordinary days, airy as an open moor. The floor was of white marble so pure it was like walking on a frozen lake. The stained-glass windows were stories limned in gold, the eyes of the knights and magicians formed by sapphires or emeralds or chocolate opals.

Tonight, the hall was decorated for Hallowtide. There were turnips carved into faces, scarecrows temporarily dragged in from farmers' fields, ravens in cages waiting to be hand-fed harvest seeds and soul cakes. There were hundreds of candles upon every surface, most unlit, as the tradition was for revelers to light a candle after each dance they danced, so that as the evening wore on, the hall would brighten. Tables heaped with food lined the walls—white buns soft as clouds spread with creamy cheeses, whole carrots and cabbages stewed in goose fat, crispy duck with roasted plums, and trays of fresh oysters wriggling in their shells. There were squares of expensive salt cheese all the way from Langorelle, skewered and ready for toasting over the fire. There were plum puddings swimming in custard, candied ginger and chocolate-covered chestnuts, raspberry pudding with cream, and steaming apple crumbles.

Autumn's stomach was in knots. Normally, she counted the days to Hallowtide—all the Malogs did, apart from Gran, of course, who had no patience for dressing up, dancing, or any of the rest of it. Kyffin was already there, somewhere, while Jack was back at the cottage nursing a pretend stomachache. He would have the unhappy responsibility of feigning shock if Gran happened to discover that the gwyllions were missing. They'd left the stall door open and off its hinge to suggest a crafty prison break.

Autumn was shocked by how quickly her brothers had jumped to her aid. It was unprecedented. They'd never helped her with anything important. . . . But then, she couldn't remember ever asking them to. Autumn had always had the boggart, and Winter, of course—what use did she have for older brothers? But now the boggart was gone, and the brothers who had always lurked in the background—mildly unpleasant but harmless, like lumpy couches—had revealed unexpected uses.

It was confusing. Fortunately, she and Emys had been arguing all day, which took some of the strangeness off.

"All right, we're in," she said, craning her neck to look for Cai. She hadn't seen him since that night in the Gentlewood. "You can clear off."

Emys snorted. "Don't think I don't want to—I'm never doing you a favor again. But I'm not leaving you with that thing. Things."

"I've got Cai. And I'm a better Speaker than you are. Get lost."

"Why do you have to be such a brat, Autumn?"

"Why are you such a wuss? If you ever stumbled into a real adventure, you'd wet yourself."

"Fine. Go take your pet monster to the party. And if it bites your head off and eats your brains, see if I care."

"At least if a monster ate *my* brains, people could tell the difference."

"I don't want to have anything to do with you for the rest of the night."

"I thought you weren't doing me any more favors."

"Autumn!" There was Cai, waving to her by the croaking ravens. He had been talking to Winifred and Bryony, both of whom actually smiled at Autumn—though Winifred's smile was the indulgent sort you might give to a favorite pet.

Cai made his way over, and Autumn met him halfway, the gwyllions trailing in her wake. Emys folded his arms and fumed. Still, she could sense his voice in the gwyllions' heads. He was keeping an eye on them anyway, the big whiner. She felt a little prickle of gratitude and told herself it was just her nervousness.

"You look pretty," Cai said, politely ignoring her huge, threadbare cloak and gazing instead at her dress. It was an all right dress, Autumn supposed—light blue with a darker blue pattern of tiny flowers, unfortunately faded and much darned, for Gran couldn't exactly afford to buy her a new dress every Hallowtide. She didn't look half as nice as Cai, in his gold-trimmed cloak and mask edged with pearls.

"Thanks for the mask," she said, pushing it up. She could see Cai better without it, and she faltered. "Cai?"

"I know." He kept smiling, but it didn't touch his eyes. He lowered his voice. "Pretend everything's fine. My sister's coming."

"Your sister?" Autumn had a moment of blankness before her memory kicked in. She'd forgotten Cai had a sister.

She gripped Cai's arm. It wasn't that he looked ill—it was that he didn't look like *Cai*. The sharpness was still there, and he moved like a shadow. And his eyes—

Autumn swallowed. She could see the forest in Cai's eyes. The waving boughs; the meadows of bluebells. It was as if the Gentlewood was looking out from his face.

A girl of eight or nine came bounding through the crowd. Autumn couldn't tell whether she was a magician or not; the air seemed to brighten when she neared, but that could have been the ferocity of her smile. She was pretty and plump with long hair the same glossy dark as Cai's. When she saw Autumn, the smile slid from her face.

"Are you dancing with *her*?" she demanded. "You promised to dance with me."

"Blue, this is Autumn," Cai said. "We have something important to do tonight. But I'll be back to dance with you later, promise."

The little girl's expression darkened into a sulk that reminded Autumn of the boggart.

"Dance with me *now*," she said. Autumn stared at her, but Cai only smiled at his sister's rudeness, as you would at a growling kitten.

"I can't," he said seriously. "You see, I'm on a quest."

Blue looked suspicious. "What sort of quest?"

"I have to find ten shooting stars before dawn, to use in an important enchantment. Maybe you can help me."

He murmured to his staff, and a cloud of starlight formed above Blue's head. She gave a squeal of delight. The cloud rippled, and the tiny stars trapped there began to fall. Blue darted this way and that, trying to catch them. One streaked across the room, and she ran after it, giggling, without a backward glance.

"Is she a magician?" Autumn said.

"Yes—a moon magician. She's going to start school soon."

"Isn't that unusual?" Autumn said. "Your parents aren't magic, but both of you are?"

"Actually, it often happens that way. There are a lot of theories. Some magicians think that there are people who have magic but aren't able to use it—it's dormant, in other words. They'll never be magicians themselves, but if they marry someone like them, they can pass it on to their kids. If non-magicians have a magician child, their next child is usually magic, too." Cai looked around. "My parents are here. But if I introduce you to my dad, he'll talk your ear off for an hour." His voice was exasperated but affectionate. "Come on."

Autumn let Cai lead her through the hall, feeling as if she were lit by her own cloud of starlight. Everybody stared at them, servants and students and masters alike. Even the ravens murmured and croaked as they passed. Many of the students called out to Cai, and quite a few of them blushed when he greeted them back in his calm, polite voice.

Gawain, standing with a knot of junior apprentices, clapped Cai on the shoulder in a proud, possessive sort of way. "Who's this?" he asked, giving Autumn a puzzled look.

Autumn fixed Gawain with a glower that made him take a step back. Cai said quickly, "I have to talk to Autumn about something, Gawain. Excuse us—"

"Is your friend all right?" The girl at Gawain's side gazed past Autumn with rounded eyes.

Autumn turned. She stifled a yelp. The cloak of gwyllions was writhing, and one of the boots was turned nearly backward.

The Lords and Ladies do not enjoy this confinement, one of the gwyllions said. *It is too hot.*

The Lords and Ladies are fortunate not to be on the bottom, said the lowest gwyllion. *The Lords and Ladies must pay more attention to their weight.*

What rudeness! Perhaps the Lords and Ladies should build up their strength. Their muscles have grown enfeebled.

The upper third of the gwyllion lurched forward, while the boots rattled and made hissing noises. Several students were frozen in place, staring.

Autumn forced a laugh, and carefully patted the gwyllion's back. "Ah, my brother isn't much of a dancer." *Stop that stop that stop that,* she hissed.

The gwyllions stilled a little. There was still far too much movement, though, in the stomach region—not an area that was supposed to move, as a general rule.

"What's he supposed to be?" the girl said, spilling punch on her dress as she leaned her entire body away from the gwyllions. To Autumn's horror, the tip of the topmost gwyllion's beak was protruding from the hood.

"Well, a gwyllion, of course," Autumn said, giving Cai a meaningful look. His eyes widened. "What do you think?" She forced a laugh.

The girl laughed too, equally forced. "Gawain, let's get some punch."

Gawain frowned. He wasn't looking at the gwyllions, having discounted the figure in the servant's cloak at first glance. "But you already have—"

"So nice to meet you," the girl said to Autumn, dragging Gawain away.

Cai's mouth had fallen open. "Autumn, how—why—"

"Just keep smiling," she muttered. She plastered a large grin on her own face as she gripped the edge of the gwyllions' cloak. "Come on, *Jack*."

If anything, the onlookers seemed more horrified when the gwyllions started walking. The left boot was turned completely around now, but the figure in the cloak seemed not to notice this terrible deformity and kept walking with that mincing, ominous stride. Two students actually leaped out of its way.

Finally, they were standing in a sufficiently shadowy alcove. By that time, Cai seemed to have figured things out a little. "They're going to lead us to the cloud tower?" he said. "Why?"

"We made a deal," Autumn said. Into Cai's mind, she added, *Which I'm not going to keep. After they lead us to the cloud tower, you have to get rid of them.*

Cai gave an infinitesimal nod. "I see. Well, it's a good thing, I suppose—that map has been a headache. It puts the third cloud tower next to the vegetable patch, but I can't find any trace of it. I was going to say we should look there anyway, but if they know where it is . . ."

It's the boy from the tower, one of the gwyllions murmured.

Pretty starlight boy, another crooned. *The Lords and Ladies are pleased to see him again.*

Yes, yes, ever so pleased.

Autumn shushed them. She turned to Cai. "What happened to you?"

"I knew you would notice," Cai said. "Nobody else seems to."

Autumn stepped back, eyeing him critically. "You look the same. But you also look different. I can't explain it. It's like there's two of you."

"I don't look entirely the same." Cai glanced over his shoulder, then pulled off his gloves.

Autumn gasped. Little black shadows flickered beneath Cai's skin. They crept all the way up to his elbows, where they faded.

"When did this happen?" Autumn demanded, grabbing his hands.

"It started after we got back from the Gentlewood," Cai said. "It's gotten worse. I don't know what's going on. Why is it happening now?" He was trembling.

"Oh, Cai," Autumn said. She hugged him, surprising herself. "It's going to be all right. We'll figure this out together."

Cai hugged her back. "Autumn, I'm so glad you're my friend."

Autumn's eyes prickled. She drew back, feeling suddenly

awkward. "What are sidekicks for, anyway?" She blushed to the roots of her hair. "Course, I don't mean that. I could never be your sidekick. I'm just a beastkeeper."

"*Just?*" Cai shook his head, smiling a little, which Autumn was glad to see. "I don't think that word has anything to do with you, Autumn."

She looked away, worried that the force of her blush would set her hair on fire. "You magicians and your nonsense," she muttered.

"There's something else," Cai said. "I'm hungry."

"Oh," Autumn said blankly. Then, when she realized from the look on Cai's face that he didn't mean hunger of the common kind, "*Oh.* What for?"

"That's the problem." He looked as if he might be ill. "I don't know."

This was unwelcome news, but Autumn hid her worry as best as she could. "We'll figure that out, too. Monsters eat all kinds of things." *Mostly children*, she thought but did not say. "Look at the boggart. He eats anything. Meat. Sap from the Gentlewood. And you know people make all sorts of strange offerings to boggarts—the stories say they have a particular liking for maidens' tears."

"Really?" Cai looked relieved. He paused. "Actually, that's gross."

"Cai, are you sure you're well enough to look for Winter tonight?" Saying it made Autumn ache. She felt torn in two between her worry for Cai and her longing for Winter.

He lifted his strange eyes to hers. "I made you a promise," he said, his voice hard with determination. "We're going to find your brother. Tonight."

"Autumn!" Ceredwen dashed up to them, nearly skipping. She wore the pretty pink dress she'd worn to last year's Hallowtide and had woven herself a pair of wings from branches and raven feathers, which also adorned her mask. When she saw Cai, she gasped and dropped into a curtsy.

"You're not supposed to do that on Hallowtide," Autumn reminded her. On Hallowtide, everyone was equal. At least on the surface—all that food didn't cook itself, and so only a few of the cooks had the day off. The rest crept between the kitchens and the banquet hall like ghosts, keeping the tables well stocked.

Ceredwen blushed, but she was bubbling with excitement, and it was stronger than her fear of Cai. "Autumn, one of the bards heard me singing, and she offered to take me on as her apprentice!"

Autumn was sure she'd misheard. "The bard *what*?"

"Can you imagine?" Ceri hopped up and down. "Bards travel all over Eryree—I'll get to see the whole kingdom! Sometimes they even visit the Southern Realms. Think of all the songs I'll learn!"

"Congratulations," Cai said kindly. He had stealthily replaced his gloves.

Autumn shook her head. "But Ceri, you're not a bard. You don't know any instruments. And servants aren't taught to read."

"I was," Ceredwen said. "The head housekeeper did it as a favor to Mum. She knew I always wanted to be a bard. And the bard said all you really need to know at first is the triple-stringed willow harp, and that's dead easy. She's going to teach me."

Autumn still didn't understand. "But what if she finds out you're a servant?"

Ceredwen's smile faltered. "She already knows that. She doesn't mind. She only cares that I can sing and read music. Some of the bards used to be servants. Others are minor nobles. They're all sorts."

"You'll be great," Cai said. "When do you leave?"

"Tomorrow. Oh, there's the bard now—I'm going to see if she needs more honey wine. I have to look after her, now that I'm her apprentice and all." And Ceredwen skipped away.

Autumn watched her go. "You shouldn't do that," she said to Cai.

"What?"

"Give her false hope. It's not very nice."

"Hope?" Cai said, blinking. "What does hope have to do with anything? She has what she wants."

Autumn shook her head. "It won't last. She doesn't know anything about music."

"She'll learn." Cai seemed so puzzled that Autumn fell silent. It would be strange not to have Ceredwen at Inglenook.

But even stranger was the thought of Ceredwen wandering across Eryree with a troupe of bards. Bards weren't as beloved as magicians, but they were respected. They weren't just entertainers, but the keepers of Eryree's history.

Was it true that some bards had once been servants? Autumn couldn't believe it. All the servants she knew had always been servants, and so had their parents. She felt as if she'd been told that the sky could turn green if it felt like it.

Cai blinked. "Where are the gwyllions?"

Autumn whirled. *There* were the gwyllions—they had shuffled to the tables of food. The students gathered there watched the cloaked figure with confusion that deepened to horror as the topmost gwyllion began to tear at a mincemeat pie with its face.

Rude not to share, the lowest gwyllion said.

The Lords and Ladies can wait their turn, the topmost gwyllion said. Bits of pastry flew through the air. The watching students backed slowly away.

What impertinence! the lowest gwyllion said. *The Lords and Ladies wait for nothing.* It stamped its boots, and then, with an awful jerking motion, the figure leaped onto the table like an ungainly seal taking to land. Pie crust and oyster shells went everywhere. Somebody screamed. An entire pudding sailed into the air and landed on Gawain's head.

Fortunately, Autumn and Cai arrived before anything worse could transpire. "Oh, Jack," Autumn said with a breathless laugh, dragging the cloak of gwyllions off the table. "Your appetite has gotten the better of you!"

"I'll help you get him cleaned up," Cai said.

They dragged the gwyllions away, grins plastered to their faces, leaving a small crowd of magicians staring after them.

In the corridor beyond the banquet hall, Autumn sagged against the wall, consumed by helpless laughter. Even Cai smiled, lighting his too-pale cheeks.

"Did you see Gawain's face?" Autumn snorted.

"Yes," Cai said. "I have to say, blancmange suits him."

Autumn turned to the gwyllions. *It's time. Will you take us to the other tower?*

The Lords and Ladies will have what is theirs, the gwyllion crooned, a reply Autumn did not care for. But she knew monsters, and she knew that sometimes they used riddles simply to frighten.

The cloaked figure tore itself in three, leaving behind a pile of boots and fabric covered in custard. The gwyllions soared up the stairs.

Cai and Autumn ran after them. Then they went down some other stairs, then through a door that Autumn had never seen before, hidden behind a dragon tapestry.

"What is this place?" Autumn said. They were in a long corridor full of nonsensical staircases going up, then down, then up again. Some were plushly carpeted, while others were bare wood.

"Nothing," Cai called back. "Just where the masters store the stairs they don't want anymore. Doors, too."

Autumn noticed how Cai's feet did not entirely touch the ground anymore. He moved like the boggart now, like the wisps, and he didn't seem aware of the change. She felt her worry deepen.

The gwyllions scratched and shoved their way through a door carved with vines and snakes. To Autumn's astonishment, they were in the corridor leading to the Silver Tower.

"B-but—" she stuttered. "But this should be on the other side of the castle!"

"That door we went through is a portal," Cai said. "The gwyllions must have smelled it. There are portals scattered all over. I know the school so well it's like having a map in my head."

"What a jumble your head must be," Autumn said.

Cai frowned. "But what are we doing here?"

Autumn turned to the three gwyllions, who had alighted at the foot of the dark stair leading to the Silver Tower. *This is the way to the broken tower,* she said. *You promised to take us to the tower that isn't broken.*

Poor blind child, the gwyllions said. *One is two, and two is one. The Lords and Ladies led you right.*

Cai's eyes widened. "Oh! A folding spell. Of course! Why didn't I think of that?"

Autumn stared at him blankly.

"Remember how I said the cloud tower was folded into the sky?" Cai went on. "That's how those magicians hid it, long ago. Well, maybe there's another tower folded into that tower.

Basically, it would mean that the two towers are in the same place, but on different magical planes." He mimed folding. "Have you ever made a paper crane? It's like that. Folds inside of folds."

Autumn was silent. "I think I need to sit down," she said.

"I'm sorry," Cai said. "I know it's strange. The castle's a mess of magic, like I said—spells upon spells, half of them forgotten or tangled up in strange ways."

"Magicians!" Autumn groaned. "You even need housekeepers to tidy your enchantments."

She rubbed her eyes, feeling indescribably lost. This wasn't her world. This was so far from her world that she wouldn't be able to see her world with a telescope.

"So the other tower is here?" she said, focusing on the part she had understood. "Can we get to it?"

"I'll try," Cai said.

He turned and murmured to his staff. It sputtered fitfully before glowing brighter. Strands of starlight spilled over the stairway threshold, but it was strange starlight with tiny filaments of shadow threaded through it.

Cai gave his staff a shake.

"Have you been having trouble with your magic?" Autumn asked, keeping her voice as calm as possible.

"Not trouble exactly. But some spells are harder." Cai's mouth tightened. "I'm sorry."

"Will you ever stop apologizing for things you didn't do?" she said frostily. Cai hadn't chosen to turn back into a monster on the one night she needed him the most. But she couldn't help wondering how many gwyllions had survived the boggart's flame, and if they would be in a mood to let them pass through the cloud tower unchallenged. It seemed unlikely.

In the end, though, Cai seemed to finish whatever spell he had been casting. The starlight soaked into the threshold, leaving only a faint luminescence. The gwyllions hissed and took flight, disappearing up the dark staircase. Cai went next, beckoning her on.

Autumn swallowed. If there was one thing she knew, it was that you should never let monsters lead you anywhere. And yet here she was.

Autumn's grip tightened on her walking stick. It was a strange thing—neither the moss nor the mushrooms that sprouted along the grain of the wood seemed troubled by the loss of their damp forest home. In fact, Autumn had spied several new mushrooms poking their heads out of a knothole. For some reason, the stick gave her courage. She was going to find Winter, no matter the danger.

I'm coming, Winter, she thought. *I'm coming.*

The stairs were just as Autumn remembered. The Silver Tower was the same, too—there were the empty floors and the empty furniture covered with sheets. They climbed and climbed until they reached the floor with the common room and the gaping fireplace.

"This looks the same," Autumn said. "We're still in the Silver Tower, Cai."

"No, we're not. Look." He took her hand and pulled her through the enchanted fireplace.

"Oh!" Autumn exclaimed when they reached the other side. She spun around, specks of lingering magic floating off her cloak. This cloud tower was unbroken—there was the winding staircase leading up and up, and the patchy stone walls. There was no rubble, no leaning walls. And Autumn remembered, suddenly, that the boggart had broken the common room windows in the Silver Tower—and yet the common room they had just passed through had been undamaged.

"This really is a different tower," Autumn murmured.

Cai looked around. "Where did the gwyllions go?"

Autumn had no answer to that. The only sound came from the wind, and the shadows were only shadows. She took Cai's hand.

As they climbed, other differences became apparent. This tower, whatever it was called, was more decayed than the Silver Tower. The wind and clouds rippled through it, and sometimes the tower would groan ominously.

Light gleamed above them. "What's that?" Autumn said.

Cai leaned against the wall, breathing hard. "Are you all right?" she asked.

He nodded but didn't meet her gaze. "I can keep going."

"Not what I asked." She hefted his staff and took his arm. "Come on."

They climbed the last few steps. To Autumn's astonishment, the light seemed to be cast by lanterns. They reached the next floor, and the wind died away.

Autumn froze. They were standing in a luxuriously furnished circular room. A massive desk scattered with glittering papers anchored one end, facing the wall so that the occupant could gaze into the night sky. The floor was a stone mosaic of Eryree, the Gentlewood, and the wintry expanse of the Boreal Wastes. Several of the stones appeared to be gold, or perhaps the mosaic was enchanted. Dark, silken curtains fluttered in a soft breeze, and lanterns drifted in midair.

"What is this doing here?" Cai said, as if the room was a stray cat that had wandered inside unexpectedly. "This looks like Headmaster Neath's office. Doesn't it?"

"How would I know?" Autumn said. "You think he's inviting me up for tea and a chat all the time, like he does with you?" Then she stopped dead. "Wait, Cai—I'm not allowed to be in the headmaster's office! None of the servants are, except the head housekeeper."

"Calm down," Cai said. "The headmaster never leaves the masque before dawn. Besides, I don't think this is really his office."

Autumn's fear ebbed, and she could think again. "You're right. His office is in the Northmost Tower, isn't it? Is this another one of the gwyllions' illusions?"

"I don't think they're powerful enough for something like this." Cai tapped one of the lanterns as it floated by. "No, I think this is a reflection spell."

Autumn groaned.

"It's sort of the opposite of a folding spell," Cai said. "A folding spell hides something inside something else. A reflecting spell creates two of something, in different places."

Autumn's head hurt. "Why would any decent person need two of an office?"

Cai walked over to the desk and flipped through the papers. "Well, the headmaster keeps this one a secret. I've been in his other office a hundred times, and he never mentioned it. Maybe he uses this one to cast enchantments he doesn't want anyone knowing about."

"I guess not." Autumn shivered. "He hid it inside a tower hidden inside another tower. But what sort of magic is he doing, if it has to be kept secret?"

Cai was frowning at the papers. "What is this? Spirit magic? Spells for ensnaring the soul? Why would he . . . ?"

Autumn traced the spine on the huge book the headmaster had left open and facedown on his desk. "The . . . Long . . . Winters . . . of . . . Eryree," she sounded out slowly. "The Long Winters? I remember Gran mentioning those."

Cai nodded distractedly. "We study them in history class. They started eighteen years ago, lasted five. Five years in a row when the snows started in September and kept on until June. All sorts of monsters came south from the Boreal Wastes looking for food, including the Hollow Dragon."

"Hmm." Something about the dates tugged at her, though she didn't know what. She flipped *The Long Winters* over and found a messy but recognizable sketch of the Hollow Dragon staring back at her. The headmaster had filled all the empty spaces of the page with tiny, crammed-together notes that Autumn couldn't read. She closed the book.

Something drew her away from Cai. A feeling she recognized, which made her heart pound and her throat clench. Across from the desk there was a half set of stairs leading down to a glass observatory. It was shrouded in cloud, which parted to reveal the sweep of the mountain and Inglenook far below, awash in light. Someone was lighting fireworks, which opened and closed like eyes. Above the fireplace in the wall was a large mirror with a gilt frame.

And before the fire were half a dozen people seated calmly in armchairs.

Autumn didn't recognize the faces she could see. There was a girl with two long braids, and an older man in a magician's cloak. None of the people moved, or seemed to notice her. Her heart beat like a bird trapped in her chest as she walked to the chair closest to the fire and beheld the slender figure seated there.

She cried out. Instantly, she was at Winter's side, and pulling him into her arms.

"I knew you were alive," she sobbed. His hair, identical to her own, tickled her cheek. "I knew. I *knew*."

"Autumn." Cai was at her side, drawing her back. "Autumn. Look at him."

"What?" She was going to shove Cai through the window. Why was he pulling her away from Winter? But even as she thought it, her mind was registering how Winter hadn't moved or spoken, the strange chill in his skin. His eyes, open but glassy.

"What's wrong with him?" She crouched before her twin. "Winter, it's me. It's Autumn. I found you, like I promised I would."

Winter's boots were gone, as was his cloak, and his tunic was torn. Autumn took off Gran's cloak and wrapped it around him, trying to rub feeling back into his arms. He was so cold! And something else was off—what was it?

"Cai," Autumn murmured. "He's smaller than me—look!" She pressed her palm to Winter's, stretching their fingers out.

Cai nodded. He was murmuring some spell that brought color to Winter's cheeks. "He hasn't aged since he disappeared. He's alive, but frozen in time."

Cai moved among the other seated figures, shining star-light in their faces. He looked pale but determined—a hero going about his hero business. Only the picture was off. He had removed his gloves, and the shadows swam beneath his skin. They looked less like shadows and more like waving leaves, as if the forest was inside him.

"That's Master Arte," Cai said, motioning to the man. "He vanished into the Gentlewood three years ago."

Autumn barely heard him. She couldn't stop looking at Winter.

"Cai, this isn't *him*," she said. "It's just his body."

Cai nodded. "That must have something to do with the headmaster's soul-snaring spells."

"You think he's trying to put Winter's soul back into his body?" Autumn gazed at the still figures around the fire. "But where did his soul go? How did they get like this?"

Cai shook his head, perplexed. His starlight gleamed off the mirror over the fireplace. He took off his fancy cloak and used it to clean the glass. "Call Winter with the Speech."

Autumn didn't hear him at first. Her despair was a knot in her chest pulling painfully at every inch of her. "We're nowhere near the bay window."

"Maybe that doesn't matter, if he can move between places. Remember the spellprint down in the kitchens."

Autumn was on her feet in a heartbeat. She banged her palms against the mirror, shouting *Winter!* over and over again.

Cai grabbed her arm. "You're going to break it."

Autumn shoved him off. *Winter!*

She punched the glass. A crack appeared, and she felt a distant pain in her knuckles. She ignored it. *Winter!*

She gathered up everything inside her, like she had with the Hollow Dragon. She gathered it up and wove it into a net big enough to cover all of Inglenook and cast it wide.

Winter.

The ground shook. Cai stumbled. Autumn, panting and sweaty, felt a moment of terror. Had she done that? She looked at the mirror.

Winter gazed back at her.

Autumn, he cried, *I'm here!*

I know! Autumn pressed her hands against the glass. *I'm going to get you out. Just hold on.*

Winter pressed his palms against hers. *What did you do? I can't feel the other mirrors. I think I'm trapped in this one.*

I don't know, Autumn said. *But it doesn't matter which mirror you're in. Cai and I will get you out.*

Cai? Winter's mouth fell open. *Cai Morrigan is here?*

Yes, and he's going to rescue you, Autumn said proudly. *He rescues everyone.* "You *are* going to rescue him, aren't you?"

"I'm going to try," Cai said, gripping his staff of starlight. Autumn felt a rush of relief and pride that Cai was there, that he was her friend and was going to help her.

The Dark, Winter said. His voice was fragmented.

What? Autumn said. But Winter was looking over his shoulder at something and didn't respond.

"I need to know what did this to him," Cai said. "If it was magician or monster. I need to know where the spell began so that I can follow its trail."

The Dark, Winter said. *Can't run. Stuck . . .*

What?

To Autumn's horror, the mirror went black. When it cleared, Winter was still there, but there was something . . . *on* him. That was what Autumn thought she saw, anyway. A thing of darkness that could barely be called a thing, wrapped around him like a smothering blanket. It had no shape, nor any beginning or end; it was simply *dark*, and yet somehow it was terribly alive.

Winter! Autumn cried.

Cai had seen the darkness too. His incantation dashed watery waves of starlight against the glass. But the light was dulled by the new shadows woven through it, and when it dripped away, the darkness remained. Now Winter was so faded that he could barely be seen. It was as if the darkness was eating him—not piece by piece, but shade by shade.

"Cai, do something!"

Cai began another incantation. This time, bursts of starlight filled the air like bees, buzzing and crackling. Cai lifted his staff, and they exploded against the glass, a cacophony of light. But the darkness remained, and Winter grew dimmer. Autumn couldn't hear his voice anymore. She pounded and pounded on the glass even as it cut her hands.

Cai let out a cry of frustration. He threw his staff aside and plunged his hands into the mirror.

It was like watching someone dive into a November lake skinned over with ice. The mirror cracked but didn't come apart. Cai grabbed hold of something—Autumn couldn't see what, through the light and the strangeness of it all—and *pulled*.

Autumn's eyes were dazzled, and she tried to blink it away. Cai had taken a step back. Before him hovered . . . something. A ripple in the air, a tendril of clear smoke.

It was Winter. Autumn knew it in her bones.

"Autumn, stay back." Cai's voice was strange.

She stared. "Cai, what—"

Silly children, a dark voice crooned. Autumn looked up, a scream rising in her throat. The roof of the observatory was clustered with monstrous shapes—the three gwyllions perched on the metal beams between the glass panels, staring down at them. With them were half a dozen more, all staring, a terrible eagerness in their eyeless gazes.

The Lords and Ladies will take what is theirs, the gwyllion said. *Vengeance.*

The white-haired child will be devoured, soul from skin, another added contentedly. *But the Lords and Ladies need not dirty their own claws.*

No, sirs and madams, a third chimed in. *The hungry child will do it for us.*

Her own friend! the first gwyllion exclaimed. *What a delightful vengeance it will be. The Lords and Ladies are creative in their vengeances.*

Most creative and noble.

Horror bloomed in Autumn's heart. "Cai?" she whispered.

"Stay back," he said. Autumn drew in her breath. If she hadn't known the figure standing before her was Cai, she would never have recognized him. It wasn't just the leafy darkness rippling beneath his skin—it was his eyes, which held a terrible hunger.

And Autumn knew then that Cai wasn't the sort of monster who ate hearts or tears.

He was the kind who ate souls.

"Cai, no!" Autumn cried. Winter's soul drifted about, a slightly fuzzy patch of air. That was what had made Cai change—the sight of the soul, or the smell of it. (*Do souls have a smell?* some part of Autumn wondered dazedly.) Now his hunger had taken control of him.

She lunged for her walking stick—she didn't know what she intended to do with it, exactly, only that she needed it. *Cai*, she shouted, *stay away from Winter!*

She struck the floor with her stick as she said it. Cai blinked, and some of himself returned to his eyes. But then he looked back at Winter's drifting soul, and it was gone.

Cai, stop! Autumn struck the floor again. But it was like when she had tried to command him in the Silver Tower—she felt as if she was banging her fists against a stone wall. Whatever Cai was, he was something stronger than her.

No.

Autumn drew herself to her feet. She would *not* give up— not now, not ever. In desperation, she called to Winter in the Speech. She could sense him, confused and adrift, not understanding where he was. He floated toward his body, then stopped, as if he didn't recognize it.

I'm here, she said, reaching for him blindly. *Trust me. We have to do this together.*

The ripple in the air that was Winter seemed to shiver. Cai stepped forward. He didn't touch the ground at all now but glided like the boggart.

Autumn gathered her strength and Winter's together, and found that it added up to more than she could have ever imagined. Then she let the command fall like a clap of thunder.

Back.

The word thrummed through the air and into the floor. Cai flew backward. He struck the glass wall of the observatory, cracking it, and slid to the ground.

Even as he hit the wall, Autumn was moving. She planted herself between Cai and Winter's body, still motionless in the chair.

"Autumn," Cai murmured. He was himself again, Autumn thought, but there was still too much of the forest in his eyes. Autumn didn't know who would win—Cai or that terrible hunger. Cai's gaze drifted to Winter and seemed to harden. Autumn gripped her stick.

Light flared. Autumn cried out, throwing her arm over her face. Glass shattered, and a gust of chill wind lashed her face. Autumn opened her eyes.

Cai had vanished. The pane of glass was gone, opening the observatory to the night. A glimmer of light fled from the tower, darted over the magic-lit castle and the craggy mountainside, and was gone.

21

In Which a Boy
Is Put Back Together

Autumn couldn't move. She stood by the broken pane, the wind pulling at her hair and clothes, staring in the direction Cai had gone. Everything seemed to have slowed, including her ability to think. She couldn't wrap her mind around what had happened. Half the gwyllions had taken off after Cai, while the others wheeled overhead, filling the air with confused mutterings.

"Autumn?" a voice said.

Autumn whirled. "Winter!"

He had fallen out of the armchair and was propping himself up on his hands. Autumn lunged forward and drew him close.

"Autumn." Winter's voice was dry, and he coughed. "I knew—I knew you—"

"Of course you did." Tears slid down her face. "Winter."

"That's my name," he said in a voice full of wonderment. "I

almost forgot it." He was shivering so hard Autumn worried he would come apart. She drew Gran's cloak tighter around him and kissed his head a dozen times. His hair was as soft as rabbit down.

"I was at the edge of the forest," he said. "I remember! I remember."

"You don't have to talk now," Autumn said. "Can you stand? We have to get you home so Gran can look at you. I bet she forces a quart of her cure-all down your throat."

She was laughing and crying, shaking almost as badly as Winter. Nothing felt real. The gwyllions were forgotten— even Cai was forgotten.

She had found Winter at last.

But Winter kept talking, the words spilling out like water from a burst dam. "Autumn, I forgot everything when I was in the mirrors. I forgot Gran. I almost forgot you! And I forgot about the Hollow Dragon."

Autumn sucked in her breath. "So the Hollow Dragon *did* get you? And here I was, sure it was something else."

Winter nodded. "I was at the edge of the forest, gathering the wisps. But one of them wandered into the Gentlewood, so I followed it—I went as far as the toadstool ring. I wasn't afraid, because how many times have we gone to the toadstool ring and met nothing worse than a dozy troll? The Hollow Dragon was so quiet, I didn't hear him coming. I just heard someone singing, quiet and lovely. I didn't see him until he was right there. His eyes were like two flames in the dark."

The words kept pouring out. "He swallowed me in one gulp," Winter said. "It was so hot—I knew it was hot, but I couldn't feel it. And the Hollow Dragon mustn't have chewed me up before he swallowed, because I don't remember that either." He looked down at himself. "I'm not chewed at all, am I?"

Autumn's mouth was dry. "And here I thought those old snags were confused. I tried to follow your path, but I couldn't work it out. How did you end up in Inglenook? And all—all pulled apart?"

"I don't know. Everything went dark after that dragon swallowed me. When I woke up, I wasn't in the forest anymore. I was here in Inglenook, stuck in the mirrors."

"Someone brought you back," Autumn murmured. "That's the only explanation. Someone got you away from the Hollow Dragon and brought you back here in pieces. But who? The headmaster?"

Winter pushed himself up. The shaking was less, but he was still far too pale for Autumn's liking. "I thought you said Cai Morrigan was here."

Autumn swallowed. "He was. He's been helping me—he pulled you out of the glass. He's not some snooty magician, Winter. He's all right—he's some sort of monster. He lost control of himself back there." She let out her breath. "Oh, he's going to hate himself for that. Poor Cai."

Winter nodded. "I thought I sensed something . . . Something bad."

"He's not bad." Her eyes welled with unexpected tears. "He's my friend."

Winter looked thoughtful. "He felt familiar somehow. I can't put my finger on it." He gazed at the motionless figures by the fire. "What about them? We have to help them too."

"We will," Autumn promised, though she had no idea how, without Cai. "Right now, we have to get you home. Come on."

"What's that?" Winter gazed past her, toward the upper level of the headmaster's office.

"What?" But a second later, Autumn heard it. Someone was coming up the tower stairs. Someone with two heavy feet and a staff that struck the ground with every second step.

"Get behind me." Autumn placed herself in front of Winter, her heart thudding. She gripped the walking stick until it hurt. Was it Cai? If it was, would he be her friend again, or was he returning to devour both their souls?

Winter, behind her, squeezed her hand. Autumn felt the weight of fear lessen. Whatever happened, he was with her. She squared her shoulders and faced the figure pacing across the floor of the headmaster's office.

"Ah," a voice said. "I guessed I might find you here one of these days. Got no sense in your head at all, do you, girl?"

It was Gran.

22

In Which the Boggart
Is a Little Bit Human

Autumn blinked, unable to understand how Gran, so much a part of the mountains and the forest, could be standing there in the headmaster's office, now or at any other time. "How—what—"

"Give me a minute, now," Gran said. She wheezed and leaned against the railing leading down to the observatory. "Ay! All those stairs don't get any easier over time, and that's the truth."

A dark shape skimmed over Autumn's head, tearing out several strands of her hair. *The Lords and Ladies will take what is theirs!*

Autumn shrieked and hefted her walking stick. But Gran didn't blink. She hobbled down the short flight of stairs to the observatory, leaning against her own stick. "The Lords and Ladies can mind their business," she growled, "else they'll get a kick in their royal behinds."

The gwyllion hissed. *It's the rude old hag. The Lords and Ladies will teach her to bow to her betters, won't they?*

"Oh, go soak your heads, you overgrown turkeys. *Go on, GET*," Gran added in the Speech, her voice like a clap of thunder.

The gwyllion flapped backward as if lifted by a powerful wind. *Such disrespect!* it managed before it was wafted through the broken pane and into the night. The other gwyllions followed after it in a great huff, their beaks clacking.

"Hope they didn't give you any bother, girl," Gran said, eyeing the broken pane. "I ordered them to keep to the other tower so they don't trouble the headmaster, but some folk never learn to listen, do they?"

"Gran?" Winter stepped out from behind Autumn.

Gran froze. Autumn didn't think she'd ever seen her so thunderstruck. In that moment, she looked old and thin in a way she hadn't before, as if some of the substance had gone out of her. "Winter?" she whispered. "Is that my boy? My old eyes are playing tricks."

"It's me, Gran."

"Cai pulled him out of the mirror," Autumn said. "He pulled him out, and then he ran off because—because . . . Oh, Gran, it's a very long story. I don't know what to do. I think Cai needs our help as much as these people do."

Gran seemed not to hear a word. She knelt and pulled Winter into her arms.

She held him for a very long time. When she finally drew back, her face was wet. "Is that really my boy? You came back to us?"

Winter had tears on his face, too. "I came back. Thanks to Autumn."

"And the Hero of Eryree, I hear?" Gran wiped her nose on her sleeve and pinned Autumn with a hard look.

Autumn shook her head. She couldn't bear to talk about Cai in that moment. "Gran, what are you doing here?"

"Oho. Think you get to ask the questions first, do you, girl?" She looked back at Winter, and her gaze softened. "Though I do suppose you've earned the right to some answers. I come here every night, child, to check on my grandson." Her gaze shifted from Winter to the motionless people in the armchairs, and a shudder went through her. "Or what remained of him, that is."

"Every night?" Autumn goggled. "Does the headmaster know?"

Gran blew out a gusty breath. "Course he knows. Think I've got the magic to cut through his silly spells without his say-so? He lets me come and go as I like."

Autumn's voice shook with anger. "You knew all along Winter was here. Why didn't you tell me?"

Gran heaved another sigh and said, "All right. I'll give you the tale from the beginning. But first, we're going home. Your brother needs food and rest."

"I've rested enough." Winter was pale but determined.

"And I'm not leaving Maddie and the others until we pull them out, too."

"Good grief! They're beyond our help, child. Don't you think I would have put you back together long ago if I could, and them others too?" Gran shook her head. "Maybe if you hear the story, you'll believe me. Come along."

She led them to the headmaster's desk. She seated Winter in the magnificent chair of oak and blue velvet. Autumn fussed over Winter, drawing Gran's cloak tighter and getting him strawberry tea from one of the pots on a shelf. It was as fresh and hot as if newly brewed.

"Where do I start?" Gran said. "I suppose with my little scuffle with the Hollow Dragon."

Autumn's mouth fell open. "*You* rescued Winter and brought him here?"

Gran snorted. "Who else? When your brother disappeared that night, I went after him. Found him in that old mushroom ring. But there was one problem—it wasn't all him."

Autumn's heart sped up. "Not all him?"

"The Hollow Dragon, you see," Gran said, "is a soul-eating monster."

Autumn gripped the edge of the desk. Her heart was so loud it drowned out almost everything else. "A soul-eating monster."

Winter's brow was furrowed. He didn't notice Autumn's expression. "So it—it ate my soul?" He touched his chest, as if feeling for teeth marks.

"In a manner of speaking. When that creature takes a soul,

he don't eat it right away. He gathers and feeds on it bit by bit till there's nothing left but scraps. You know what that means?"

Winter thought. "That the souls can be rescued?"

"That's it. After I found your body, I followed the Hollow Dragon's trail and I fought him. I got your soul back and trapped it in a mirror the headmaster gave me—he'd enchanted it for that purpose, see."

Autumn let out a soft *"Ah."*

Gran squinted at her. "Figured that part out, did you?"

"I saw Winter once," Autumn explained. "In one of the castle windows. Cai guessed it was that sort of enchantment. But he didn't think anyone remembered how to cast it."

"Some magics are best forgotten." Gran shook her head. "Though I can't deny that old spell came in handy. Anyway, I collected Winter's body and his soul both and brought them to Inglenook. I've rescued others the same way over the years—as many as I could." She gestured toward the observatory and the motionless figures. "There was only one problem."

"The headmaster couldn't figure out how to put them back together," Autumn murmured.

Gran shook her head. "No. And worse yet, the spell doesn't stick. Glass isn't a soul's natural habitat. The soul starts to die. Eventually it fades altogether."

Autumn clung to Winter. She had come so close to losing him. "Why, Gran? Why didn't you *tell* me?"

Gran's creased face softened. "I think you already know the answer, child. 'Cause I didn't see any prospect of saving him.

Oh, Headmaster Neath was full of promises, he was. Swore he'd figure out a way to put all these folks back together. Made it sound as easy as joining up pieces in a jigsaw puzzle. I hoped. But as the years went by, my hope got fainter and fainter. Neath's a clever boy. But some monsters, well—they're beyond cleverness."

Autumn drew a ragged breath. "Gran, Cai put Winter back together. He pulled him out of the mirror."

Gran gave Autumn a long look. "I didn't know he could do that. But then, there's a lot about their kind we don't know."

Autumn's mouth was dry as ash. "They're alike, aren't they? Cai and the Hollow Dragon?"

"Very like," Gran agreed, "as they're brothers."

"Brothers!" Winter cried.

Autumn, though, said nothing. She was thinking over everything that had happened. "You knew about him all along," she said.

"That I did," Gran said. "I was the one who brought him here, after all, when he was a babe. The headmaster wanted him to be part of the menagerie."

Autumn reeled. Cai, part of the menagerie? Like Amfidzel, or the other monsters Gran captured when they were young? It was a moment before she could speak. "What is he?"

"That I can't say," Gran said. "There are many Forgotten Beasts—beings so old and strange that we humans don't remember their names, or maybe we never named them. But what I can say is that his kind is bodiless—like the boggart. But unlike boggarts, Cai's folk often like to possess living creatures."

"I know," Autumn murmured. "Cai and I saw the Hollow Dragon in the woods. But Gran, that dragon was dead. *Really* dead."

Gran nodded. She sat down on the edge of the desk. "Thirteen years ago, during the last and worst Long Winter, Cai's parents were making all sorts of trouble—not his human parents, mind, but those he was born to. They stole dozens of souls from the villages up north. The king sent magicians and soldiers to kill them—Headmaster Neath among them. They thought they'd succeeded. But in truth, they only killed the dragons those monsters were possessing. Cai's folks kept on taking souls. That was when the headmaster came to me."

Winter's eyes were round. "To you, Gran?"

Gran grimaced. "Now, I'm not normally one to be part of the heroic goings-on in Eryree. I mind my business and leave that nonsense to magicians and knights. But the headmaster and I have always gotten on just fine, and he knew I could help. He gathered up a handful of magicians, and together we went into the Gentlewood. I helped them track down Cai's parents. Then they killed them properly dead."

Autumn pressed her hand to her mouth. "They killed Cai's parents?"

"Forgotten Beasts who were feasting on countless souls like your brother," Gran said. "And yes, they were Cai's parents. You can be glad they're gone and sad for Cai, child. Both those things can be true."

Autumn gripped Winter's hand tighter.

"There was one problem, though," Gran said. "Those two Forgotten Beasts the magicians killed? They weren't alone. They had their children with them."

Autumn and Winter drew in their breath.

"Now, I could sense they were children," Gran said. "Though they were in the bodies of full-grown dragons, like their parents. One was older. The other was brand-new. Born only a few days before, I thought."

"Cai's afraid of dragons," Autumn murmured. "He can't even get near one without seeing a lot of awful visions. Oh!" She sucked in her breath. "His visions . . . Those are visions of the past, not the future. They're memories."

Gran nodded slowly. "It fits. He saw his parents killed in front of him. I imagine something like that would stick to a person, even if he was just a baby. Anyway, the older child escaped, still wearing that awful dead dragon. But the younger was easy prey, and the magicians snared it with a spell. The headmaster was delighted. He wanted the students at Inglenook to study Cai like they would study any other monster, and train to fight him."

Autumn hung on Gran's every word. "But if these Forgotten Beasts were as strong as all that, wasn't it a bad idea to bring one to the menagerie?"

"You don't think I told the headmaster that?" Gran said with a humorless laugh. "He heard me out, but he's a celebrated magician, and too sure of his own wisdom. And what do you think happened? We brought Cai here, still wearing his dragon skin, and we could barely contain him. And of course, as the days passed, he grew hungrier and hungrier. It was clearly only a matter of time before he escaped and took some poor child's soul for his dinner. The headmaster's plan was in shambles. Or so I thought. I thought, surely he'll just kill the monster and be done with it."

Gran drew a deep breath. "Well, it just so happened that one of the servants had recently given birth to a magician. A little boy. The headmaster decided it was the perfect solution. The child was only servant-born, and if he died, what did it matter? And so—without telling me beforehand, not that I could have stopped him if he had—he put the monster-child in the magician-child's body and bound him there with the child's own magic. Bound him so well that not even the Hollow Dragon himself would recognize him if their paths crossed."

"Oh, Cai," Autumn whispered.

"Oh, Cai, indeed," Gran said. "Anyway, that's the long and short of it. The headmaster thought he might still study the monster as he grew up, but there was no longer anything monstrous about him—he acted like the child he thought he was. And then that ridiculous seer made that prophecy at his bedside, and suddenly Cai Morrigan the servants' child became Cai Morrigan, savior of Eryree."

Winter was watching Autumn worriedly. He could sense what she was feeling.

You already knew Cai was a monster, she told herself, knotting her shaking hands. *This doesn't change anything, not really.*

But she knew it did. It changed everything.

"Cai can't kill his own brother," Autumn said.

"Can't he?" Gran said. "The Hollow Dragon is destroying Eryree bit by bit, and he's wilier than his parents, harder to catch. He wants to find his baby brother, but he doesn't know where to look. His fury and hatred of magicians, who killed his parents and stole the only family he had left, is polluting the forest. The Gentlewood is spreading faster, and it's growing angry—just last week, one of the king's magicians was strangled by a willow. Soldiers talk of strange morasses that open suddenly and swallow them whole. That forest has always been a wily old thing, but there's a viciousness to it now that wasn't there before. My own gran, may she rest easy in her grave, wouldn't recognize her old Fairyland now, it's grown so full of shadows."

Autumn clung to her twin. "What do we do? Cai needs our help."

"The Hero of Eryree needs us, does he?" Gran snorted. "There's something I didn't see coming. You'd best tell me everything. From the beginning."

Autumn told the story as quickly as she could. Gran asked no questions, merely harrumphed at unexpected moments.

"Why is Cai changing now, Gran?" Autumn said.

"Your journey into the Gentlewood brought it out of him somehow," Gran said. "Maybe seeing his brother again made some part of him remember what he is."

Autumn slammed her hand against the arm of the chair. "This is all the headmaster's fault. None of this would be happening if he'd just let Cai and his brother go!"

She was startled by her own words. The headmaster was a magician. The headmaster was the *headmaster*. A few short weeks ago, she wouldn't have even considered having an opinion on any of his grand adventures or secret plots. Headmaster Neath had likely never even spared a glance for his youngest beastkeeper—in a sense, he was as far away from her as the king in his palace, or a hero in a ballad sung in another room while she cleaned a chimney.

But now she was part of that ballad, wasn't she? Cai was her friend, and so he'd tangled her up in it, or she'd tangled herself. The story didn't just belong to people like the headmaster anymore. Maybe it never had.

Gran was nodding. "You may be right. But the headmaster isn't a bad man. Or if he is, he's only bad in the ordinary way, the human way. His worst crime was keeping hedgewitches out of Inglenook, when we could have done good."

Autumn drew in her breath. "You know about hedgewitches?"

Gran rolled her eyes. "Has it never occurred to you, child, that I've spent a few more years on this earth than you? You can't surprise me. Headmaster Neath wasn't the one who kicked hedgewitches out of Inglenook, but like all those headmasters before him, he never bothered asking if it was the right thing to do." She sighed. "The trouble is, most magicians think alike. Battles and enchantments are all they understand. Sure, you can kill monsters, trap them, take their children. But that only feeds them, really. What keeps them at bay is facing them, having a conversation, sitting down to tea."

Winter had been listening quietly to the conversation, a pale, still presence. He was often like that—even if he had questions, he rarely asked them. He said to Autumn, "We need to find Cai."

Autumn started. She had a hundred questions about hedge-witches, but Winter was right. Their eyes met, and she saw his uncertainty.

"Cai's my friend," she assured him. "He won't hurt you."

He nodded slowly. "If you care about him, so do I. But I also care about the people still trapped in the mirrors. It seems like Cai is the only one who can save them. Will he?"

"Of course." Autumn felt dizzy. It was too much all at once. "He saves everyone. We'll find him."

She went to the window Cai had crashed through only a few moments ago. The wind rippled through the broken pane, sharp with cold and tangled with leaves and pine needles.

Autumn paused. Leaves swirled around Inglenook far below. The torches guttered in the suddenly fierce wind. It was coming from the Gentlewood. The trees writhed and tossed their branches.

Winter came to her side. "I don't know," she said in response to the question in his eyes. "But I don't like it." She took his hand and pulled him toward the stairs.

"Ah, ah!" Gran called. "Where do you think you're going with that boy? He's not well enough for one of your mad adventures."

Autumn and Winter exchanged looks. "Sorry, Gran," they said together, and then they ran for the stairs.

"Hey!" Gran called after them. "Oh, when I get my hands on you two—"

Autumn kept a firm hold on Winter's hand. She wanted him to rest, too, but she wasn't letting him out of her sight ever again, and she had things to do now. *They* had things to do.

Joy whispered through her. How lonely she had been without Winter! How strange it had felt to be Just Autumn.

And now, at long last, she had him back.

They chattered all the way down the stairs—a much easier and faster direction to travel than up. Autumn talked most, of course, telling him everything that she hadn't told Gran. Winter told Autumn a little about the strange gray land of the mirrors—she pieced together the rest from his silences.

"I'm sorry I didn't find you sooner," she said when they came to the bottom of the stairs. "I'm so sorry."

Winter's face was flushed. He looked better than he had in the tower, as if each breath was a stitch knitting him back together. "In the mirrors," he said, "the others all forgot their names. But I never forgot mine. Do you know why? I think it's because you never did. You were always out there, carrying my name around inside you." His gaze drifted. "Most people don't have that, you know. Someone who would never stop looking for them, even when there was no hope at all. I think we're lucky."

Autumn's face scrunched up. It was the most words Winter had ever spoken at once. She wrapped him in another hug.

When they found their way back to the banquet hall, everything was in confusion. Many of the servants and students were still dancing. Wind snatched at the music, tangled with twigs and other forest detritus. It was coming from the foyer doors, propped open with stones, where a group of magicians clustered. They cast worried looks at the writhing forest and seemed to be debating what to do about it, but few revelers were paying attention to them. The ravens had been loosed from their cages and were perched on the tables, nipping the food and croaking mournfully, and the music had a wilder aspect now. The bards sang a naughty sea shanty, and many joined in when they got to the naughtiest bits. Older boys chased giggling girls through the whirling dancers.

"Autumn."

Autumn spun around. Standing behind her was none other than her dear boggart, dressed in a cloak of midnight trimmed with red and green jewels and a neat black suit with black gloves. His mask, pushed up on his head, was pure gold, edged with black fur and what looked eerily like real cat ears, though larger than any cat's Autumn had seen. Naturally, he was more magnificent than any of the magicians.

Autumn leaped into his arms. Then she pulled back and shoved him.

"Where have you been?" she demanded. "I've been looking everywhere! Cai and I could have used your help tonight."

"Hi, boggart," Winter said.

The boggart looked astonished. His face split into a smile—whenever the boggart smiled, he seemed surprised by it, as if he'd never done it before. The room warmed, and several students looked up, confused by the summer breeze and the scents of wildflowers and baking bread and other wonderful smells that appeared from nowhere.

Winter hugged the boggart, too.

"But this is perfect," the boggart said. In his happiness, his child-shape flickered like a guttering flame. "Now you won't miss Cai."

"*Miss* him?" Autumn said.

"Emys," the boggart said. Autumn turned—sure enough, there was Emys, staring at Winter with mouth agape. Kyffin, at his elbow, let out an inarticulate cry and gave Winter such a hug that he lifted him clear off the ground.

"Come on." The boggart grabbed Autumn's hand and swept her into the dancers.

"Boggart!" Autumn twisted, trying to keep an eye on Winter. Masked figures in colorful cloaks swirled about them like strange birds. "I don't want to—"

"I have something important to tell you," he said. "Do you know about Lyn Uskrime?"

Autumn looked back at him, baffled. The careening dancers made paths for the two of them, or perhaps the boggart made them.

"It's a lake in the Gentlewood," he said. "Far to the north, near the snow line. Near enough that the lake is frozen most of the year, and perfect for skating, but not so near that the trees forget how to blossom. A dragon used to live there, and she planted hundreds of pear trees that lean over the lake and drop flowers onto the ice. There's a beach covered in white pebbles, perfect for a dock. At night, the sky fills up with all sorts of colors, like ribbons."

"Why are you telling me this?" The lights of hundreds of candles blurred as the boggart spun her around. Autumn wanted to run back to Winter, but something in the boggart's eyes stopped her. She grabbed his chin and tilted his head, examining him. "You look different. You're still sick, aren't you? Why did you run off when you weren't well?"

The boggart shook free and spun her deeper into the dancers. Several couples stumbled as Autumn and the boggart passed, as if an invisible wind had knocked them out of the way.

"The Hollow Dragon is on his way," the boggart said. "He'll be here any moment."

Autumn went rigid. "How do you know that?"

"Because I said it was all right."

Autumn's eyes traveled over the boggart. She'd never seen

him like this—he never looked exactly like a boy even in his boy shape, not really; there was always something sly and boggartish about him that gave the game away. But she couldn't see that now. He looked angry and pleased with himself in a childlike way, as if he'd just shoved another boy into a mud puddle.

The truth sank into Autumn like a damp chill. "You invited him."

The boggart didn't answer.

Autumn's thoughts whirled. "Is that—is that why the Hollow Dragon has never attacked Inglenook? Because you're here? I thought it was because of all the magicians!"

"Magicians!" The boggart tsked. Some of the mischief returned to his eyes—mischief of a darker sort. "No, he's angry enough to fight the magicians. But Inglenook is my territory, and by our laws, the laws of the Folk, he can't come near it. He might want to fight the magicians, but there isn't a monster in Eryree stupid enough to fight me."

Autumn thought of how the Hollow Dragon had never come close to Inglenook, keeping only to the forest. And all along, it had been the boggart keeping him away!

"Why?" she murmured.

"The Hollow Dragon is looking for someone," the boggart said. "He's been looking for nearly thirteen years. I think it's time he found him. I think it would be better for everyone if he took him away."

As the boggart spoke, the room darkened and the air chilled.

Autumn felt something inside her break. "Cai," she whispered.

"It's all right," the boggart said. "I would never let the Hollow Dragon hurt you. It won't matter when he destroys Inglenook, because you and I will go and live at Lyn Uskrime. It's beautiful there—you'll like it. You can skate and play in the orchards all day and I'll build you a castle with a hundred windows, just like I promised." He smiled. "Winter can come. And the others, if they like. I would never abandon any of you. You're my family."

Autumn felt as if the wild music was inside her, drumming the breath from her lungs. She was sick. She was furious. She was a hundred things at once. She was dimly aware that the boggart, in his agitation, was pulling the wind along with him, and that the dancers were standing back, staring at them.

Autumn felt the fury win, radiating from her head down to her toes. She wrenched out of the boggart's grip and grabbed him by the shoulders. Then she shoved him through the dancers, who were blasted out of the way like dandelion seeds in a gale, and into the wall.

"You listen to me," she hissed. "You uninvite that monster right now. You tell him to leave and never come back. How dare you let him destroy Inglenook? How dare you let him hurt my friend?"

"Autumn, Autumn." The boggart looked frightened now—Autumn had never spoken to him like this before. "Cai isn't your friend—I am. That's why I brought the Hollow

Dragon here—I did it for you. It will be better when Cai's gone. You'll see."

Voices shouted in the distance. The musicians played on, but the dancers were breaking apart, rushing toward the windows and into the foyer. Leaves, brown and wet, swirled into the hall.

"My friend," Autumn murmured. Her mouth was dry as ash. "Have you ever truly been my friend, boggart?"

"Autumn—"

"You send that monster away," she said. "Or I'll—I'll banish you from the family."

The boggart looked astonished. "You can't."

Autumn's heart thudded. "You're right. I can't. But I can make your life miserable. I can have Gran take down the old beastkeepers' hut. I can order you to leave every time I see you, and even if you don't have to obey the command, you'll still feel it."

Then she said the worst thing that could be said to a boggart, the only thing they truly feared. "I can ignore you."

The boggart's face went from astonished to black. His fury made him lose his shape, becoming a wolf and then a dragon and then nothing, just his natural shapeless self. Autumn turned away, and he followed her.

No, she said, putting every ounce of her anger into the word. The boggart staggered back, more from surprise than the strength of the blow. Autumn hadn't given him an order in the Speech since she was little, when she used to tell him to build snowmen for her or become a horse or a hare or a falcon and race her down the mountainside, and the boggart would pretend that she could make him do anything.

The boggart let out a howl so terrible that the remaining dancers stuttered to a chaotic stop, and the harpists dropped their instruments with a clang. The entire crowd stared at her. But Autumn kept walking and didn't look back.

"Autumn!"

Winter found her among the swirl of revelers. Some clustered around the windows, while others streamed into the foyer. Light bloomed on the lawn outside, and several of the window-gazers cried out. The musicians started up again, no doubt guessing that whatever was happening was part of the ordinary wildness of Hallowtide. It was chaos.

Autumn spied Emys and Kyffin by the windows. "Come on," she said, pulling on Winter's hand. He followed unquestioningly.

They discovered the source of the light as soon as they stepped outside. A ragged line of magicians had formed on the mountainside, staffs blazing as they chanted some spell. Their light became a wall that drifted down Mythroor toward—what? Autumn couldn't see. The blaze of light made the shadows beyond seem thicker, heavier—her eyes couldn't pierce them. The forest clustered at the base of the mountain, a well of darkness.

"There," Winter murmured.

Autumn squinted. At first, she saw only a ripple of movement. Then she tasted ash on the air, and she knew.

The Hollow Dragon floated up the mountainside. His claws brushed the grass, and the decaying dragon skin fluttered in the wind. He was a towering shadow lit by two glowing points of light. Leaves, branches, even entire trees swirled around him. And drifting behind him like a net of fish behind a boat came an army of monsters.

23

In Which Autumn Wades into the Stars

Autumn's heart faltered. There were wisps and humming dragons, tiny and drifting like reflected lights on a dark sea. But there were also gwarthegs, wild gwarthegs, lowing in their terribly human voices. And there were monsters Autumn didn't recognize, which seemed to be made of sticks and ivy and gnarled bark. Lower-order monsters, all—she saw no large dragons or gwyllions.

"Why are they following him?" Winter asked.

"It's like the forest, I think," Autumn said. "The Hollow Dragon's anger poisoned them."

The wisps threw themselves at the wall of light. At first it seemed as if it would hold, but then it began to fray. The Hollow Dragon breathed a cloud of sparks and ash into it, and it tore. The monsters kept coming, moving higher and higher up the mountainside.

More magicians had joined the ragged group defending the school. They began weaving a fresh wall, but they were scared and clumsy. The Hollow Dragon's wisps circled, biting and pulling at their hair. Their magic overflowed and spilled down the mountainside like too much paint layered onto a canvas. There was no organization, and Autumn wondered if any of the magicians had ever believed the school could be attacked. Students ran about like lost lambs.

"Where's Cai?" someone cried.

"Why isn't he here?"

Headmaster Neath strode forward, his silver-and-gold hair streaming behind him. He looked like a wall himself, noble and strong. She could hear the sighs of relief from the assembled students. A few weeks ago, Autumn might have sighed with them.

Now, though, as he went to meet the monster Autumn had fought in the Gentlewood, she stopped seeing him as some hero in a ballad, or a distant constellation. He was just a man, an old man, and she didn't think he could stop the Hollow Dragon.

The headmaster gave a cry and thrust his staff into the air. It flared once, painting the mountainside with light. He turned the staff around and around in a complicated pattern, releasing a stream of light. It wove itself into a cloud of silver arrows flecked with bone-white feathers.

But Headmaster Neath was so focused on the towering

Hollow Dragon that he couldn't see anything else. Even when Autumn screamed a warning, he didn't glance back.

Suddenly, he started and gave his leg a shake. A humming dragon tumbled free, its teeth bright with the headmaster's blood.

The headmaster sank to one knee, his staff slipping from his grip. The cloud of arrows wavered, then with a sound like glass breaking, they fell to the ground and melted against the grass. They joined the river of light spilling down the mountainside, wasted magic that the monsters took little notice of.

The Hollow Dragon didn't slow. He reached the headmaster, halfway up the mountainside, now fallen onto his hands and knees. Then the Hollow Dragon simply glided over him, the folds and flaps of dragon skin shrouding him from view for three painful heartbeats. When the Hollow Dragon passed, the headmaster lay motionless in the grass. Autumn didn't have to wonder whether the Hollow Dragon had taken his soul. She could see it in the headmaster's pale face, his blinking, empty eyes that stared at nothing.

"Look." Winter tugged at her cloak.

Autumn cried out. Inglenook's ghost tree had caught fire. At least half the magicians who had been weaving the wall raced toward it instinctively. Now the wall was wavering.

A harp sputtered into song. Ceredwen sat on the flat, grassy lawn outside the banquet hall, strumming an old shanty. Her playing grew louder and more confident, drowning out the bells of the gwarthegs trundling up the mountain. Several magicians blinked as if awakening from a daydream. Two bards joined Ceredwen, and the music swelled. Ceredwen met Autumn's eyes and nodded.

Autumn turned back to the Hollow Dragon. She flexed her fingers on her walking stick. They were shaking.

"Autumn," Winter said, watching her face, "are you going to fight Cai's brother?"

The shaking in Autumn's fingers spread down into the rest of her. "Someone has to."

"But the prophecy isn't about you."

"No," she agreed. "But I'm the one who's here."

She turned and ran down the mountainside.

She darted past the magicians, who took no notice of her at first, perhaps because they didn't, as a habit, take notice of girls in servants' cloaks. But then they started noticing and shouting at her.

It wasn't just the Hollow Dragon that made Autumn's bones quake. It was striding past all those magicians. Putting herself between them and that monster, as if *she* was the hero. A part of her wanted to dive into the nearest gorse bush, prickles and all. She wasn't anyone important. She was a beastkeeper.

A beastkeeper who can stop that monster, a little voice said. *If that doesn't make someone important, what does?*

And so Autumn kept going, until the magicians' voices faded into the distance. She stepped carefully into the river of magic, which rippled and frothed about her feet. It had a slower, stickier quality than water. In places it was warm—sunlight, she guessed. In others, it had the ghostly glimmer of stars.

She waded on. She came to a current of firelight, painfully hot, and sucked in her breath. Each step she took made a little splash. The drops of light floated into the air like fireflies.

The Hollow Dragon paused. She could feel him watching her. The strains of Ceredwen's song tumbled down the mountainside, muffled and broken by the wind. Did the Hollow Dragon remember Autumn from the forest? There were deep scrapes in his decaying hide that she didn't recall seeing before, which must have been the work of the folded dragon.

Autumn swallowed hard. She waded deeper into the river of light, to where the waves lapped against her knees. Then she planted herself between the Hollow Dragon and the magicians and didn't move.

That's right, she told the Hollow Dragon. *You stay there.*

He let out a long, slow, hot breath. Autumn tried not to flinch. The Hollow Dragon's breath didn't smell like an ordinary monster's—which was about as pleasant as you'd expect, on the whole. It smelled like dry deserts inhabited by nothing but bones.

Autumn thumped her walking stick against the ground. It sent up a great mist of light.

Go back to the forest, she said. *And let the headmaster go!*

The Hollow Dragon cocked his huge head. Autumn could

feel him pushing against her command. It was like raising her hands to a tremendous wave breaking on a beach and expecting the wave to meekly retreat. She was trying very hard not to run away.

Wherrrre, the Hollow Dragon said. At first, Autumn thought it was a moan, not a word. It was a voice like wind through a lonely mountain pass.

Wherrrre.

Nowhere, Autumn said grimly. *Your brother isn't here. Go back to the forest.*

The Hollow Dragon roared. Autumn couldn't stop herself that time—she clapped her hands over her ears. The Hollow Dragon took a great breath and *blew*.

A cloud of ash and fire gusted toward the school. The windows in the banquet hall and two classrooms shattered, and fire bloomed inside. People screamed, and smoke poured out of the hall.

Inglenook was burning.

Go back, Autumn cried.

But the Hollow Dragon wasn't listening anymore. He glided up the mountainside, and Autumn heard a fresh wave of screams from the magicians behind her. A spell exploded above Autumn's head like a firecracker, leaving her dazed. She fell onto her hands and knees amid the river of light, and it washed over her.

A strong arm wrapped around her shoulders and hauled her

to her feet. Autumn was coughing, and starlight dripped from her nose—she'd inhaled a mouthful of it. Her throat burned.

"Winter," she murmured.

"No," Emys's voice said. His face was pale and grim. He let go of her and yelled at the Hollow Dragon, *Leave here at once!*

The Hollow Dragon slowed. He cocked his huge head at them.

"I'm here." Winter's hand slipped into Autumn's. Kyffin was right behind him. He strode forward and began shouting at the Hollow Dragon in the Speech, his commands jarring against Emys's.

Autumn met Winter's eyes. He nodded. She knew they were both thinking of that moment in the tower.

"Together," Autumn murmured.

Hands linked, they faced the Hollow Dragon and cried, *Back.*

The Hollow Dragon shuddered. He stopped advancing and simply stared at them, the folds of his skin rippling in the wind. Another spell exploded above them, but Autumn didn't flinch this time.

Back, she and Winter said.

"Oh, you're in for it now," said a voice behind them.

"Gran!" Autumn cried.

"Don't stop, girl." Gran's glare was fixed on the Hollow Dragon. She looked winded—as well she would, Autumn thought guiltily, for she and Winter had left Gran to hobble down from the cloud tower alone—but otherwise just as foreboding as always. Behind her was Jack, his red face a mask of terror.

"What are you doing here?" Autumn demanded.

"I heard screaming," Jack said.

"Found him wandering around the mountainside," Gran said. "Can't go nowhere without stumbling across one of you moppets. Can't any of you stay where I put you? Like cats, you are."

The Hollow Dragon roared, and Gran slammed her walking stick into the river of light—it was gnarled and bent like Autumn's, half-covered in green lichen. "I won't have any of that!" she declared.

Wherrre, moaned the Hollow Dragon.

Gran looked at Autumn and Winter. "You two had the right of it. Together, now."

Autumn took Winter's hand again. Gran took Winter's other hand, and Jack's.

Go back, they said.

The command rang through Autumn and into the earth. The mountain trembled, and a golden mist rose off the river of spilled magic. The Hollow Dragon fell back a pace.

But he didn't retreat.

"He's stronger than before." Gran's voice was grim. "I see what he's up to, the varmint. He's put a bit of himself in all them other monsters—he's possessing them, too, in a way.

That means we're not just fighting him—we're fighting the lot of them." She poked Emys and Kyffin with her stick. "Get over here, you two."

Autumn's brothers fell back. Emys took Autumn's other hand, and Kyffin took his.

Back, the Malogs said together.

The Hollow Dragon roared. Another spell exploded overhead, and Autumn chanced a look over her shoulder. The magicians had strung together another wall of light, though it had a patchy, piecemeal appearance. They stared down at the Malogs in mute astonishment. Humming dragons swirled around them, wanting to bite, to tear. But they couldn't break through the Malogs' command.

Autumn?

At first, Autumn thought the voice belonged to the Hollow Dragon. It sounded like him, gusty and strange. But it was coming from a place past the Hollow Dragon and to the right, almost at the tree line.

"Gran can hold him off," Autumn whispered to Winter. "Follow me."

Winter looked into her face and nodded once.

Autumn pulled out of Emys's grip and ran. Emys called after them, but they didn't stop. Autumn ran until the jagged wall of shadow that was the forest began to separate into distinct trunks. And there, in the shadow of a birch grove, was Cai.

"I'm sorry, Autumn," he said. His eyes were red.

Autumn laughed, surprising herself. "See, that's how I know you're still *you*."

"Don't come closer," he said, holding up a hand in warning. "I don't—"

"Oh, Cai," Autumn said. She pulled him into a fierce hug. "How many times do I have to tell you that you're not scary?"

Cai hugged her back. "I don't know what to do," he said. "After I—I went to the forest. I thought about just walking until I collapsed, and never coming back. I feel so awful about what I did."

"You pulled Winter out of the mirror, that's what you did," Autumn said. "You rescued him like you rescue everybody."

She drew back. Cai's eyes were forest-colored again, the brown of bare willow boughs. "This is Winter," she said. "Winter, this is Cai."

Winter came forward uncertainly, his white hair like a beacon in the darkness. Cai's face broke into a smile that chased the darkness away. Winter smiled back.

"I'm—" Cai began.

"Sorry," Autumn finished. "Winter, Cai is very sorry. Okay? Cai, we don't have time for you to spend half the night apologizing. I have to tell you something." She exchanged a look with Winter. "We should probably sit down."

So, as magic spilled down the mountainside and the fire in Inglenook flamed ever brighter, they sat among the birches. Autumn told Cai what Gran had told her.

When she was finished, Cai was silent.

"I know," he said quietly. "I remember what happened now. I've been having strange dreams since we went into the Gentlewood. I wanted to believe that was all they were—dreams. But they're not. I remember the magicians killing my parents. I remember it all."

Autumn took his hand.

Cai leaned forward suddenly. "I have to leave. That's the only way to stop the Hollow Dragon"—he swallowed—"to stop my brother from attacking Eryree. That's what he wants, isn't it? Me. But I don't know *how* to leave. How do I step outside my body?"

"You don't have to go anywhere," Autumn said. Her voice was so furious that Cai started. "Who says you do? You can stay here if you like—plenty of monsters live with humans. Stop thinking about what you *have* to do for once."

Cai gazed at her. "I don't know how."

"Come on." Autumn dragged him to his feet. "Surely you must have some idea tucked away in that messy magician's brain of yours about how to fight the Hollow Dragon."

Cai gazed up at the stars. "There is something," he murmured. "But I don't think I'm strong enough. It's how—it's how Headmaster Neath killed my parents."

"You can borrow some of my strength," Autumn said. "I've got lots."

"Autumn," Winter murmured. He had been watching their

conversation in silence, and for once, Autumn couldn't tell what he was thinking.

"No." Cai shrank back, shaking his head. "I couldn't do that. It's too dangerous."

"Why?"

"Borrowing another person's strength is *always* dangerous," Cai said. "And especially now, with me—being the way that I am." He shuddered. "I can *see* your soul, Autumn."

"And I suppose it looks like a ham sandwich to you," Autumn said. "It doesn't matter. You'd never hurt me."

"Cai!"

A small shape came racing down the mountainside through the waving grass, clutching her skirt around her knees. "Cai!"

"Blue!" Cai exclaimed. "What are you doing here? You have to go back to the castle."

Blue stopped. Her face was red, and her hair was coming out of its braid. She glared ferociously at Autumn and Winter. "Where did you go?" she demanded. "You were supposed to dance 'The Ballad of Luad' with me. Then you vanished, and now the magicians are scared of some monster." She said it with a curl of her lip, as if she were more annoyed with the Hollow Dragon for interrupting the masque than afraid of him.

"I'm all right," Cai said. "But you have to go back to the castle now. Go find Dad."

She stared at him. "You seem different. What's going on? And why do you look like you're going somewhere?" She gave

Autumn another death glare. "Are *those two* trying to take you away? Are they telling you to fight the monster? I don't like it when you fight monsters. Why is it always you who has to?"

"You don't have to worry," Cai said. A look of determination came into his eyes as he gazed at his sister. "We'll dance the ballad later, Blue. There's something I have to do first."

He looked at Autumn, and she nodded. He lifted his face to the stars again. Autumn tried to work out what he was looking at. Cai's staff blazed brighter and brighter. It wasn't blinding, but she was certain the magicians up at Inglenook would notice it.

The ground began to rumble.

"Cai?" Autumn said. She realized she should have asked Cai what he was planning. He didn't reply. A filament of starlight loosed itself from Cai's staff and circled around Autumn's wrist. She felt a strange tug somewhere in her chest. Then, suddenly, she was very tired.

"Oh." She wobbled a little. Winter grabbed her shoulder.

"Are you all right?"

Autumn nodded. The mountain rumbled again. Light flared overhead, so bright that Autumn had a moment of confusion—was it already sunrise?

She screamed.

Whirling above them was a star. It was enormous, glittering and gleaming and white as bone. Its long tail streaked behind it as it traced a circular path around and around the mountain. Cai was rotating his staff, for the star was attached to it somehow, as if with a lasso.

His eyes met Autumn's. She turned to Winter, and he nodded. Winter said something to Cai that Autumn couldn't hear, and Cai touched Winter's shoulder.

Autumn took Cai's other hand, and they walked back to Inglenook.

"Wait!" Blue cried. "Cai, don't!"

"It's all right," Winter's voice murmured. "Stay here." Autumn heard no more than that.

She watched Cai. "You don't have to kill him, you know. As he's your brother and all. You can just scare him away."

Cai's hand tightened on his staff. "I don't think that's enough."

"Why? Because the prophecy says something different?" Autumn stamped her foot. "Cai, forget the prophecy. You know what I think? I think prophecies only come true because people believe in them. They're like paths. If you stay on the path, you'll get to where it wants you to go. But you don't have to. You can go any way you want—over the moors or the mountains, or up into the clouds. Like we did, remember?"

A smile broke across Cai's face. Like the boggart, he seemed surprised by it. To Autumn's astonishment, he kissed her cheek.

"You're right," he said. "You're wiser than any magician I've ever met, Autumn."

Autumn's cheeks burned. "What nonsense" was all she could get out.

They had reached the river of magic. The star was still

circling the mountain, its tail so bright that it formed a ring of fire. The Hollow Dragon had closed some of the distance between him and the Malogs, but Gran hadn't fallen back. She'd shoved the others behind her and stood there like a boulder.

The magicians up by the castle had seen Cai below. A murmur went up, and Autumn could sense the relief in it—here was their hero, blazing with light at their darkest hour. A smattering of cheers could be heard, and a few people yelled Cai's name. The person yelling the loudest was Gawain, whose face was stricken. He seemed to be trying to break free from the magicians holding him back so he could race to his friend's side. Winifred was one of those restraining him, her face wet with tears.

Cai looked at Autumn. She nodded, squeezing his hand.

Stop, Cai said.

The Hollow Dragon shuddered. He whipped around—a disconcerting thing, for Autumn had the sense that the thing inside the dead dragon turned before the dragon did and regarded them through the back of its head.

Cai was pale and shaky, the usual signs of an impending faint. Autumn tried to send a little more of her strength in his direction. She couldn't tell whether it worked, but Cai kept his feet.

That's right, Cai said to the Hollow Dragon. *I'm here.*

The dragon gave a strange cry, a sort of chuffing sound that reminded Autumn oddly of Choo. He drifted down the mountain, away from Gran, hesitating every few yards.

Cai? Autumn said. The Hollow Dragon was close enough now that she could feel its breath on her face. Cai stood frozen, his eyes full of shadows and waving boughs. The magicians assembled above stared down at them in awe.

"I hear it," Cai murmured.

Autumn couldn't stop staring at the star's fiery path. "What?"

"The song," Cai said. He smiled at her. In his eyes was a strange light that didn't come from the star. "It's beautiful."

The thread of magic connecting Autumn to Cai snapped.

"No!" she cried. She hadn't snapped the thread—had she?

Cai fell to his knees. Winter was there suddenly, drawing Autumn back.

"It's all right," Winter said.

Autumn stared at him, aghast. "Did *you* do that? Did you separate us?"

Winter gazed back at her sadly. "I had to, Autumn. I knew you'd never be able to. It's the right thing to do—Cai knows."

The star that had been circling Mythroor slowed. Autumn thought she caught the shimmer of something in the air—a thread like the one that had connected her to Cai, this one joining Cai's staff to the star. The star, no longer having enough magic to propel it, recoiled against the thread. The thread pulled taut, and then the star was falling, falling in a blaze of gold and silver. The star hit Cai squarely in the chest and burst apart in shower after shower of light. Autumn screamed.

But Cai was a star magician, and starlight couldn't hurt him. Or at least, it couldn't hurt the boy who should have been Cai Morrigan, the boy whose face Cai had been wearing since they were babies. That boy sagged to the ground, and another boy, bodiless now, drifted out of the explosion of starlight and tasted the air.

"Cai!" Autumn screamed. She could barely separate him from the shifting shadows and light.

The star had sliced across the Hollow Dragon's side as it careened past, and now dragon scales floated through the air like jewels. The monster gave a shuddering roar, and then it folded to the ground.

Something rose out of the limp dragonskin. A ripple of shadowy motion that joined Cai as he hovered glittering in the air. The two ripples whirled around each other, one laced with ash and embers, the other glazed with starlight, and then they darted into the gloom of the Gentlewood.

Autumn didn't even look at the boy lying limply on the grass, starlight pooling around him. That boy wasn't Cai, and never had been.

Autumn ran.

She ran so hard her feet churned up mud and grass. She tripped over a hillock and was up and running again before she even felt the pain.

"Cai!" she yelled. "Cai!"

She jumped over the ancient stone fence that had been worn down to a scattering of stones, and the tangle of gorse and mushroomed stumps that lined Glammary Crag. She knew the shape of Mythroor better than her own palm.

But she forgot about the mud.

Just below the crag was a tremendous puddle that only went dry at the height of summer. Autumn's left boot sank into it up to the ankle, but this didn't stop her, for her downward momentum was too great. She came free of the boot and kept going, rolling over and over.

When Autumn finally came to a stop, she was covered in mud and leaves and wet. Her cloak was torn, and her palms were bloody. She let out a low groan, the only sound she could manage.

Some time later she became aware of a familiar presence at her elbow, and a familiar hand on her back. She didn't raise her head. Then, some time after that, a cold nose nuzzled her and a warm tongue smelling strongly of trout licked her cheek. Strong hands wrapped around her shoulders and lifted her out of the mud. She became aware that her teeth were clacking from the cold. She didn't understand what she was seeing for a moment—the view was oddly hazy, and her eyelashes were tangled with something wet and cold. Then she realized that it was snowing.

"Cai's gone," she said, or tried to say. Through her tears and running nose and the mess of mud stuck to her face, it didn't really sound like words. Winter took her hand.

"I know he is, child," Gran said. "I know."

Choo gave a whine. He was staring into the dark forest, his tail whipping back and forth.

"What about Inglenook?" Emys's voice said from somewhere behind Autumn. "The fires—"

Gran snorted. "Let's leave the magicians to clean up their own mess. I think we've done enough for one night, don't you?"

And she lifted Autumn as easily as a lamb and carried her home through the gentle snowfall, Choo and her brothers trailing behind.

24

In Which They Go Back to Where They Began

Autumn sat in the grass amid the wan February sunlight, muttering to herself. Cloud shadows drifted by every few minutes, darkening the book in her lap—which was giving her enough trouble as it was—and draining the warmth from the air. She pulled up the hood of her Inglenook cloak.

She sat on the lawn below the school, keeping an eye on Amfidzel puttering about below. It was nearly three months after Hallowtide. The school looked much the same up there on the mountainside, puffing smoke as usual, but it didn't *feel* the same. Ever since Headmaster Neath had recovered, he'd been making a flurry of changes at Inglenook. Among them, reading lessons for all the servants.

Autumn glared down at her book, as if that might convince it to speak. She didn't think she would ever be much of a reader. Still, she couldn't deny that it was a satisfying thing to pick up a book and see words rather than a labyrinth of black scratches. It made her a little less annoyed with Winter for suggesting to Headmaster Neath that all the Inglenook servants be given a proper education. The headmaster was suddenly falling all over himself with eagerness to grant the Malogs' every request—which was nice but extremely disconcerting. Gran had twice chased away a small army of carpenters who had descended upon the cottage with measuring tapes, all sent by the headmaster to build them a nice addition. Autumn suspected Gran would relent eventually, if only out of exhaustion.

The Gentlewood rocked in the breeze. Autumn often found herself gazing at it these days. The sunlight made the dark, wet boughs glimmer as if enchanted.

She forced her gaze back to the book, though she was no longer reading it. It was strange. She had thought that when she found Winter, she would be happy—all the way happy, not just mostly happy. Gran had said that was just the way happiness worked much of the time, that it was like a slippery fish that kept darting just out of reach. Autumn had been so annoyed that she'd stomped out to the garden and worn a trench in Gran's potato patch. She'd felt a little better after that.

She didn't have to look up to know that Winter was behind her. He crouched on the grass, regarding her book with a wry smile. With him was Choo, who snuffled at the strange object in Autumn's hands, puzzled.

"Didn't you finish chapter three yesterday?" Winter said.

"Shush," Autumn replied. "I had to go back. The story wasn't making sense. Can't you just tell me what happens?"

"No," Winter said happily. "Are you ready to go?"

Autumn nodded with relief and shoved the book into her pack. Together, she and Winter dashed down the mountain path with Choo barking at their heels. The days were growing longer, and though it was nearly suppertime, sunlight lingered in the sky. They passed Inglenook's ghost tree, or what remained of it. Amfidzel paced around the tree with a rake in her mouth while Jack looked on. The fire in the Hollow Dragon's throat had burned hotter and faster than ordinary fire. The tree was a charcoal shell now, but Amfidzel had sniffed out a seed, dormant but alive, near the dripline. She intended to plant it beside the mother hawthorn and nurse it to life. The dragon wasn't acting out of kindness; as a gardener, she had been horrified by the loss of such a venerable old tree. Autumn hoped she would have more success with hawthorns than she did with roses.

"Wait!" a small yet surprisingly commanding voice yelled. "Wait!"

Autumn heaved a sigh. Blue raced down the mountainside toward them, her dark hair streaming in the wind. The girl had started her lessons at Inglenook a month ago. Her staff held only an ember of moonlight at the tip, for she hadn't yet learned how to gather it properly. She didn't seem to have noticed, though, for she held the staff like a queen's scepter.

"You're going into the forest," she said. "I'm coming with you."

"Blue, it's not—" Autumn began, but the little girl marched ahead of them without a backward glance. Autumn looked at Winter, who raised his eyebrows.

Blue came to a halt at the forest's edge and glared at the trees as if expecting them to leap out of her way. "Over here," Autumn called, indicating the path that was little more than a stain in the ground, invisible unless you knew where to look. Blue hustled over to it as if she'd known where it was all along.

The forest was quiet. The bluebells swayed against the patchy snow, which had turned wet and muddy in the chill February rains. It was that awkward time when spring seemed to come and go, one day dotting the bare boughs with tiny buds that sparkled with melted frost, the next dashing for cover as winter roared back to life.

The Gentlewood was slowly returning to its old cantankerous self. Monsters that had been stirred from long slumbers by the Hollow Dragon's rage had gone back to their blankets of moss. Dragons were less prickly and more preoccupied with their gardens. Trees tucked their roots back into the ground. The forest itself seemed asleep, the way it used to in the winter. That didn't mean the monsters had left, or that the paths were any less inclined to trickery. But the fury and hatred that had soaked into the bones of the forest like poisonous rain was gone. Gran said she didn't think the king's knights would have any trouble pruning the trees back from Eryree's borders this year.

Autumn and Winter left the path and wove through the trees to the bit of clearing that had once housed a garden—now rather sad and trodden on, apart from the honeysuckle, which could survive anything, including dragon combat. The folded dragon was alive, but Gran said he was hurt, and would likely sleep until he was well again.

After a few moments and a lot of crashing, Blue emerged from the forest behind them, her cheeks red and her hair snagged with twigs. She didn't pause to pat Choo as he ran hopping circles around her, and he hopped all the more, delighted by his own anticipation.

"This is where you meet him?" Blue surveyed the clearing with disdain, as if she had expected a reception room.

"I don't meet him anywhere," Autumn said, trying to keep the annoyance from her voice. She knew she should feel sorry for Blue, who after all had known Cai better than Autumn had, but the little girl had a way of repelling sympathy, like rain off a duck.

Blue's eyes narrowed. "Your brother said you visit him."

"Which brother?"

She frowned. "The one who looks like he was hit on the head."

Autumn sighed. "That's wishful thinking. I haven't seen Cai since Hallowtide."

"Then why do you come here?"

Autumn didn't have an answer to that. She knew that Cai had gone back to his forest as he'd always longed to do. That he had family who loved him, even if that family was a soul-eating monster.

And yet.

And yet *someone* had smashed the mirror in the headmaster's second office and rescued the people slumbering by the fire a few days after Hallowtide. They had come wandering down the stairs, a little unsteady on their feet but decidedly alive and whole.

And *someone* had given back the headmaster's soul late that night as he lay sprawled in the grass, collecting frost, while the masters and students raced to and fro, enchanting the lingering monsters and putting out fires.

And *someone* had left a neat pile of children's books on the front step of the beastkeepers' cottage on Midwinter's Eve. Jack thought they had been left there by the Spirit of Winter, because he still believed in the Spirit of Winter, the skinny, bearded old man who traveled across Eryree on the longest night of the year, borne by the icy winds, bringing gifts for well-behaved children.

Autumn had no proof that Cai had done any of those things. But she'd had no proof that Winter was still alive, not really.

Sometimes hope was just as important as proof.

And so she waited.

After a while, Blue began to shiver. The forest air was wet, and the cold had a way of seeping inside you.

"You can go back to the castle," Autumn said. "He's probably not going to come."

Blue glowered at Autumn. "He's *my* brother. Not yours."

Autumn bit her tongue. Blue was one of the most ferociously spoiled children she'd ever met—which was saying something, given that she worked at Inglenook. She often had the sense that the little girl had never heard the word *no* in her life. She suspected it was largely Cai's doing.

"You have all sorts of brothers," Blue said, an odd heat in her voice. "Now I don't even have one. Why do you get so many, when I don't have one?"

Autumn was astonished into silence. She'd had no idea that her overabundance of brothers was something anybody else would want, let alone be jealous about. "You have a brother," she said finally. "You have Cai."

"Him!" Blue crossed her arms. "I haven't decided if he's my brother or not."

"That's not something you get to decide," Autumn said. "Trust me."

"Is too," Blue said mulishly. "He might be my brother, or he might not. But I know Cai's my brother. The *real* Cai, the one who left."

Autumn pressed her lips together. She knew what Blue meant. Cai—whom she'd taken to thinking of as the Other Cai—had come to visit her a few days after Hallowtide. He had been like a newborn baby, if newborn babies could speak and weave complicated enchantments. He had thanked her for rescuing him. He had no memory of anything before that night, apart from a few fragments here and there. Autumn had felt sorry for him, but all the same, she wished he hadn't come. He was a perfectly nice boy, and when he left, he had smiled at her. His smile was warm and lopsided. It was a good smile. It wasn't Cai's smile.

Her Cai was gone.

Blue glared into the forest. "I'm going to find him, you know. I'll find him and bring him back."

Autumn suppressed a sigh. "How are you going to do that?"

The girl glowered. She didn't have an answer, and she knew it. "You'll see," she finally spat. Then she picked up her skirts and fled through the forest, back toward Inglenook, making a fearsome noise through the undergrowth. Autumn and Winter exchanged one of their shared looks, the kind with words in them that they didn't need to speak, and he followed Blue on quiet feet.

Autumn tucked her legs beneath her, shivering as the stony cold soaked into her skin. She wished the boggart was there. But even though she'd forgiven the boggart for what he'd done—because how could you not forgive a monster for being monstrous?—he was avoiding her. He slept and slept, folding himself up under the floor of the cottage, where he could absorb the warmth of the fireplace, or sometimes in the chimney, from which he would emerge stinking of wood-smoke. Gran said that he felt guilty and didn't know what to do about it. If true, he was the first boggart to feel guilty in the history of boggarts, and Autumn didn't blame him for his confusion. She supposed that just as Cai was going to have to learn how to be a monster, the boggart would have to learn how to be human.

Autumn's thoughts were just turning to the warmth of the beastkeepers' cottage, and dinner, when Choo sneezed.

Autumn stiffened. Choo sat gazing into the forest, panting but alert. Despite his stillness, excitement ran through the lines of his body. He sat like that in front of the door a few minutes before Gran got home. Only now there was no door; there was a forest of trees with spaces between them, spaces filled with shadow that deepened like the sea. The birds were silent, as if holding their breath.

Autumn?

Autumn was on her feet in an instant. "Cai!"

She wanted to lunge forward and hug him—a ridiculous urge. Instead, her heart in her throat, she darted back and forth before the trees. She couldn't see a thing.

"Where are you?" Frustrated, she stamped her foot. "You're not hiding, are you? Cai!"

No, he said a little sheepishly. *Sorry. I didn't want to startle you.*

Something rustled among the branches in a deliberate sort of way, drawing Autumn's gaze. She squinted. There wasn't much to see, though, apart from a blur of motion. Cai had a little bit more substance than the boggart, but only a little. It was a shadowy, shifting kind of substance, like tree branches waving in the night, the dark opposite of his old starlight glimmer. Choo ran happy circles around the blurry space.

I'm sorry, Cai said. *I can't stay very long. It's too dangerous. I'm dangerous. And my brother's still angry at the magicians.*

Autumn could practically *hear* him blushing. Could a shadow blush?

She burst into tears.

Autumn, Cai said, *it's all right.*

"No, it isn't," she blubbered. "I said I would help you fight the Hollow Dragon. But I didn't do anything."

Of course you did! Cai sounded bewildered. He flickered a little in the fading light. *I needed you, Autumn. Without you, I never would have gone back to where I belong. To where I began. I never would have been free.*

"Free," Autumn repeated. Her tears were drying, leaving behind a cold, dull emptiness. Cai had what he wanted now.

To leave.

Cai flitted back and forth. His thoughts were all muddled, and Autumn knew he was searching for a way to comfort her, to make things right, like he always did. She felt a stab of surprise from his direction. *You're wearing an Inglenook cloak!* he said. *Is it—*

"It's mine." Autumn looked down at her sleeves. "After everything that happened on Hallowtide, the king decided that hedgewitches have to be taught at Inglenook again. He sent knights across Eryree, looking for teachers. Apparently there's a few folks who still remember the old ways, though they don't call themselves hedgewitches anymore. As soon as they track them down, us Malogs are going to start our studies, along with any other hedgewitch kids they find."

Oh, Autumn, Cai said. *I'm so glad.*

Autumn said nothing.

Isn't that what you wanted? Cai said. *I saw how you always looked at Inglenook.*

"It's what I wanted." Indeed, the thought of attending classes at Inglenook filled her with such astonishment at times that she felt like Choo, ready to run delighted circles round and round the castle. She thought of Sir Emerick's words about wanting to want something. In truth, she'd always known what she wanted, she just hadn't let herself feel it. She still struggled with it, sometimes, for it all seemed like much more than she deserved, little more real than a dream. The feeling was fading, but she wondered if it would ever go away for good.

"Just turns out that I want a lot of things," she said. "More than I thought."

I hope the others aren't being horrible.

"How did you guess?" She sighed. "Not *exactly* horrible, I suppose."

For the most part, the other Inglenook students didn't seem to know what to make of her. If Gawain or Winifred caught her eye, they looked away again. The rest mostly kept on ignoring her, as if she were still just a servant and Hallowtide had never happened—some even seemed to be making a point of it, as if by joining them she'd given them some grievous insult. She'd overheard one boy making fun of the way she talked.

They'll come around, Cai said. *Actually, I take that back. Some of them will come around. I don't know if you'd noticed, but Inglenook's full of snobs.*

Autumn let out a snort of laughter. Still, she couldn't help thinking how much nicer it would have been to have a friend among all those magicians.

Cai was quiet for a moment. *I miss you, Autumn.*

"I miss you, too," she whispered. "Why did you come back?"

I came to say goodbye.

"Oh." Autumn's hands knotted in her lap. "Where are you going?"

North. Far from Eryree. Far from any people.

"The Boreal Wastes?"

I think so. He still sounded like Cai, thoughtful and calm, tapping a book with his fingertip. *But so deep into the Wastes that they stop being the Wastes and become the blank place on the maps. The rest of our family lives there.*

– 340 –

"I don't understand," Autumn said. "Why don't you just stay here, Cai?"

I can't. He settled on the patch of grass beside Choo, who flopped onto his back with delight. *Not just because I love the forest. Because I don't want to hurt anyone.*

Autumn wiped her face on her sleeve. "You stupid hero."

I guess so, Cai said with a sigh. *Autumn, will you do one more thing for me?*

"Course I will. Anything."

Will you look after Blue? His voice caught. *She doesn't have anyone else here.*

Autumn nodded. She thought for a moment. "She has the other Cai."

Right. He sounded awkward. *I keep forgetting about him. How strange is that? What's he like?*

Autumn sighed. "He's all right, I guess."

He could probably use a friend, too.

"You just can't stop worrying about other people, can you? Winter's already made friends with him. They get along like fire and hay—the other Cai likes to talk, and Winter likes to listen. They've both been through a lot, and Gran says it's good for them to be friends." Autumn sat up straighter. "Cai, you have to do something for me too."

Of course.

"You have to promise to visit me." Cai started to speak, but Autumn spoke over him. "I know you have to go. I don't mean soon. But one day. Because you're my best friend, and when I think about never seeing you again—" She swallowed.

I know, Cai said quietly.

"Promise that you'll visit," she said. "Even if it's just when I'm very old and my hair is even whiter than it is now. You can be my omen."

Autumn—

"Promise," she said fiercely.

I promise.

Something rustled deeper in the forest. *I have to go*, Cai said. She could sense the forest pulling at him, even now. But the old longing in his voice wasn't mixed with worry anymore. He didn't have to worry about the forest now—he was part of it.

You make me wish I could stay, Cai said. *You're the only person who's ever done that, apart from Blue.*

Autumn felt a gentle touch on her hand like a cool wind. Then the forest went still. Birds returned to the trees, murmuring their sleepy twilight songs.

She sat there for a long time. The forest was darkness woven into darkness, the only light coming from the few stars poking through the treetops.

Something rustled through the underbrush. She whirled around, thinking Cai had changed his mind. But it was just a fox, an old one by the looks of it. He studied her for a long moment with his golden eyes, one paw in the air, trying to decide if she was friend or foe. He seemed to make up his mind and trotted across the clearing, so close she could have caught him in her arms, before disappearing into the darkness.

A little later, someone settled on the rock beside her. "You missed supper," Winter said. "Don't worry, though. I managed to wrestle some fish and potatoes away from Emys."

Autumn sniffled into his shoulder. A thought occurred to her, prompted by her growling stomach. "Is there any seabread left?"

"I hid the loaf Seren brought over this morning. It's under your bed."

Autumn laughed. She drew back and gave him a look. "Did you know Cai would visit me today?"

Winter raised his eyebrows a little. "I know everything about you."

Autumn snorted. "Including my future."

"Oh, sure. Knowing the future's the easiest thing in the world." Winter tapped his temple mysteriously. "I can see your future right now. It's wet."

"Wet?"

Winter leaped off the rock and sent a snowball flying. It hit her square in the face.

Autumn was up almost as soon as the snowball connected. Winter had a head start, but she caught up to him easily—though he was almost her size again, her legs were still longer than his. She tripped him, sending him sprawling into a snowbank. He yelped and threw another snowball, which went wide. Choo ran circles around them, barking madly, while the Gentlewood grumbled and rustled its leaves at the noise, and they ran laughing and shouting back to the cottage.